AN EARL IN WOLF'S CLOTHING

EMILY WINDSOR

SENARA
PRESS

ISBN: 978-1-9161139-0-9

ASIN: B075ZP4ZL9

This book is written using British English spelling.

For our dear Tansy.
The duchess in wolf's clothing.

THE RULES OF THE ROGUE SERIES

An Earl in Wolf's Clothing (Book 1)

Merry Christmas, my Viscount (Book 2 - Novella)

Let Sleeping Dukes Lie (Book 3)

Marquess to a Flame (Book 4)

CONTENTS

PROLOGUE

LADY TROWBRIDGE'S BALL, LONDON. EARLY JUNE 1813. ALMOST MIDNIGHT.

"Oh, Lord Winterbourne, never have I seen such a–"

Sophie hurriedly closed the door on the amorous couple, willing her mind to forget the scene that had seared into her eyeballs.

Sneaking through the hallways in search of her betrothed – or nearly betrothed she should say until the formal announcement – was most enlightening.

Never would she have guessed that so many scurrilous activities took place whilst everyone else was partaking of supper. Earlier, a murky room had disclosed some missing bachelors surrounded by a thick cloud of smoke, decks of cards and a stack of money – they hadn't noticed her swift withdrawal either.

The enormous and rather gaudy lacquered longcase clock proudly announced its knowledge of the midnight hour, causing Sophie's hand to pause on another door handle. Perhaps she should just press her ear to the panel this time?

A feminine giggle emanated followed by a rumble of male laughter, a sound far too gruff for her nearly betrothed, so she hastily gathered her skirts and marched on.

At midnight, her father had expected to formally announce her engagement to the Earl of Kelmarsh, and yet the alluring man was missing. Sophie had hunted everywhere for him and although the search had proved educative in certain matters, it was now becoming a little irksome.

"Lost your earl, have you?" came a low cackle from behind, and Sophie closed her eyes in sufferance. "Really, Miss Beckford," the female continued to the back of Sophie's head, "you'll have to attach a piece of string to him."

Slowly turning, she met Miss Rachel Harper's laughing green gaze. The lady wore a bold yellow gown with matching turban covering blonde curls. Considerably taller than herself, this giant daffodil ought to have made Sophie feel dainty – but no. Instead, she felt dowdy, pale and plump.

Rather like a pigeon trapped by a brightly feathered parrot.

"I'm sure I will find him soon enough, Miss Harper."

"Well, a gentleman like that, Miss Beckford. I expect he couldn't be bothered to keep his eyes open long enough to find a more suitable match."

Sophie drew a sharp breath at the direct insult – to both herself and her nearly betrothed. The earl's propensity for falling asleep anywhere was well known and had earned him the sobriquet of the Lazy Lord, but generally his idiosyncrasy was tolerated, at times deemed amusing. The previous year, Rowlandson had even produced a caricature of the Earl of Kelmarsh dozing to one of the Prince Regent's speeches. The epithet had read: *Lucky is the Lord allowed to slumber in Prinny's presence...*

"I believe I saw your own Mr Maydrum enter another room with a...female, so perhaps you should look to your own," Sophie declared, wishing she was better at witty ripostes as barely a ripple of anguish crossed the lady's pretty face.

"Men will be men, my dear Miss Beckford. You'd better learn that quickly."

Miss Harper sauntered past, elbowing Sophie's arm none too gently, but at the last moment turned her head, breath close. "I happened to notice your earl near the library earlier. Good luck."

The lady's tone of malice produced a shiver within and Sophie wished she wasn't such a mouse.

Her first London Season had been a horrid shock and the subsequent five hadn't been any better. She'd felt so eager at eighteen years – for the dancing, the music and the...shopping. But then Sophie had discovered the etiquette, the crowds, the rivalry, and she'd begun to grit her teeth through the endless society events.

That was until this year and...Abraham. The Earl of Kelmarsh disliked his given name, believing it hideously old-fashioned, and always shortened it. Sophie rather liked the full version – solemn and strong.

Despite serious misgivings at following Miss Harper's advice, she strode towards the library as best she could in a satin frilly ballgown with pale-pink gauze over-dress.

Miss Harper was simply jealous, of course. Bram was an

earl and a fine-looking one at that. His character, although unassuming, was of a gentle nature, kind and...yes, intelligent, for despite his unfortunate snoozing foible and occasional sluggish demeanour, she often discerned a sharp gleam to his eye. It wasn't obvious, she acknowledged, as his silver-rimmed spectacles obscured one's view.

Sophie had only seen him once without his spectacles but it was a moment she would always remember. On readying himself to propose marriage, he'd removed them. She'd been surprised, shocked and mildly amused – would he be able to see to propose or would he ask the chaise to join him in holy matrimony?

After setting his spectacles on the sideboard, he'd prowled over to her.

And then she'd seen them.

Eyes of the deepest sapphire blue – so unusual with his chestnut-brown hair. She knew it was a cliché but they *did* remind her of the ocean. Years ago, on a hot summer boat crossing to Ireland, the sea had glinted that same colour. Not shallow pools or grey expanse, but a deep cerulean.

Coquettish laughter filled the hallway, and Sophie squeezed herself into an alcove as a couple weaved their way past.

Evidently, she should have explored the back rooms more often during her five Seasons of balls and routs as they were truly fascinating. But good girls didn't, and she supposed all these lurid goings-on were the reason why not.

As the voices faded, she set forth once more, her slippers soundless on the marble floor.

Would Bram embrace her when she found him? Kiss her? The thought produced a shiver of anticipation within.

They'd first kissed after she'd accepted his proposal, and it hadn't been at all what she'd expected.

Thinking she knew Bram's nature, she'd expected a tentative, lazy peck. That assumption had been terribly flawed.

His darkened eyes had neared and glinted with a mysterious light. One firm hand had caught her nape and those lips had descended. Fierce and passionate. The man had kissed like a god.

Not that she'd been kissed by a god, or in fact anyone else before...not like that. Their mouths had met in perfect coordination despite her total lack of experience. A low rumble had sounded in Bram's throat and he'd pressed closer, his whole body–

A door slammed somewhere as the library loomed ahead.

Luckily, the hostess's daughter was a friend and hence Sophie knew the vague layout of this townhouse; otherwise she might have been days, lost and wandering the Trowbridge residence.

She lifted her fist to knock as opening doors unannounced, she now felt, was a somewhat foolish occupation, but before her knuckles could meet the surface, a low purring giggle oozed from within. Sophie sighed. Another amorous couple and no Bram, she'd have to–

"Celeste, not now."

Sophie froze at the voice, stiller than the statue of Hephaestus currently growling his marble displeasure from a plinth to one side.

"You did not say that last time, *mon tigre*," the teasing French accent fawned. "In fact, you ask for more, *non?*"

5

Sophie's sharp breath echoed through the hall, and she thrust her ear to the door. Surely she was mistaken…

A faint sound of rustling. A female sigh. That familiar male voice again.

"Celeste." But this time with a pleading tone.

Sophie closed her eyes as a nagging ache began to tingle her body. She tamped it down.

It wasn't.

It couldn't be.

"Mon chou. We do a little bit, hmm, Bram?"

The pain erupted, sharp and unforgiving.

"I am neither a tiger, cabbage nor sweet bun, Celeste, but an almost betrothed man. You know why I am here."

Relief swamped Sophie. He didn't want the unknown French cat. All would be well.

"Mon Dieu! A tedious plump Englishwoman could never satisfy you. Dull and boring. I see her – no wonder you fall asleep all the time." A pause. "Shall I make a little chitty-chat with her?"

For a moment, there was absolute silence. Surely he would refute the harlot's wicked words, for although she and Bram had never spoken of love, they had a strong affection and in time–

"Men need an heir," the male voice imperiously stated, "and she is perfect. Do not interfere."

"Ah, you *romantique* Englishmen. You marry her for the wide childbearing hips, *oui?"*

Another pause ensued.

"Correct," he said. "I do not want a wife that craves excitement. Quiet and humdrum suits me perfectly."

Sophie brought her forehead softly against the door, fingers unclenching and trailing slowly down the wood:

willing the voices to stop, willing herself to move away and not hear any more.

A broodmare. All he wanted was a wretched broodmare.

"Oh, you wicked man!" The female tittered. "I see her look at you tonight – *pathétique*. She looked, how you say, smitten as a kitten."

"Exactly as it should be. Now, where were we?"

Despite turning her back to the door, the words still filtered through, and Sophie ripped off her pink satin gloves, to tug at the engagement ring on her finger.

"I shall be at the Clarendon," the relentless female continued. "Is the only place for a decent meal in London – French chef, *bien sûr*. Come to me then," she growled, low and impassioned, "and bring your friend."

Sophie yanked viciously, the silver raking her knuckles.

"It won't be till at least the early hours," Bram warned. "Damn ball goes on a bit."

The ring tore off, gouging her skin, blood smearing her finger.

"I cannot wait. Is your friend also handsome? Perhaps we can–"

Heaving herself away, Sophie was surprised no tears came. Her body felt too numb, too dazed.

The equally cuckolded Hephaestus leered in delight, and staggering up to him, she slipped the ring over his pointing finger, dropping her torn gloves behind the plinth.

An ornate gilt mirror hung on the wall behind him and Sophie stared at her reflection.

How pale she was and how very, very stupid. "Men will be men," she repeated to her emotionless features. "You'd better learn that quickly."

Two weeks later...

A GLIMMERING OCEAN reflected the cloudless sky – unusual for Wales but such was the day.

The water appeared limpid and inviting, yet sickness and anger roiled within Bram at the sight.

He'd lost her.

Sophie. His graceful swan amongst all the quacking ducklings.

The packet boat to Ireland that carried his beloved was no longer visible to the eye, not even a dot on the flat horizon. Leaning back on the harbour wall at Milford Haven, he wrenched off his spectacles and fisted his hands over tired eyes.

A host of people could be blamed: his superior for the instruction to meet with the woman; Celeste for insisting it took place that night; the Beckford butler who'd these last days maintained Sophie was indisposed when in fact the family had already departed for Wales; himself for all the bloody pretence.

"Yer've no need to worry, sir," a jovial Welsh accent assured. "There's another boat to Waterford, there is, same time next week."

Bram dropped his arms, bending to peer blearily at the swarthy fisherman. "I was five hours late. My horse lost a shoe. I didn't even know she'd gone. I'd thought to give her time but... It's all a gargantuan cock-up." He was rambling, but thirty hours without sleep did that to a man; he ought to know.

A firm palm slapped his back, inducing a cough. "Get some sleep at Nelson's inn. Sit in the admiral's very same chair, yer can – if yer slip the landlord some coin. Catch next Thursday's boat. Then do some grovelling and yer'll get her back in no time."

Bram frowned at the very un-Welsh name for the hostelry. Surely it should be Evans or Thomas? "I can't go to Ireland," Bram replied, the words catching.

Indeed, why couldn't Sophie have gone to Scotland? There, he was still hunted by the Clan MacDougall and had been threatened with disembowelment if he ever crossed the border again.

But he would have gone, for Sophie.

Or she could have stayed in beautiful green Wales? Or Cornwall if she really had to... But Ireland of all places.

He gazed at the calm blue expanse. It was impossible.

"In a bit of trouble over there, are yer?"

He nodded, not in the mood to explain.

"Well, my friend, looks like yer goose is cooked, eh? *Beth yw ynfytyn*." With that unhelpful summation and no doubt a Welsh goodbye, the fisherman meandered off to fiddle with some nets.

Bram scraped the back of his head against the stone wall, relishing the pain, and dug a hand in his waistcoat pocket to pull out the ring he'd discovered on a Greek god's finger that fateful night.

The ruby and sapphire double heart jewel glinted in the rich sunlight.

It had taken him an entire day to choose the perfect engagement gift and on Sophie's hand, it had looked exquisite. The ruby like her – warm, tender and luscious. He was the sapphire – cold, opaque and now undeserving of its exquisite partner. Yet the two gems suited, melding perfectly beneath a coronet of diamonds.

Dragging himself from the wall, he replaced his spectacles and pocketed the ring. He may not be able to set foot on Irish soil, but Bram knew people that could. People that could watch, carry gifts and warn off any hovering suitors in subtle and...less subtle ways.

Sophie would have to return to England some day, and when she did...

He'd be ready.

1

THE PURSUIT BEGINS...

NEARLY ONE YEAR LATER. ALMACK'S ASSEMBLY ROOMS. LATE APRIL.

"There's no icing. I can't eat cake without icing. It's like tea without cream, gambling without money, a woman without–"

Bram growled deep in his throat, halting Lord Winterbourne's words, but then hastily converted it to a cough as Lady Sefton glared at him from across this crammed temple of exclusivity. "I didn't ask you to come to Almack's with me. You merely had to procure the vouchers and, although I am grateful, your continued whining will get us thrown out. Damnation!" he muttered through gritted teeth as he noticed Winterbourne delving deep into a coat pocket. "What are you doing?"

A small silver hip flask appeared and before Bram could protest, a slug of clear liquid was dumped into his lemonade. He shifted from foot to foot and sniffed it gingerly.

"Gin! Blast it, Jack, we're not allowed to drink here. It's a bastion of soberness and–"

"No, no, 'tis fine. Lord Bosbury tried adding brandy last week but it tinged the lemonade, and Emily noticed. She was terribly annoyed. Gin's much more befitting. Besides" – he lowered his voice to a waggish whisper – "I know Lady Jersey *very* well." The man waved his hand at said lady and she coyly shook a finger at him from her exalted position. "How d'you think I got the vouchers? I know things about the patronesses that would steam your spectacles up for a week."

Bram shook a weary head at Jack Winterbourne's devilry. He'd been asked by their superior, Sir Asher Rainham, to take the roguish marquess under his wing as a last, very last, favour. The chap was new to the profession of spying but had been engaged by Asher for his knowledge of seemingly everybody – be they duchess, dairymaid or actress – as long as they were female.

Dejected at the lacklustre fare, Jack nevertheless started gnawing on the nude cake so Bram took the opportunity of brief silence to search the crowded room. The sublime to the ridiculous could be found at this showy affair. A wave of white-clad debutantes amid a sea of multicoloured silks – it pained the eyes to look.

Craning his head, Bram could just make out Sophie's walnut-brown curls bobbing with the dancers and, despite the chatter of voices and dreadful orchestra, he discerned her peal of laughter tormenting him.

"Stop staring at Miss Beckford," Jack admonished. "You know my family motto."

Yes, Bram did. After all, he'd been told it ad nauseam.

Never run after a woman.

And probably, to Jack's delight, he was going to follow that advice.

Bram wasn't going to run after Sophie. No, he was going to charge, hurl and stampede his way to her until she had no option but to fall powerless into his arms.

Since arriving back in London two weeks previous, Sophie had refused to see him, speak to him or indeed even look at him. It was as if he didn't exist. So here he was at Almack's, his attendance tonight not a coincidence.

"Now you're looking fraught and not at all like the Lazy Lord," Jack observed.

Bram let his features fall to their normal sleepy expression. The two of them must make a strange pairing, he thought: the Lazy Lord and the...Lecherous one. Nobody seemed to care though, just delighted to add another pair of noblemen to the Almack's Marriage Mart; another two poor fools to nibble on their austere fare and feign enjoyment.

Glugging the revolting mix of lemonade and gin, he eyed Sophie and her dance partner as they came to the end of the line.

"She's thinner."

"Hmm. Looks most becoming to me," Jack said, scrutinising.

"She's lost a softness to her face that she had a year ago..." Or to be more precise, ten months, two weeks and three days, he added silently, knowing exactly what Jack would make of that admission.

Currently, she was twirling far too happily with some young coxcomb, who was failing dismally in trying not to gaze at her magnificent assets.

The blaggard gave her a salacious grin, and Bram

wondered if Sir Asher would turn a blind eye to one of his spies killing an innocent prigstar. He could do it with the coxcomb's own badly tied cravat; there were thirty-six, possibly thirty-seven, ways one might accomplish death by neckcloth. And after all, this whole mess had been Asher's fault to begin with. "It will take but a moment," he'd said. "Celeste will only meet with someone trusted," he'd cajoled.

That woman had been a pain in the arse all those years ago in France and she hadn't changed. Unfortunately, she was also an exceedingly useful double agent.

"Abraham! I repeat, don't stare at Miss Beckford."

"*Never* call me that, goddamn it." He turned to Jack, scowling. "And how am I supposed to get her back if I'm not allowed to do anything? Why can't I look at her?"

"Rule number twenty-six."

"Don't tell me you have a list of rules for this type of thing?" he said, incredulous.

"Well, not written down, no. It's all in the old knowledge box." Jack tapped his forehead and winked. "You've broken about five already, but since you're new to this—"

"Lud, you make me sound like a greenhorn. I'll have you know I was bedding women and" – Bram dropped his voice – "engaged in service of the Crown when you were in the nursery."

"Hah. You're no more than four years older than me, and I was very precocious. But have you ever had to chase after a woman? Totally different prospect."

Well, Jack had him there. His liaisons in past years had always been brief and usually with women in the same profession. Everyone knew you could end up with a knife in the back at any moment and pleasure was taken when the chance arose.

Sophie had been the one to knock all that into a cocked hat. The one to remind him of what he really wanted. What he'd always wanted...

The orchestra ceased its infernal racket and his beloved Sophie curtsied to the goggling bugger. Not only that, but she smiled and let the fellow lead her from the dance floor whilst Bram downed the rest of his...refreshment.

Previously, Sophie had always worn frilly pinks and whites as befitting a debutante, but tonight she wore a duck-egg blue gown with matching gloves, and the colour made her fair skin and deep-chocolate hair glow. The lines of her dress were also much simpler and the style suited her. She seemed more confident, more assured, and he wondered at the change.

Had she acquired an ardent suitor in Ireland? It would have been difficult as he'd kept a close eye on her via his contacts and received regular reports. Three male annoyances had been taken care of with eighty guineas and a thoroughbred stallion.

An itch at the immorality of all those underhand deeds prickled his conscience. But he was a spy after all, and that wasn't particularly moral either.

"What's your advice then, Jack?" He cracked his knuckles, earning another glare from Lady Sefton, but he returned a sleepy grin and she smiled sweetly. Bram was sure he would regret asking Jack for assistance, but desperate fools called for a rogue's rules. Sophie was having nothing to do with him, and he was at a loss.

"Don't bother explaining – just be domineering. Women like that. They want us men to be assertive, impulsive and carnal."

"My 'persona' is none of those. I'm supposed to be quiet, idle, nondescript...so people forget about me."

"Are you saying your nearly betrothed never knew the real you?"

"Well, no, I suppose she didn't. But sometimes I sensed..." What could he say? After having so many 'personas' over so many years, he wasn't quite sure who the real him was any more. But Sophie had seemed to see beyond. She hadn't laughed with the others when she'd found him *allegedly* dozing in a chair but asked if he was well. Neither had she smirked as he'd *purportedly* lost his train of thought talking to a suspect traitor – Sophie had gently touched his hand, not in pity but in affection, and he'd never felt such gut-wrenching desire.

"Have you asked Sir Asher for permission to tell her the truth? From your pathetic ramblings, she doesn't seem a flibberty chit."

"I did, nigh on a year ago, but we were rather busy being at war. I asked again a few weeks back when peace was declared and he said it was under consideration but..."

Unfortunately, allegiance to the Crown and keeping your trap shut had been drilled into Bram since childhood. You never knew who may be placed in danger – colleagues, family, friends...wife.

Silence was indeed golden.

"Well..." Jack tapped his foot and polished off his own drink with a grimace. "Looks like I'll have my work cut out then."

"GLASS EYES IS GAWKING at you again."

"Don't call him–" Sophie stopped herself. She no longer

defended the Earl of Kelmarsh as he had lost that right. Instead, she shrugged and smiled at her cousin Aideen. "The earl can gawk all he wants. I don't know what he's doing here anyhow. He detests Almack's."

Aideen grinned back. "Nothing like having a grand time in front of a former suitor. He looked like he'd swallowed pond water when you danced with Stanton."

"You couldn't tell that from here."

"His fists were clenched and his posture taut. I agree those spectacles make it difficult to see his eyes but the jaw was tight."

"Goodness. You do notice things."

"I used to observe Da very closely to see how much I could get away with. When you're stuck in the Irish countryside most of your life, there isn't much else to do. Know who Kelmarsh's friend is? Very handsome."

Fiddling with her fan, Sophie breathed deeply and willed her rising flush to subside. "That is the Marquess of Winterbourne. An utter rake, although I hear he is not one to debauch innocents." Unfortunately, her own memory was not so forgiving and the image of the marquess with his appreciative paramour that fateful night a year ago returned to haunt her.

She glanced up, catching Lord Winterbourne's eye. He gave a roguish grin and said something to Kelmarsh, who turned his face in their direction.

Breath caught in her throat.

Sophie had purposely not noticed him tonight, reliant wholly on Aideen's commentary for his whereabouts.

"He's thinner."

"Lord Winterbourne?"

"No, Br– The Earl of Kelmarsh. He's lost a gentleness to his face."

"Let's hope he pines away then, till he's merely a wraith."

Truly, he did look somewhat different. His pose for once was neither indolent nor heavy-eyed but...alert. Thinner in face, the change made him look sharper, keener. He'd also forsaken his customary grey attire for black and the sombre colour caused him to appear almost dangerous. Which was ridiculous.

"He certainly wasn't pining for me a year ago so to blazes with him."

"That's the spirit, my dear cousin Sophie. May the seven terriers of hell sit on the spool of his breast and bark at his soul-case for eternity."

Before she could fathom that most descriptive of curses, Aideen was whisked away for a dance, and Sophie at last had the chance to breathe. Her cousin was a love but she did tend to exhaust the senses.

It had been Aideen, however, who had borne the brunt of Sophie's sobbing a year ago and for that she would always be grateful.

After Sophie's direful discovery at the ball, Mama had taken one look at her face and enclosed her within gentle arms. Papa had grumbled oaths under his breath and announced that the whole family were to visit relatives in Ireland. No questions were asked of their beloved daughter, her need to escape being understood.

Numbness had enveloped her during the long coach journey through Wales. Detachment had taken hold on the boat voyage. Only when she'd been reunited with Aideen in Waterford, listening to her cousin curse men to the four winds, those midnight-black curls blowing in the Irish gale, had all feeling returned.

But those feelings had been horrendous. Sophie had known she'd felt deep affection for Bram, but losing him had compelled her to admit that she'd loved him: his caring nature, the sly humour, that passionate kiss, his intelligence which for some reason he suppressed.

And now, well, she realised that although time did not entirely erase love, it had certainly been forever ruined by his actions and words that night.

Back in London, feeling rested and renewed, she now hoped to wholly enjoy this Season's pleasures with Aideen, and receiving vouchers for Almack's had certainly been an agreeable start.

If only Kelmarsh had not been here tonight.

"I say, Miss Beckford, that is a ferocious frown. Is someone bothering you?" Stanton asked, proffering a rather small glass of lemonade. "I'll beat him all hollow, if you require."

Smiling blandly, Sophie took in the man's form. She peered closer. The fellow was a dear but the earl would flatten him. Despite Kelmarsh's lax demeanour and slenderness, he was strong and muscular. Asking him once what he did as a pastime to keep so trim, he'd replied that he enjoyed hunting. She'd always wondered at the dichotomy, him seemingly too gentle, too languid for the ardent sport of pursuit.

"No matter, Mr Stanton. Simply a stray thought."

The fellow smiled, eyes engrossed in her bosom, and Sophie wished she *had* asked him to approach Kelmarsh.

"Daughter, dearest?" The scent of flowers reached her first and she turned to see Mama approach. "You've ripped your hem, love. Go and get it fixed before you trip. I'll keep Mr Stanton…amused." Her mother gave him a quelling stare and he anxiously tugged at his cravat.

Who needed a man to bruise an ogling suitor when Mama was around? Still striking in her fifty-fourth year, she was dressed in pale pink and resembled an autumn rose, her blond hair slowly turning soft white. She remained a fearsome adversary to any over-ardent suitor.

Squinting at the dancers, Sophie spied Aideen continuing to haul the poor young man around the floor, so she weaved her way amongst the spectators towards the door. About to step through, a tingling sensation at the base of her spine made her glance back. The room was still heaving and the chatter phenomenally loud, but she felt… watched, eyes inspecting from the shadows.

Furtively, she peeped over to where Kelmarsh and Winterbourne were previously standing, but they'd disappeared, two empty lemonade glasses discarded on a side table the sole remaining evidence.

Sophie shivered. "Pah, the seven terriers of hell to you all," she mumbled, elegantly stamping her way to the retiring room.

2

A PAINFUL REUNION.

*B*ram waited and watched from the half-open door in the hallway. How long did it take to pin up a hem, for God's sake?

"Where the bloody hell are you, Sophie," he muttered to himself.

Now past the hour of eleven, Jack had deserted him for the delights, if one could call it that, of a Covent Garden gaming hell. His cohort had heard the Almack's patronesses closed the doors to newcomers at eleven on the chime, and Jack had worried that meant he'd be locked in – no escape.

All fine with Bram as it meant Sophie was a prisoner too. Of course, he had to be careful with this hastily cooked-up plan. Grab the wrong woman in the dim candlelight and he'd look a total buffoon.

A couple of girls made their way from the retiring room, giggling. Lud, they seemed so young. Lady Sefton had prodded Bram in the direction of "ideal countess material" after Jack had hastily left. But they'd been children, barely above seventeen. How in hades was he supposed to converse with a girl of school years?

Thankfully, his current persona meant all he had to do was look vaguely heavy-eyed and nod at appropriate moments. It had been Sir Asher who had invented this sleepy persona and he had to say it was the most enjoyable thus far.

Never had he been one for chatter, and after his time in France four years previous, he'd relished the peace of mingling amongst the ton whilst being unassuming and congenial. Neither had he used methods of seduction for his work – he left that stratagem to Jack and his ilk.

Bram was the quiet one. The one you trusted and forgot.

A distant footstep sounded down the hall, and gently he removed his silver wire spectacles, popping them into his waistcoat pocket.

WHO WOULD HAVE THOUGHT Almack's could be a trifle eerie?

The maid had taken an age to hem her dress, although Sophie had to admit the mend was perfection.

Eventually, she'd been the only one left in the retiring room, and after smothering herself in lavender to out-drench Stanton's eau de onion, she was headed back to the ballroom. Now the hallway lay deserted, candles fluttering in an unknown breeze.

Music wafted through the air as the orchestra embarked upon a country reel – no wonder the hall had emptied. One couldn't snare a husband loitering in the corridors... although discovering a perfidious nearly betrothed was a different matter.

Pausing in front of a large mirror, she adjusted the

delicate sleeve of her blue gown. Cousin Aideen was a marvel at choosing colour and dresses, and as soon as she'd noticed Sophie's extensive pink gown collection, she had started a campaign Wellington would have been envious of. After convincing an easily convinced Sophie, her cousin had slowly worn down Mama's resistance and finally a weary Papa's, until a new, more flattering selection had been ordered.

Turning towards the laughter and music, a swift dark movement in the corner of the mirror caused her to spin. A black shadow rose from nowhere and before she had time to shriek, a large bare hand clamped over her mouth and dragged her backwards into the opposite room, the door slamming behind them.

She kicked and struggled but the fiend was at her back, preventing her pummels from being effective.

"Sophie, love. Don't fight me. You'll hurt yourself."

On recognising the abductor's voice, she raised her foot and stamped down with all her might. Had he been wearing boots, the effect would have been negligible, but all the men were in dancing slippers, and her feet, she acknowledged, were not dainty.

"Fu– Blast it, Sophie."

This course of action had the desired result and, despite his curses, Bram's arms released her. She pulled away, whirling to face him.

"Lord Kelmarsh! What is the meaning of this disgraceful act?"

His eyes rose from peering at his injured foot and she saw him clearly for the first time in a year.

Only one candle burned in this room, and he appeared fatigued in its solitary glow. Fine lines traced their way beneath his blue eyes, although in this light, the azure irises were as pitch as the sea on a moonless night. A faint grey marred the chestnut hair at his temple and, as she had commented to Aideen, he seemed leaner.

Of course, none of those observations made any difference to the sheer attractiveness of his face – his sensual lips, slightly stubbled firm chin and long eyelashes.

"You aren't wearing your spectacles." Oh, what an idiotic first line for a treacherous nearly betrothed.

"I don't need them with you, Sophie."

What did that mean? That she was fat enough he couldn't miss her? Or that he could smell his way to her? The lavender was a little overpowering, and although she had lost some weight whilst in Ireland, she was still notably curved in the bosom, hip and derrière.

"Why not?"

Bram stalked up to her. Stalked! The man never stalked. He languidly roamed, or lazily strode if absolutely necessary. Now standing close, she could smell his scent; at least that hadn't changed. Coffee and clove. It had always produced a rush of pleasure in her body, and she was horribly ashamed to find it still did.

"Because you are always in my head. My heart. I see you always."

Oh, good answer, she thought, deliberately bashing down hard on the small thrill that came with those words.

Heartless cad! Pity he hadn't defended her with such sentiments to his little French cat in the library that night.

"Words are easy, Lord Kelmarsh. Actions are more revealing and I believe yours revealed more than enough a year ago."

"You never let me explain." His jaw was tense as her

cousin had noted, but now she could see his eyes and they glittered angrily. "You ran away. Returned my letters."

"Are you surprised, *mon tigre*?"

He winced. Good. That conversation in the library had been committed to Sophie's memory, burned in deep for future use, for remembrance in dire circumstances...such as these.

"It was not as you thought," he growled.

Although not immensely tall, his body still managed to loom over her and while she didn't feel frightened – after all, this was gentle Bram – she became suddenly aware they were alone...together...in a room. A quiet, lonely room that contained various unrelated items of furniture, and was obviously a storage area for chairs and whatnot. A room unlikely to be disturbed or ventured into. She contemplated her blue silk slippers and observed the tips of his own footwear brushing hers.

Oh...he was *that* close.

Spinning away, she took herself to feign disinterest by the window and look upon the London night. Carriages grumbled along, and a few hawkers and female flower sellers milled about in the street below, some rather inadequately dressed for spring.

"What is your explanation then? You have forced me in here against my will but I'm prepared to listen."

"Sophie, I know this sounds absurd but I cannot tell you...not yet. But you must believe me when I say that nothing untoward happened."

Sophie turned from the industrious street, her face incredulous. "That's it? Well, I'm glad I didn't waste my time staying in England to hear such...such...pudding-headed nonsense."

"Do you know, Sophie," he said, cocking his head, "Ireland has changed you. I noticed it when you danced."

She sighed. He was the fifth person to say that and it simply wasn't true. Ireland hadn't changed her, London had.

In the country, growing up, she had always felt relatively spirited, not bold like Aideen, but comfortable and happy. Coming here for her first Season six years ago had shattered that confidence.

London, which in the country seemed so exciting, had instead been fraught. Rules. Status. Jealousy. Gowns trodden on, malicious gossip and people you didn't know gazing at you through quizzing glasses, evaluating your worth.

Then there was the city itself. Even living in the midst of Mayfair, one couldn't miss the limbless soldiers, the tired women and the gaunt children. Having been raised in an idyllic countryside village in Hampshire, she'd been too protected, too cosseted, and the gritty shock of London had shaken her to the core.

Each year she had longed to return to the country until she'd met the man standing before her.

And then he too had disappointed her.

"No," she stated, "I am as I was before any of this. Before I became disillusioned, quiet and...mouse-like."

"You were never a mouse, Sophie. Quiet maybe, but that is not a negative trait. I thought... I thought you a..."

"Yes?" He couldn't stop there! Thought her what? A deer? Rabbit? Pigeon?

"A swan. A graceful swan amongst all the quacking geese and ducks."

Oh.

"Maybe a mute swan, then," she managed to say through the lump in her throat.

A smile finally broke his features and he stalked, yes stalked, over to her again.

Clearing her throat, Sophie backed away, reminding herself that this was kind, gentle but treacherous and deceitful Bram.

"Lord Kelmarsh... Bram. There is no need to talk of the past." She continued to back away as he prowled closer still. "We will remain acquaintances." The wall met her back. Nowhere to go. "And now part as...acquaintances."

His right palm lifted to press against the wall.

"No, Sophie. Acquaintances is not what I had in mind at all."

Desperately, Bram strove to recall the advice given him by the roguish marquess but it was all becoming shrouded in a haze with Sophie's close proximity. He tried not to look at her bosom, which was heaving in air quite dramatically, and instead focused on her soft cinnamon eyes, currently glaring daggers at him.

Bram realised she must loathe him, but surely not all fondness had been obliterated by that night. Some might say they hadn't courted long enough to call their regard for each other anything stronger than affection.

Those 'some' were wrong. In the past year without Sophie, he'd felt but half alive.

The previous June, happiness had been so close, so tantalisingly near, and yet it had been snatched away. But not again.

Bending to whisper, he watched Sophie lick her lips.

"I cannot yet tell you the truth of that night, but soon. And then you can ask me anything. You will always receive my honesty from this day forward. But for now, I repeat, nothing was as it appeared."

Her breathing hitched as Jack predicted it would, and he pressed a finger to her soft mouth. It was time to implement the plan – impulsive, carnal, assertive.

"Sophie Beckford, I want you. You are mine just as I belong to you. This feeling between us has not diminished. You must be able to sense it also – drawing us closer. No more running. I once told you I liked hunting... Well, I am going to pursue you. I am going to capture you. And I *will* have you."

Sophie's pupils dilated with the direct words as Jack had also suggested they might and Bram could feel the scorching heat rise between their bodies. Those words were intended to make her melt, but that rogue hadn't mentioned what they would do to him.

They made him feel... Primal. Eager. Hungry. They conjured up tousled sheets, Sophie stripped naked, her luscious curves arching across his bed.

No longer could he bear it and leaned yet closer, all but touching. He bent his head, his lips almost–

"Bloody hellfire!"

Pain. Dire, inconceivable pain burst from his loins and surged throughout his body. He staggered back, bent double, clutching his ballocks as he dropped to one knee.

"What utter drivel, Abraham Walcott," he distantly heard Sophie yell through his agony. "You are the most untrustworthy carbuncle London has ever known."

The door slammed and even though agony now radiated

to every limb, he managed a chuckle. Jack's advice may have been hopeless rot, but a woman that could send one of Asher's spies crumbling to his knees was most definitely worth the chase. He would not be giving up on Sophie Beckford.

This pursuit was only just beginning.

"ARE YOU WELL?"

The Irish lilt brought Sophie from the fuming stupor she found herself in whilst standing by a curtained window of the assembly room.

"I met Br… I mean Kelmarsh, on the way back from the retiring room." She wouldn't detail the abduction as Aideen would likely finish the man off.

"And?"

"He blathered on about pursuing and capturing me."

Her cousin's pretty, obsidian eyes flashed. "Licked the blarney stone, has he?"

"Well, he couldn't be bothered to come to Ireland after me, so I doubt it."

"True enough, although he did send letters." Aideen pursed her lips and pushed them to one side, scrunching her nose. "Maybe we should have opened some of them before their return and to be sure, the later ones didn't kindle well. As for those divine presents…"

Sophie grumbled under her breath. She wouldn't think about *those*.

"So, what did you say?" Aideen chomped on a thin piece of bread and then peered at it suspiciously. "My dog could make better than this."

"Hush, cousin! We'll have our vouchers withdrawn."

"Blah. Not worth coming here anyway, no champagne. Tell me about the earl."

"Well, he was saying all these passionate things but all I heard were his words from that night. Calling me humdrum whilst he arranged a tryst with *Celeste*." She spat the name as a weather-beaten gentleman limped past, giving her a queer look.

"And?"

"I...er, did what you taught me."

"Mary, Joseph and all the handsome carpenters, what did you do? Which one? Cheat at cards? Slap his face?" Aideen gasped. "You didn't?"

"I did. Right in the... As you showed me," Sophie whispered.

"The ballocks, cods and tallywags?"

"Are there three of them? I thought–" She never got any further as she was squeezed in a fierce hug.

"That's my Sophie. You show the scoundrel what he can do with his gibber."

She returned the hug, feeling the warmth and camaraderie embrace her as it had done last year when freshly arrived in Ireland, but all of a sudden, she spied Kelmarsh over Aideen's shoulder. He'd donned his spectacles again and his expression was sleepy as Lady Jersey chatted on, but observing his posture, she noted the crooked stance and clenched fists.

Uninvited, his passionate words returned: "I want you. You are mine. I *will* have you."

3

'SILENCE IS A TRUE FRIEND WHO NEVER BETRAYS.' (CONFUCIOUS)

"*Y*our plan the other night was ridiculous. If being close to Sophie didn't addle my brain so much, I would have realised it."

Jack's eyes narrowed in hurt. "I have a good friend who ended up marrying the woman he grabbed in the dark, so I'll have you know it *does* work."

"And did that woman also knee him in the nutmegs?" Bram grouched. "If not, stubble it."

Silence followed so whoever Jack was talking about had obviously received a more positive response. Preposterous plan – his groin still ached two days later.

The two of them were seated outside Sir Asher Rainham's office in Whitehall having both been summoned. His department filled a small annexe, and though Asher's official title had something to do with diplomacy, key people in the government were aware of his work as one of the principal spy coordinators. Napoleon might have been sent to Elba with peace proclaimed, but the office seemed busier than ever with men rushing hither and thither.

Banishing the French bugger to a secluded island may seem a clever idea, but Bram suspected getting him to stay there would be a different matter. Little Boney had many supporters and they would be gathering their strength.

Another secretary rushed into Asher's office and Bram settled back, knowing they might be waiting some while.

Sophie would be receiving her tenth gift today. It was the best by far.

Every month, on the day they were due to be married, he had sent a present. At first, he'd commissioned small items, female fripperies and suchlike, but a written report he'd obtained concerning their reception had forced him to change tack. He'd needed to send items she couldn't–

"Isn't that Rigid Rake?" Jack's hushed question interrupted his musings.

Indeed, Alexander Westhide, the Duke of Rakecombe, was striding down the hallway with a frowning countenance and a posture upright and stiff – as usual.

Rakecombe nodded in Bram's direction as he passed and stalked headlong into Asher's office without so much as a knock.

"Is he... No." Jack shook his immaculately coiffed hair. "I refuse to believe that strait-laced Rakecombe is a...a..."

"You should know by now that not all is as it seems in this business."

"I can see that, but the fellow is a stodgy, pompous rusty guts. I merely exchanged pleasantries with his god-daughter once and found myself escorted from his ball...by four footmen."

Bram hid a smirk. No, Rakecombe would not take kindly to flirtatious overtures made to his god-daughter. Rake by name was most definitely not Rake by nature. In fact, the duke was well known for being prudish, unyielding and...protective, and Jack did have a reputation after all. But such characteristics also made Rakecombe an excellent spy – always in control, dependable and tenacious.

The secretary rushed from the room and garbled in their direction, "Sir Asher requests you enter, my lords."

Raising a brow at each other, they both stirred their stumps and sauntered into their superior's private abode.

As usual, his office was immaculate. The clerks may rush about with reams of documents, but the desk was like a smoothly synchronised battleground. Quills and ink were set at regimental distances and documents aligned to the corners of the leather inlay. Asher sat behind it all, his intelligent gaze taking in the two of them.

"Good to see you both. I've asked His Grace, the Duke of Rakecombe to join us."

Bram simply repeated their nod, but Jack was more fulsome.

"Rakecombe, an irrefutable pleasure. How's your lovely god-daughter?"

Not a single flicker marred the duke's face as he sat lounging on a leather chair by the desk – a study in stillness.

"Married," he replied.

"Good, good. Excellent. Such joyous news," said the ever-affable Jack.

"Kelmarsh, about that matter." Asher interrupted the bonhomie and Bram turned. Grey strands streaked through their leader's dark hair and shadows clung around his eyes like coal sacks. "I am still looking into it, but for now we must remain silent. There are some people to talk to, and I'll let you know soon."

"Does this concern Miss Beckford?" Jack enquired. "We all know about that disaster."

"I don't," interjected Rakecombe. "I did hear you chased some wench halfway across the country but given your bachelor state, you obviously didn't catch her."

"I got as far as Milford Haven, but the packet boat had sailed."

"I warned you," Asher's low clipped tones rebuked. "I said that based on the calculations of horse versus carriage, with a head start for the Beckford family and the inevitable delays involved, you only had a thirty-seven per cent chance of catching her. Twenty-four, if it had rained. You were lucky."

Bram stared and noticed the other chaps had similar incredulous expressions. Asher Rainham really wasn't normal.

"Where's Milford Haven?" Confusion wrinkled Jack's brow.

"Wales," the duke elucidated. "If you want to be an Intelligence Officer, you'd better study a map of the country. Might be useful."

"Faugh! I've never set foot in Wales in my life. Not planning to either. My uncle visited Fishguard on business once and wanted me to accompany him. I mean, why? Whatever happened in Fishguard?"

"Actually, a cobbler's wife of that village named Jemima Nicholas single-handedly captured twelve French soldiers in '97 armed with nothing but a pitchfork. In their defence, the French were drunk."

They all turned aghast to Asher once more.

"Perhaps I will make the journey after all," Jack said, lowering himself into another plush leather chair and crossing his hessian-booted feet. "I like women with a bit of pluck."

AFTER AN INORDINATE AMOUNT of time going through various updates, Asher finally got to the business in hand. Bram glanced at the clock on the mantel. Sophie would have her present by now; would she like it, or wou–

"You all need to keep an eye out," Asher began solemnly. "A French spy known as *La Chauve-Souris* is said to be in London, looking for more victims. Bram, I know you are retiring, but if you wouldn't mind doing the usual listening, I would be indebted. Rakecombe will be the one hunting, so keep him informed."

"What does he look like, this *Chauve-Souris?*"

Asher scowled and shuffled his perfectly straight papers. "No one knows. That's the problem. The devil is infamous for kidnapping relatives of people in key positions. He then uses them for leverage. Mason's sister was taken a year ago but thankfully the man came to us first, a loyal fellow to the bone, and we were able to pass on false information."

"And the sister?" Jack asked, twirling a pocket watch between his fingers. "I presume she was rescued. Could she not give a description of the Frenchman?"

Their leader's eyes dipped to the desk. "*La Chauve-Souris* never leaves loose ends. The people kidnapped have always been found dead. Including Mason's sister. She was left on his doorstep, strangled."

Bram felt his gut clench. Maybe he should stay away from Sophie for a while longer, but the thought of losing her to another suitor was an equally terrifying prospect.

Surely now he was retiring, it was unlikely he would be a subject of interest.

Killers like *La Chauve-Souris* were why he'd kept quiet about his life as a spy – all it needed was a whisper in the wrong company or Sophie to overhear something she shouldn't.

Danger lurked in every shadow.

The sound of tinkling metal on the wooden floor distracted him and looking over, he noticed Jack had snapped the chain on his pocket watch, his knuckles white.

"Well," Bram's protégé said, popping the wrecked chain back into his waistcoat, "I expect he'd love to know we all call him *La Chauve-Souris*, the dark and shadowy *Bat*, but those two words separated mean something entirely different, don't they? *The Bald Mouse*, in fact."

"This is no joking matter, Winterbourne," Asher said with a frown.

"You misunderstand my word play. Appellations such as *La Chauve-Souris* are intended to give cachet. Did he name himself that?"

Asher nodded. "We were informed of his *nom de guerre* by a double agent."

"Then he's arrogant and puffed up. He likes the prestige and the association. Better to deflate such haughtiness at the beginning, eh, Rakecombe?"

Bram felt like the referee at a boxing match, amazed at Jack's ability to turn his mood on a sixpence, and watched until the motionless duke finally uncrossed his legs and perused Jack from hessians to horns.

"Much as I am loath to admit it, Winterbourne is correct. It might even be useful to use this more insulting sobriquet in my investigation. It could draw him out if he thinks we are smirking at him. Nothing more dangerous than laughing at a conceited man."

Sighing in relief, Bram sat back and noticed one corner of Asher's mouth curve in satisfaction. Yes, he always got the best out of his men.

"Talking of code names" – Jack turned to their superior – "have you got mine yet?"

"No. I am still considering."

Bram smiled whilst the duke's lips vaguely quirked. Everybody knew Asher chose their aliases carefully and took a disproportionate amount of time in doing so.

"I quite like Bram's. Don't suppose I can take it on when he retires?"

"Too confusing," Asher answered. "And besides, you are not a wolf."

"And Bram is?"

"The wolf in sheep's clothing. That is Kelmarsh. Everyone thinks him harmless and yet he listens, hunts patiently and only then strikes. An excellent code name."

"And Rakecombe's? What's his?"

"If you tell him, Rainham," the duke interrupted, "you will not live to see your own retirement. I have my poison cane with me."

The three of them gazed at the innocent ebony walking stick rested across Rakecombe's lap. He abruptly stood and they all reared back as he took the object in hand.

"I have matters to attend to, so if that is all?"

"Yes, yes. There are some extra details with my secretary, so take them with you."

"Fine. By the way," Rakecombe drawled, focusing on Bram, "I never thanked you for that information on

Francois. In return, I am inviting you to a rout at my mother's house three days' hence."

Bram frowned, unsure how that invitation could be classed as gratitude.

"Miss Beckford will be present," the duke continued. "Apparently, she met my god-daughter at the modiste and they became friends. I'm sure Miss Beckford is not of the mutton variety, but my relations do seem to pick up stray lambs fairly frequently." And with an enigmatic glance at Jack, the duke strolled out.

A PERCEPTIBLE TENSION filled the townhouse on Conduit Street that Sophie could not ignore.

Mama skittered around but kept diverting to saunter past a window, while her father toddled out of his study every now and then to check the post. Even her maid found an excuse to dust a shelf, which seemed strange, as she was a lady's maid and had never dusted in her life. Only Aideen seemed unaffected, studiously reading a book by another window.

Sophie both dreaded and looked forward to this date in equal measure. The twenty-second day of the month. A perfectly ordinary number. Except this was the date she and Bram had agreed upon for their wedding. It was supposed to have been an August event in St George's, and Sophie could only be thankful his duplicity had been discovered before the official announcement.

The drawing room mantel clock chimed twelve and even Aideen's eyes flickered to the window. A door slammed across the hall and Papa ambled in again, but taking in the motionless females, he coughed lightly and shuffled back out.

"Perhaps now you are in London, he won't..." Mama's words trailed off.

The whole household, Sophie was sure, felt disgust at Bram's actions, but as Mama had said upon the arrival of the eighth gift, "He may be a despicable rogue, dearest, but he's a despicable rogue with taste."

"Oh, this is ridiculous!" Sophie railed. "The blackguard has us all under a spell, waiting upon him. I shall take Aideen's sensible attitude and read a book." She flounced over to the table where her cousin sat and dropped into the seat opposite. "What are you reading, cousin?" she asked, snatching the book away.

"Er."

It was an odd response and upon inspection, Sophie realised why. "It's upside down!"

"'Tis a useful trick." Her cousin beamed, black eyes twinkling as Sophie threw the volume of poems in her general direction. "But you are right. He is a hateful scoundrel," Aideen consoled, "although you must admit his presents have always been...special. Jane wagered it will be a necklace, but personally I think it will be something unusual again."

"I don't want his presents."

"If the earl desires to waste his money, that's his concern. You can always sell them and buy a dress... several dresses...and some shoes. French silk stockings even."

Sophie ruined a nail picking at the exquisite marquetry of the table whilst her cousin recovered the poetry book and pretended to read again. Now Sophie could see that this position by the window gave Aideen a perfect view of the entire street.

During their first month in Ireland, a mysterious package had appeared on the twenty-second day, addressed to Sophie. No one had seen the messenger and neither had it been carried by the post. The small parcel had contained a pair of exquisite green silk satin gloves, embroidered with forget-me-nots. Nothing but a card had been attached, adorned with Bram's name – she'd immediately presented the gloves to her maid, Jane.

More packages had inexplicably arrived on the same day of subsequent months. A silk reticule. A cream poke bonnet adorned with ostrich feathers. A brisé fan of blond horn sticks, densely carved and pierced with flowers and foliage. Her maid had become the most richly adorned servant in Ireland.

From time to time, Sophie had believed Bram to be in Ireland himself, that he'd followed her and was waiting to explain, to declare himself.

But he never came... Only the parcels appeared, regular as clockwork.

Then the gifts changed.

On the fifth month, as though Bram knew his offerings were being passed on, he sent something impossible to ignore. A beautiful mother of pearl brooch on which two turtle doves were carved, united in love. Even her mother, who remained staunchly hostile towards Bram, allowed a small sigh at the romanticism. Sophie tucked it away out of sight in the corner of her jewellery case.

After the brooch came more gifts she could not bring herself to give away. A turquoise hand mirror. A perfume bottle of consummate workmanship. A cream silk shawl from India adorned with red flowers and a silk fringe.

Mama nibbled her fingernails and crossed to the window once again. "His last gift was so unusual. I often wonder where the rascal got it. Certainly, it appears French."

Yes indeed. Lastly there had been the ormolu swan and eagle inkstand – regal, lustrous and unforgettable.

Towards the end of her stay in Ireland, the whole house had trembled with eagerness at the arrival of the packages from Sophie's not very mysterious suitor.

Everyone had been excited except for her, as mixed in with the anticipation there'd been pain and hurt and bitterness – for all that she had lost.

"There's a man approaching with a very large box." Aideen stood, dropping the book carelessly on the table. "May Kelmarsh die in his pumps, but I have to say the English bug is persistent."

Mama quizzically mouthed the word *bug* in Sophie's direction but all she could do was shrug as the heavy brass knocker boomed the gift's arrival.

After a murmur of male voices in the hallway, there was a scratching at the drawing room door and when her mother bade them enter, a small dapper man staggered through followed closely by her father.

"I have this gift for a Miss Sophie Beckford," the man announced, setting the awkward box on the hastily cleared table. All smiles, the messenger gave swirling bows to the other ladies, until turning to Sophie, whereupon he kissed her fingers.

"Ah, our beauty for a beauty," he said enigmatically. "Lord Kelmarsh sends his felicitations." And so saying, he reached into his pocket for a card and handed it to Sophie with a flourish. Papa coughed at the impropriety but was abruptly silenced, she suspected by her mother's elbow.

My dearest Sophie,
To my silver swan of grace and charm, I bestow your
inferior.
Always, Bram.

Sophie twisted to the man in confusion, but he was busily untying the well-wrapped box, before standing back for all to see what it held.

Atop a grand plinth sat a magnificent sparkling swan. Created from silver, it appeared to swim upon a mirrored lake, its neck gracefully arching in pride.

"Oh, it's beautiful," Sophie managed through her gasp.

"Devil eat my feet, but that man's got some style...and money." Aideen's fairly ungallant but true comment was ignored as the bringer of the box rubbed his hands together.

"That is not all, ladies. Lord Kelmarsh discovered this delight in my master's Mechanical Museum. For you see, this swan is no commonplace ornament but an automaton. If I may be so bold?"

She nodded, as did everyone else, whilst the jaunty man showed his back and fiddled with the item.

Finally standing away, the swan was revealed once again and they all huddled closer as a melodious strain emanated, light and tinkling.

And then it moved.

Sophie drew breath, the sound echoed by all others in the room, as the swan reared its head, a mechanical clack accompanying its movements. The silver bill appeared to preen its feathers before the creature bent its neck to the shimmering base, and...suddenly there was a struggling silver fish in its beak. The swan raised its head in happiness, the fish ceased fighting, the music ended and all was silent.

"Oh, Sophie."

A light press on her hand and she turned to a blurry Aideen whose fingers came to wipe a tear trailing down Sophie's cheek.

"You silly goose," Aideen admonished, and Sophie couldn't help but laugh.

"No, a swan apparently," she said, tearfully handing over Bram's card.

The dapper man seemed inordinately pleased at their emotions and applied himself in explaining to her father how it worked.

"And here is the winding key," the fellow said, extending it in his hand to Sophie.

"But I thought... I thought it was just a demonstration."

The man from the museum raised a brow and smiled. "But no, sweet Miss Beckford. It is yours. Keep it safe, for I believe it will be a treasure for many years to come."

Sophie curtsied, overwhelmed by everything. The fellow bowed before departing, accompanied by her father, and Sophie stepped forward to reverently circle the swan. With a single finger, she stroked its lustrous neck.

"Well," breathed Mama, coming to stand by her side. "That certainly cannot be given to the maid. What are we to do with the man?" Rose perfume assailed her nostrils as Mama put an arm around her waist. "Is it possible you... misheard that night, daughter?" There was a hopefulness to her voice. "He does seem most sincere and earnest?"

She noted Aideen's snort from across the room, but it

was a valid question. "He said I was humdrum. Agreed with the harlot that I was pathetic. Said he was marrying me for an heir and arranged a tryst on the very eve of our betrothal. Over and over, I have tried to excuse his words, but there is no sane reason that I can think of. And besides, why did he not follow me to Ireland?"

"Oh, my love." Mama sighed and pulled her close. "Men can be so vile."

Aideen's arm encircled her from the other side as they all gazed at the dozing swan.

"Pfff," her cousin grumped. "May the devil damn them all to the well of ashes, seven miles below hell."

4

DIVIDE AND CONQUER.

*T*hree days later and Bram was in hell.

The Running Horse alehouse just off Brook Street was jovial enough, but the two men sitting either side of him were far from it.

"Can we not depart for your mother's rout yet?" Bram demanded. "She's likely to have us turfed out if we arrive foxed and rumpled."

His words had no effect other than a jaded grimace from Rakecombe. "The *mater* normally has to bribe me to grace these events, so think yourself lucky I am attending, thus giving you the opportunity to meet with Miss Beckford."

"But why a drink beforehand?"

Rakecombe idled in his seat, tapping that damn venomous cane on the floor. "Once you've been to one of her affairs, you'll understand why some Dutch courage does not go amiss. Although if I'd known Winterbourne was attending, I might have stayed away."

"Unfair, my upright Rake." Jack scowled, brushing ale

from his silk burgundy tailcoat. "I wouldn't miss Kelmarsh making an arse of himself for the world. Even put up with your puritanical droning."

"Just because I don't set out to swive anything in skir–"

"Please," Bram interjected, "drink your ale and shut your traps."

The two men huddled back in silence, Winterbourne with a studied air of nonchalance, Rakecombe with one of restrained abhorrence.

Tonight, Bram was hoping to corner Sophie and he could do without turning up bosky, but Rakecombe had sent a messenger asking if they could meet beforehand. He'd thought it was to discuss *La Chauve-Souris* – obviously not.

Over the past three days, Bram had tried endlessly to contrive a chance meeting with Sophie. He'd lingered on the corner of Conduit Street, strolled along Piccadilly and even lurked within view of the modiste – but nothing. The maids and footmen of the Beckford household had also proved resolutely unbribable. When he found out where her father got his staff, he'd have to follow suit as never had he seen such a loyal lot.

Asher always cited patience as the most important quality to possess on a hunt, and Bram usually had that in abundance, but obviously the chap had never embarked upon a pursuit of a more amorous nature. Indeed, he wasn't actually sure if Asher had a passionate bone in his body.

A comrade had once admitted she'd tried to seduce their leader. Apparently, he'd looked rather baffled and asked what she was doing, convinced her previous winter boat crossing from Spain had caused some kind of brain fever.

There was, after all, a seven in ten chance of contracting an illness on a December's night in the Bay of Biscay.

The barmaid glided over, plonking three more jugs in front of them, and Jack flipped the girl a coin and a wink, before turning back to the table.

"What's the plan tonight then?"

"None," Bram bit out. "There is no plan. You will not be planning anything."

"There's always a plan," Rakecombe drawled. "Remember Chadwick? He didn't have a plan."

"What happened to Chadwick?" Jack asked.

"Dead," they both replied.

Jack winced. "You need a plan."

Silence descended and Bram removed his spectacles to rub at his eyes. Truth be told, he did need a strategy, but nothing came to mind that could resolve this impossible situation with Sophie. Only cutting through the lies and pretence would do that and yet he was bound by honour and loyalty to keep quiet until Asher gave clearance to speak. But surely there must be something...

"Poetry."

"Capital idea, Rakecombe," Jack agreed.

"No." Bram slammed his jug to the table, ale slopping. "I am not repeating some trite slapdash words that you two have newly concocted whilst stewed to the gills."

Rakecombe leaned forward, for once a smug grin on his stern face. "I quite agree. But look to the corner. For there sits a master."

"Is it Byron?" asked Jack enthusiastically, peering around. "His stuff works a treat with the ladies."

Shaking his head, Rakecombe pointed to a dark-haired

chap in his thirtieth year or thereabouts. "Your Beckford girl isn't some lightskirt or experienced widow. She's maidenly and needs fluffier words than Byron's salacious musings and that man has just the wares. Thomas Moore."

Bram popped his spectacles back on and exhaled heavily.

AN HOUR LATER, and two hours late for the rout, Bram and his accomplices stalked towards the Rakecombe abode on Grosvenor Square.

Despite the late hour, the street appeared ignited by the amount of light spilling from the duke's townhouse; there must have been a thousand candles burning. Carriages still jostled in the street outside, disgorging society's upper echelons, just as one swaying chap was being forcibly ejected down the same steps.

"Feel free to do that to me in an hour, won't you?" Jack said. "As long as it's after Kelmarsh's recitation, of course."

"Talk to my god-daughter again and you'll acquire the tip of my cane." Rakecombe shot him a malevolent grin. "You won't feel a thing."

Bram ignored them and ran up the steps two at a time, the scrap of poetry folded in his waistcoat pocket.

The Moore poet chap had turned out to be a thoroughly pleasant fellow, having scribbled some lines in exchange for a few drinks. He'd not encountered Moore before, but recently, Bram's missions had focused on men who had pockets to let and were ripe to be plucked by the enemy. Therefore, he'd spent an inordinate amount of time dozing in gaming establishments – not the type of place to have met the latest popular bard on the literary scene.

As soon as they entered the drawing room, the chatter fell away to hushed murmurs. A deadly duke, an indolent earl and a man about town marquess swaggering in together was, Bram supposed, an unusual sight.

"Darling." A very small rotund lady flew at Rakecombe and patted his cheek. Only those watching closely saw the minute twitch of his eye at the endearment and embrace.

"Mother," he growled back, and the noise levels rose again to buzzing.

The three nobles paced a path through the ground floor, but the rout was an almighty crush. Fluttering fans clouted one's chops as the women weaved in and out, guests bellowed to be heard and men could be seen escaping to the card room – all the ton world and his wife were here.

How in the hell was he supposed to find Sophie in this?

"Ouch!"

Something hard and sharp dug into the lower part of his back, causing him to swivel and wallop whatever it was with his elbow. He heard a low yelp and grabbed hold of its source to stop them both falling to the floor.

Immediately – and he didn't give a damn if his cohorts said it was impossible – he knew who it was.

Softness. Hay meadows. Summer. Home. A tingling travelled up his arm, his hand burned and the scent of lavender fields assailed his nostrils.

Sophie.

His grip tightened. A female gasp.

The poetry plan slipped away, and what he really yearned to do, deep down, emerged in its place. He yearned to haul Sophie against his body, kiss her senseless and stride out of this place with her held in his arms.

Old-fashioned – a little.

Primitive – without doubt.

Satisfying – most definitely.

His other hand lifted to Sophie's shoulder.

"LET GO of my cousin this instant and I'll let you live."

The harshly whispered Irish lilt drew Sophie from her daze and she straightened, backing away. Bram's hand slipped from her arm whilst the other still hovered at her shoulder. She frowned and then that too fell away.

Where his fingers had gripped seemed to flame and the expression in his eyes had positively singed. They'd been so close, enough to see past the reflection of his spectacles: the azure blue had darkened to ink.

"Miss Beckford." Bram bowed, his countenance now languid. "May I introduce you to my...friends."

She glared, unable to flee, hemmed in as she was by manners, decorum and too many blasted people. Turning to his companions, she then gulped.

"I don't believe you're acquainted with the Marquess of Winterbourne," Bram was saying, and a scarlet warmed her cheeks as the rogue brushed her fingers with his lips.

"Have we met before, Miss Beckford?" he asked amiably.

"No!" she almost shouted before recovering her poise. "We've never been formally introduced, my lord."

"Hmm," he murmured, raising a dark quizzical brow.

"And His Grace, the Duke of Rakecombe." A stern visage scowled down upon her as she curtsied. Dark haired and green eyed, he was fine-looking and tall, but there was something murky about the man. Maybe it was the ridiculously forbidding expression.

Sophie twisted, dragging Aideen forward, her heels seemingly caught in the plush rug.

"May I introduce Miss Aideen Quinlan, a cousin from Ireland. She is spending the Season and summer with us."

All the gentlemen did the pretty, before Lord Winterbourne flashed a smile. "And how are you enjoying England, Miss Quinlan?"

"I find Englishmen rather sly, my lord," she said, eyes flitting to Bram. "And too close." Her gaze now rested upon the duke, who was indeed looming over her.

"Sly means handsome in Irish," Sophie said desperately, "and close means...er...tall."

Aideen was loyal to a fault, but she had never been one for etiquette and insulting a duke would end their London stay quite abruptly. Specifically this duke, as she had heard he was more than a tad haughty.

The Duke of Rakecombe, if anything, loomed yet more over her attractive cousin. "Your given name, I believe, means *little fire* in Irish," he drawled, his jade gaze inspecting.

Aideen, undeniably *a little fire*, was not to be cowed. Her black eyes slowly and, it had to be said, somewhat insultingly perused the man from foot to head.

"And Rakecombe means you're a lecher–"

"I think I hear my mother calling." Sophie hurriedly curtsied. "Gentleman," she said, hauling her cousin away from the gawping males.

"I was starting to enjoy myself," Aideen moaned as they rounded a corner. "The duke looked like he was going to...implode."

"Or strangle you...or bring our Season to an untimely

end. You can't say such things to a duke, and besides, his god-daughter is a good friend."

Aideen grumped, before linking arms with her. "Sly and close the lot of them."

"THAT WENT WELL."

Bram glowered. Why had Sophie blushed when she was introduced to Jack? Did she have a tendre for him? Women seemed to fall over their slippers for the marquess. "Have you met Sophie before? You never said."

"I do recognise her from somewhere. It will come to me."

"What do you know of Miss Beckford's cousin?" Rakecombe enquired, flicking a piece of lint from his onyx-black waistcoat. "Seems a flighty piece with a volatile temper. I'd be careful if I were you. That spitting kitten may lead your dove astray."

"You *were* rather near to her," Jack accused. "I agree she's a bit wild for your prudish tastes, Rakehell, but very pretty. Delectable red cherry lips."

Even at a rout, Rakecombe carried his cane, and Bram noticed the duke's hand clench on the top. If Jack wasn't careful, he'd be escorted from the premises in a box this time. Although they may joke, the duke did have a reputation for being more than ruthless when need be.

"Do you think one of you could distract Miss Quinlan whilst I talk to Sophie?"

"Yes," they replied in unison.

Bram wasn't quite sure whose offer to accept. "Having only spoken to Miss Quinlan for a brief moment, I believe it may require both of you. We must divide and conquer."

"Very well," Jack agreed, "but remember rule number five: no grovelling."

His accomplices headed off as Bram lounged against the frame of the Canaletto, observing the marquess follow in the ladies' direction whilst the duke sauntered towards the...card room? It was his house, however, and Bram knew who he'd wager on to find Miss Quinlan first.

5

POETRY. THE WAY TO A WOMAN'S HEART?

"*W*hy if it isn't Miss Beckford, returned from hiding."

Once, Sophie would have cringed and shrunk from the spiteful voice that halted her step, but instead a calmness settled within. She no longer allowed maliciousness to subdue her. And besides, if Sophie had Mrs Harper for a mother, mayhap Sophie would be of a similar disposition.

"Miss Harper." Sophie pivoted, her face wreathed in a welcoming smile. "It is too good to see you again." Sophie held out her hands and watched confusion pucker the girl's face.

"Oh. Yes, indeed," Miss Harper stuttered, before regaining her composure in the face of so much cordiality. "How was Ireland? Dull, I expect. All sheep and potatoes."

"Not at all. The beautiful countryside, the kind people, the laughter. I had the best of times."

"I am...glad. But it must be so difficult to be back. I mean, not that your engagement had been officially announced but..." Miss Harper trailed off whilst Sophie merely broadened her smile.

The best way to subdue malevolence, she had found, was to smile at it. People found it utterly confounding.

"Oh, you are referring to Kelmarsh and I. We remain good friends. I have just met his companions tonight. Lord Winterbourne and our host."

"You were made acquainted with the duke?"

"Hmm. A most...tall and handsome man. Have you not been introduced?"

Miss Harper looked quite sick with envy, although goodness knows why. Neither man seemed marriage material to Sophie. But a duke was a duke...

"No, not in so many words, but I'm sure my mother will arrange it. I saw the duke not a moment ago and surely would have been introduced, but he was following some dark-haired girl to the supper room."

Sophie's palms prickled. "Dark?"

"Very. Jet-black hair and eyes. Looks like a gypsy."

"Oh no. The supper room, you say?"

At Miss Harper's nod, Sophie grasped both the startled girl's hands. "Thank you so much. Such a pleasure to chat again."

Please Aideen, she beseeched the heavens as she dashed off in the direction of the supper room, not the nettle patch curse.

BRAM TRACKED Sophie's progress through the multicoloured crush of gentlefolk.

Despite his idle pose, every nerve felt alert and sensitive to her presence. A celestial blue silk rippled over her white satin under-dress, skimming a luscious body. The hem was decorated with an even deeper indigo border of net...stuff, as though she'd risen from the ocean depths. He imagined smoothing it up over her ankle, the skin peeking through the gossamer material.

Tonight, her walnut locks were caught up in some complicated curliness that begged to be ruffled.

The unschooled might find brown a monotone colour, but that was because they hadn't looked properly. They didn't see the highlights of red, mahogany and umber flashing under the candlelight.

Sophie flitted around, searching for Miss Quinlan, but she wouldn't find her as he'd seen Rakecombe carelessly stroll after her into the drawing room. He wasn't sure what the duke was up to, but the cherry-lipped cousin would be safe enough.

The one other sentry to worry about was *Mrs* Beckford. The lady had been delightful when he'd been courting Sophie, but her obvious affection for her daughter meant Bram was now without doubt *persona non-grata*.

He hoped that tonight, with the poetry, Sophie would at least listen to his apology, hear his sincerity. And maybe he'd be able to gauge her own feelings for him, even if they did remain solely resentment and scorn.

If only he could tell her all. The truth, the lies, the words... But within that course of action lay danger: to other men, to himself and especially to Sophie.

Loyalty and love came in all guises and sometimes it was silent.

An ostrich-feathered matron clattered his shoulder, not really seeing him as usual. His relaxed posture and grey attire blended him to the background – or door frame in this case, and his eyes narrowed behind the spectacles.

Watching. Waiting.

Finally his opportunity arose, as a wrinkle of annoyance marred Sophie's forehead and she stomped to the French doors to enter the coolness of the gardens.

"Wait there, Sophie," he whispered under his breath, straightening himself and cracking his knuckles. "I'm coming."

THERE WAS no sign of Aideen outside either and Sophie started to feel most worried. It wasn't that she thought the duke would hurt her cousin, quite the reverse in fact, but more that the duke could then cause some kind of fuss. She'd heard of a notorious incident some years back, where he'd given the cut direct to a viscount's daughter for inadvertently clipping his heel.

After the crush of the interior, the stillness of the night was a soothing balm to her soul and the freshness a solace for her heated body.

Routs, she had always supposed, were better than balls as they gave more chance for discourse, but never had she seen so many people packed into one house. The stairs were a positive hazard: footmen bustled with trays and ladies clogged up the steps, jostling for a better view of newcomers.

Of course, no one had failed to notice the entry of the three peers, all of them looking rather dishevelled. Sophie and Aideen had hurtled at a rapid, but lady-like, pace in the opposite direction, losing her mother to Lady Harrington and her father to piquet. But they'd been carried on a flowing tide of circulating nobles around the townhouse, only to be washed up right behind Bram.

'Twas as though they were magnets – although Ireland's lure had obviously been a tad far for Bram's lodestone.

Sophie wandered down the steps and away from the terrace, having heard the faint ripple of giggling from behind a column. The merriment reminded her of *that* night, and a slight melancholia descended. The lit path led to a small gazebo, but no doubt another couple would be trysting there so she veered off to a wooden bench situated beneath a cherry tree in fading blossom.

The seat was damp, thus she spread out a handkerchief, perched herself on the very edge and closed her eyes.

"Sophie."

Magnets. Damn magnets. And she opened them again.

He stood not six feet away.

"Lord Kelmarsh. I cannot believe this is coincidence."

Faint moonlight reflected in his spectacles, and a dove-grey tailcoat clung to his torso, matched by a silver-embroidered, equally grey waistcoat. He resembled a ghost in the night. Only his hair contradicted that metaphor...and his blue eyes of course, which were hidden as always.

"No," he finally replied, standing another pace closer. "I followed you, Sophie."

"Why?" Another step forward and she would have to crane her neck to hold his gaze, so she looked to her feet instead.

"My letters were returned, Sophie, so you never allowed me to say sorry. Sorry for the words you heard. Sorry for being late to our announcement. Sorr–"

"Sorry you were caught?"

His top boots took a long stride and the scent of coffee pervaded the spring air.

"Yes," he said tightly. "I am sorry for being caught. Because nothing of consequence took place. Celeste meant nothing. By now, we would be married and not at this ridiculous rout. We'd be–"

"Arguing? Unhappy? Unfaithful?"

Surely, he couldn't get any closer, she thought, observing his booted toes meet the edge of her gown. But it seemed he could, as suddenly he sat on the bench and turned to place both palms on her shoulders, curving her body towards his.

She gasped at the intimacy.

One of his hands slid down and slowly caressed its way along her bare collarbone until meeting her throat. Fingers gently skimmed her pulse and she willed it to stop fluttering so madly. She fought to remember last year – the hurt, the humiliation, the sadness.

But none of that was enough to force her from the bench. Maybe she did, after all, want to know what he had to say for himself. He shuffled nearer, knee now brushing hers.

"No, none of those, Sophie. We would be entwined in bed."

SHE JOLTED at his words and Bram didn't blame her. That wasn't what he meant to say, but he forgot all propriety, all plans, when he neared Sophie Beckford. He just came out with...things. Words he'd never heard put together before. Unbidden and spontaneous. Perhaps they were words of a long-ago persona he'd forgotten about.

Dragging the other hand from her shoulder, he removed his spectacles and placed them to one side.

It seemed he had struck Sophie mute with his last sentence, and she stared out with wide, dark eyes, face pale in the moonlight, lips slightly parted. Hell, he wanted to kiss her. To once again feel that strange mixed sensation of overriding lust and yet endless peace.

He could expand upon "entwined" and share the images that tormented his mind, but he didn't wish to scare her. And besides, he was aroused enough as it was. Grimacing, he shifted on the hard bench, anything to relieve the damn ache, and he forced his lips to be content with purely meeting Sophie's ear.

"Did you like the gifts, my love?" he whispered. "Every single one was bought personally for you. I spent days wandering the shops, searching for the perfect items. Some fell into my lap like that inkstand and the silver swan, as though they knew my plight and sought to help me. Others, like the brooch, took hours and hours of choosing."

She turned, her mouth so close, but he had to finish. She had to hear him.

Pressing lips to her forehead, he heard a sigh. "I wish I could compel that night away, Sophie. Purge the memory from your mind with my kiss." Her body shuddered as he gently drew breath at her skin. God, she was enchanting – just as he remembered. They fitted so very perfectly.

He could stand it no longer; his entire being thrummed with pent-up desire and want. Tracing lips over her eyes, down her cheek, he met her mouth.

It began with gentleness. He meant it to stay gentle. But the feel, the fragrance, the heat – it was all too enticing and he hauled her body tight against his, crushing her to his chest. His fingers found their way to her nape, holding firm, as he ravished her mouth, passion pounding through his body so relentless, so painful.

She didn't pull away but neither did Sophie respond with fervour until, all of a sudden, he felt the touch of a hand at his own nape, sweeping away any remnants of finesse on his part. A fist seized his hair as sweet lips softly opened beneath his, and he groaned at the sheer pleasure.

Caressing fingers down her back, he clenched at the dainty buttons of her dress. Forcing his hand onward, he brought it around her side, and finding her breast, he cupped the fulsome weight in his palm.

A guttural sound left his throat, one he hadn't heard before, and he stroked a tight nipple through the soft satin of the dress. A low moan greeted his touch as he brushed a finger upon the crest, her mouth wrenching from his.

Only panting gasps escaped them, but without those lips he suddenly remembered what he was supposed to be doing.

He didn't want to seduce Sophie into marriage; he wanted her unconditional love – free and without obligation. Anyone could stumble upon them here and she would be ruined, wrapped around each other as they were.

Reluctantly, he softened his grasp, soothing the small of her back in gentle strokes. Rakecombe's words haunted him. Sophie wasn't some experienced widow; she should be treated lightly, not mauled in such a heavy-handed manner.

Lud, he was surprised his ballocks were still intact, and he'd better fix this mess quickly because once she realised how many liberties he'd just taken, it was probable she'd never speak to him again.

The plan. Of course.

Thomas Moore.

Leaning away, he gazed into her shadowed eyes. She seemed a little stunned and he could utterly concur with the feeling, but it was time for the poetry. He held her firm and spoke.

"What the bee is to the floweret,
When he looks for honey-dew,
Through the leaves that close embower it,
That, my love, I'll be to you."

A frown had creased her forehead by the second line, and he'd considered stopping.

Had he made a fool of himself? He'd done worse – an early mission had involved pretending to be a mincing fop whilst at a French ball; it hadn't gone well as he'd been out-minced by other invitees.

She'd bitten her lip at the third line and his throat had tightened.

By the fourth line, her whole body had tensed.

However, now he'd finished, she leaned close, her lips grazing his ear, producing a shudder.

This was working. All would be well – good idea, Rakecombe.

Then she spoke, her voice a caressing whisper.

"But they say, the bee's a rover,
Who will fly, when sweets are gone,
And, when once the kiss is over,
Faithless brooks will wander on."

"What?" Bram jerked back. "I don't understand."

"I suggest, Lord Kelmarsh," she growled, all signs of befuddlement now gone, "that you read the *entire* poem when you plan to steal another's work. Thomas Moore is quite popular at the moment, and Aideen has all his melodies."

Words failed him, but actions were clear. He was going to pummel both Rakecombe and Winterbourne until they couldn't stand.

"Sophie, I…"

She fired him a quelling glare and he fell silent.

What a daft verse for Moore to give him and it wasn't even original – bloody poets!

For a brief moment, grovelling occurred, but he had a feeling rule number five could be correct in this case.

She'd knee him in the cods again.

"I meant every word, Sophie…just not the other bit."

Sighing, her shoulders drooped. "I do thank you for the presents. They were beautiful. But please, no more. It merely reminds me… So no more. If you would leave, I need to arrange my hair."

"Sophie–"

A steely determination glinted in her eyes as she stared him straight. "I beg you to leave me alone."

He wasn't sure if she meant now or permanently, and because he couldn't bear the latter, he chose to follow the former and stood. "I shall call on you, Sophie. We are not finished, not by a long shot."

A hesitant nod was her only answer and so with no words left, he turned to walk towards the candlelight and raucous din of the house.

6

A MOST CURIOUS INCIDENT.

Sophie shifted on the chaise, kicked off her slippers and leaned back against a rather lumpy cushion. Her cousin sat by the window, engrossed in a book, but Sophie's mind kept wandering from her own reading.

This morning, she had discovered something strange. Something that couldn't easily be explained.

After the lateness of the rout, they'd thankfully not had many callers and so decided to pass a congenial day with studious pursuits...or generally lolling around. A lazy day, she acknowledged, but since they'd arrived in London, their slippers had not touched the ground.

The earlier bizarre occurrence led her to flip the pages back again. She hadn't been concentrating.

"Do you think this Mr Darcy is a blackguard?" Sophie asked.

"Erm," her cousin replied, without looking up. "Well, if someone called me 'tolerable', you know what I would do. Mr Darcy has a lot of grovelling to be done, that's for sure, but there is something attractive about the conceited man. He reminds me of..."

"Who?"

No answer was forthcoming so Sophie glanced up to discover her cousin had put the book down and was gawking.

"Sophie, why have you a pair of spectacles on?"

"Hmm. Yes. Well, I found out something odd today."

"That you can't see?"

"These are Bram's spectacles."

"You filched them?" Aideen asked with glee, rubbing her hands together.

"Not really. He left them on the bench when..." Sophie needed to say no more, having already confided in Aideen about last night's exploits. And indeed, her cousin's night had been similarly interesting.

"And what's so odd then?"

"They are glass."

"Well, yes, they wou–"

"No, I mean, *glass*. Plain, ordinary glass. No magnification or whatever the opposite is. I can see perfectly in them. I've read all the way to Mr Darcy's most abysmal proposal."

"He proposes? To Elizabeth? Don't tell me any more. Does she say yes? Does he get on one knee?"

"I never took you for a romantic, Aideen."

"I'm not. I'm hoping she says no."

Sophie eyed her cousin suspiciously. Aideen was good at telling whiskers but if you knew her well, you realised she always played with a curl in her hair when fibbing, twirling the raven lock around her finger.

"Enough of the brooding Darcy," Aideen proclaimed.

"Why would Kelmarsh wear spectacles if he doesn't need them?"

"I've been puzzling over that all morning."

"Habit? Fashion? To make himself look scholarly?"

Sophie merely shook her head and pushed the frames back up her nose as they slid down once again. She recalled cursing his spectacles, as she could never tell his expression or what he was looking at.

"I believe he hides behind them."

"Does he? But why?" Aideen asked.

"That is what I don't know."

"Intriguing. They certainly formed a peculiar assemblage of bugs last night, those three peers – Lazy, Libertine and… I can't think of any L's to describe His Grace."

"Leashed? Laconic? Loner? Large and lichen-eyed?"

"No, his eyes are more like fresh spinach."

"And you say you're not a romantic."

"If I was, I would have said slimy seaweed."

Sophie burst out laughing as Aideen abandoned her chair and came to sit on the chaise, hauling Sophie's feet onto her lap. "What are you going to do about Kelmarsh?"

"I don't know. He keeps saying he has a reason for last year, but that he can't tell me yet." She took off his spectacles and handed them to her cousin, who peered through the lenses suspiciously as Sophie continued. "I wanted to hurt him last night. I let him kiss me because I had a mad plan. I wanted him to want me so much…and then I would spurn him. But then that ridiculous poem…"

"Sophie Beckford, there is not a vengeful bone in your body. That's why we all love you. Always managing to see the good in everyone. If the devil appeared from the county of hell, you'd probably ask if he wanted a cup of tea and tell him he'd been unfairly maligned."

"I'm not a paragon of virtue."

"Of course not. No one is. And anyway, that very trait can turn against you. Too trusting, too…"

"Easily duped?"

"Not now, my dearest cousin. Not after incapacitating an earl in the thingumbobs. Some characteristics we are born with, and others we have to learn through experience, which you certainly have. But the Holy Almighty should probably have blended the two of us. We would have been the perfect woman."

"God forbid," a voice mumbled, and they both looked up to see Papa gazing fondly at them. "My dears, Lord Winterbourne has sent you both half a garden of roses. Red for you, Aideen, and white for Sophie. There is also an invite to Gunter's confectioners for three days' hence. From what I know, the marquess is a rogue, but a decent rogue, so feel free to accept or reject as you wish." And he ambled out again.

Aideen rolled her eyes and slumped on the chaise. "The other two are certain to be there. The three of them seem joined at the hip. Do we dare?"

Nabbing the spectacles back, Sophie placed them atop her nose. "Why not? We are in London to enjoy ourselves and if they wish to buy us expensive ices, so be it. However, we'd better continue reading, as the heroine in this book has many a superb retort for arrogant, self-important, treacherous men."

"THE MOTH!"

Bram was late for the meeting with Asher but could hear Jack Winterbourne all the way down the corridor.

"Why can't I have something fearsome…like a bear or a lion. Not bloody *Moth*."

Knocking, a voice bade him enter and closing the door behind him, he glimpsed Rakecombe failing to suppress a smirk, Asher amused and Jack looking very disgruntled.

"You have your code name then?"

Jack sent him a disgusted scowl. "You got Wolf and I get Moth."

"We're not in this endeavour for the code names, Jack."

"I know that! I myself expounded on the use of sobriquets and the cachet they evoke, so no need to repeat my blasted words. But don't tell me you weren't pleased with Wolf. Moths are so easily killed for God's sake."

"Actually," Asher interjected, "they are wonderful inhabitants of the night. Light on the wing, silent in flight, quick and inventive. Masters of disguise. They hide their true self behind a façade of imitation."

Rakecombe sneered. "They also have a habit of flying too close to burning candles."

"Hmm," Asher murmured, fingers steepled under his chin.

Jack narrowed his eyes. "Still don't know your code name, Rakehell. But I wager it's likewise deficient, as otherwise you would have said. You wait till we have a mission together."

"I'd rather get ki–"

"Gentlemen. And I say that loosely. If we could get to the matter in hand."

The matter in hand was *La Chauve-Souris*, but although

Bram had wandered the hells and clubs all the nights since their last meeting, he'd heard nothing. People were oft surprised to learn he was a member of the three gentlemen's clubs – White's at eighteen years, Brooks's at twenty-three and Boodle's at twenty-five. Memberships discreetly arranged by Asher or, when he was alive, Bram's father.

Rakecombe, who operated in the more shadowy parts of London, hadn't turned up trumps either and Bram could detect the frustration leaching from his tall frame.

"I heard from Lady Falkirk," Jack was saying, "that a chap was asking a little too closely about her late husband's family. It was at her...*special* masquerade, so I've no facial description, I'm afraid, but short and spider-shanked. Could be coincidence."

"No such thing as coincidence. Remember Chadwick?"

"What else happened to that unfortunate fellow?"

"Ambushed," the three of them replied in unison.

"Anyhow, good work, Winterbourne. That's why you're the Moth. You gather information on the wing."

"Wasn't on the wing. I was on my bac–"

"If that is all?" Rakecombe grouched as he stood. "I've better things to do than listen to Winterbourne's smutty ramblings."

"I have some documents for you. Wait here one moment." Asher rose from his chair and strolled from the room.

"So, the rout," Jack began, "did your beloved wilt at the poetry? I lost that cousin and ended up in the card room playing piquet with Mr Beckford. Terribly nice fellow."

"That bloody poem has a second verse and she knew it too. All about unfaithfulness."

A cackle from Rakecombe and Bram glared. "I'm not

listening to either of you ever again or following any more of your *rules*." He stood, donning his gloves. "Although my thanks to you, Rakecombe, for occupying Miss Quinlan."

"She's a minx," he replied disdainfully. "Do you know, I trailed her all the way around the ground floor twice, the staircase thrice and then to the supper room. Lost her once in the portrait hall and then, without warning, she was there at my side, smirking."

"And you the shadowy spy. Did she say anything?"

There was a short pause and then a mumble, "Asked me why I was following her."

Bram suppressed his own guffaw of laughter but Jack didn't bother. "And?"

"I said I'd never followed a woman in my life."

"And? Any more?" He suspected there was so much more.

"She cursed me. Odious girl. I should've had her ejected and would have done so if not for her being Miss Beckford's cousin."

"I suppose those cherry-red lips and wild gypsy hair had no bearing?" Jack said, a sly glint in his eye.

"She's Irish."

"Pot, kettle and same burned arses," Jack retorted. "Your mother is of Welsh descent if I remember my Debrett's."

"Is she?" Bram had always wondered what that Welsh fisherman had said to him, standing on the harbour front nigh on a year past. For some reason, he'd always remembered it. "Can you understand the lingo? What does '*ynfytyn*' mean? Goodbye or something?"

"Imbecile."

"No need to be nasty," Jack said with a grin, and rising to join them, he straightened his already impeccably straight coat. "Rakehell showed his gratitude to you by inviting *us* to his rout, and I will show mine by inviting you both to Gunter's."

The duke threw Jack a contemptuous snarl. "I do not partake of ices. They are for children."

"Shame. Just Bram with Miss Beckford, and the alluring Miss Quinlan all to myself. Had a word with Mr Beckford last night over piquet, so it's all above board and proper. But you are correct, Rakehell, you would indeed be a fifth wheel."

'PLAY THE PART AND YOU SHALL BECOME.' (UNKNOWN)

$\mathcal{T}$rudging up his townhouse steps at three in the morning was becoming stale, thought Bram, as the yawning Tomkinson took his coat, gloves and hat.

"You should retire for the night," he instructed the butler. "I'll see to the lamps." The weary fellow didn't argue, well used to Bram's lifestyle, instead merely nodding whilst he found homes for the damp apparel.

The study looked remarkably cosy as Bram passed the half-open door, a single candle still burning, so he decided on a brief tipple before retiring himself. It was an old habit, and in past years he'd needed the liquor to quieten the thrumming of his body after a mission. These days, he felt nothing but weariness and a vague ache to his back.

After pulling at his boots and shrugging off the tight grey waistcoat, he collapsed into the high-backed leather armchair in the corner – all the better to view his two favourite paintings.

Prior to allowing himself such a luxury, he closed his

eyes and quaffed some very fine port, the sticky, sweet liquid soothing his parched throat.

Since the rout, he'd spent the days pursuing Sophie and the nights listening to absolute waffle, hoping for anything useful regarding the French spy. He'd not had much success with his amorous pursuit but the hunt for the Frenchman had seen some progress.

Exceedingly late the previous night in Boodle's, he'd heard talk of Jack's over-inquisitive masquerade man. Apparently, the fellow had lost heavily in one of the gaming hells off Covent Garden and had been seen leaving in the company of Lord Doverstone – a pleasant young cub and the son of an important minister. Bram had relayed the information to Rakecombe, glad he wasn't getting too involved in this one – a nasty piece of work by all accounts.

Sophie, on the other hand, always seemed to be one step ahead of him, and was proving more difficult to accidently happen upon than Hemlock Henri. Of course, that deadly chap wasn't meeting anyone after a fatal encounter with Rakecombe's cane.

Yesterday, Bram had managed to call upon the Beckford household, gaining entry on Winterbourne's coat tails. It had not been a congenial morning. Sophie's mother had constantly sniffed her displeasure, Mr Beckford's piercing gaze had speared right through him and Sophie had been surrounded by a host of suitors, including that goggling Stanton from Almack's.

Never did he think to say it, but thank God for Jack and his Gunter's invite, as otherwise he'd be utterly in the woods. Of course, trying to talk to Sophie in a tea shop would hardly be intimate and one always had to have a back-up plan.

Interrogating the Beckford kitchen boy after yesterday's disastrous morning call, he had gained knowledge they'd all be attending Drury Lane Theatre in a couple of nights' time. Maybe the privacy of a candlelit box would be more conducive to conversation, although he'd heard sapscull Stanton was also to attend – another matter to take care of when he was there.

Opening his eyes, he gazed at his retirement.

One painting was of his estate, land and a country manor he hadn't seen in years and of which he solely had fond memories. Although the reports from his trusted estate manager were always glowing, he'd probably find the house itself could do with more than a few repairs when he finally took up residence.

In bygone years as a boy, when his parents had been on Crown missions afar, he had spent blissful summers there. Riding, reading and helping the villagers with the harvest – idyllic times. Bram found he had a curious talent for crop management, and he'd adored the wide-open spaces, the smell of hay. Also, in a most un-earl-like way, he had discovered the enjoyment of getting his hands dirty. He would have received the hiding of his life if he'd told his parents he'd spent half the summer of his fourteenth year digging up potatoes.

The estate kept a good supply of flourishing livestock – sheep, pigs and the occasional cow – but it had been the goats he'd loved the best. Sheep had appeared half-witted to him as a boy, cows too slow and pigs too slothful, but the goats had those intelligent eyes – they knew exactly the mischief they caused.

Neither of his parents had enjoyed the countryside, preferring the hustle and cramped alleyways of the City.

And, of course, the Kelmarsh family had been in the service of the Crown since Domesday, so London was where they belonged...as he'd been told endlessly.

He pulled his eyes from the tranquil painting to the smaller one beside it. Not his best, Bram acknowledged, as he'd never quite been able to capture Sophie's expression and he'd rushed it. Painting would be another pastime to catch up on when entrenched on his estate, rusticating.

Of course, this peaceful future all depended on a certain lady. It wouldn't be the same if he had to quote Propertius to the pigs and paint only landscapes. Sophie needed to be there – walking the fields, discussing the crops, reading together, loving together.

Lately, he wondered if she had changed her mind about living in the country. On returning from Ireland, she now seemed more at home in London, enjoying all its attractions, whereas a year ago, she'd confided that she disliked the noise, the dirt and the hemmed-in feeling – exactly like himself.

What did he have to offer if Sophie preferred a different way of life now?

The portrait depicted a slightly plumper girl, and he was mightily glad she hadn't lost weight from her lush backside and generous breasts. Certainly, that princox Stanton seemed to agree, and at his height he did have a perfect view.

Bram scrutinised her hair: the colour wasn't quite right either as he'd had trouble with the browns and had swirled them all together until she resembled a squirrel. At the Kelmarsh estate, he would take his time. Study every strand closely and measure every delectable inch with his fingers.

Closing his eyes again, he wondered if he'd fallen in love

with Sophie instantly, or whether it had taken time. Was it even possible to just hear a voice once and *know*?

He'd been feigning a doze at the Wilshire's annual ball. A meeting had been discovered between two suspected traitors and Bram had settled down on the chaise in the corner of the study – himself a study of fatigue, drunkenness and sloth. The rendezvous had indeed taken place and noticing Bram, they'd even joked about his indolence and askew cravat. Bram had snored slightly and they'd left him alone, letting him into all sorts of secrets.

Soon after they'd departed and Bram had been about to rise, the door had opened again. He'd closed his eyes and wilted back onto the plush blue velvet.

A single pair of light feet had entered and crossed the room, the smell of fresh fields drifting in their wake. He'd kept his eyes closed and used other senses to build a picture.

Lavender and hay, so probably young. Lots of rustling, so a fairly frilly dress, probably white. A light step, so waif-like.

And then it spoke.

"I hate you," it said and the mere sound shot pure lust down his body, landing in his groin. "I hate you, too," it continued.

The female's voice was breathy – it reminded him of satin sheets and rumpled hair. It reminded him of soft skin and exactly how long it was since he'd been with a woman.

But who exactly was she talking to? He'd heard no more than one set of steps.

"Men only ever look at you. I hate you both. And I also hate pink ruffles. I resemble a pig. A pig with child."

Bram had to look.

Opening one eye, he glimpsed a girl with rich coffee-coloured hair prodding her bosoms – a look of utter loathing on her face. Yes, the ruffles were a little excessive, but as to the rest of her diatribe, he certainly couldn't agree.

She was scowling into a mirror set above the fireplace, and so he had the benefit of being able to see both front and back of the girl. Her bosom was indeed impressive, and he couldn't blame chaps for staring. Two lovely slopes of alabaster skin that made his hands – and other parts – twitch. Pink silk clung to a lush rump and, compelling his eye to rise, he surveyed her glossy walnut ringlets. He was too far away to see her eye colour, but she'd clear soft skin, rose lips and a pretty but angry face.

The bosoms were prodded again in distaste, and Bram shifted uncomfortably, wishing the girl would stop doing that. She whirled around at the movement and he hurriedly shut his eye – it was beginning to water anyway.

A stirring of air cooled him and then he felt a soft prod on his arm. The scent of meadows deepened to early summer – ripe but fresh.

"Excuse me, sir. But are you well?"

He almost arched at her touch. Nobody in the four years he'd used this persona had ever shown any concern for his welfare. There'd been laughter at his expense, smirking, light shoves but mostly he'd been ignored. Which was exactly what he wanted and exactly how it should be, it being the haughty ton and all that.

"Sir?" she said again, lightly shaking him.

What was the girl about? Propriety dictated she should leave. He could be some drunken mauler about to kiss her. Or a penniless fortune hunter after a tidy dowry. Did she have no sense of self-preservation?

Sleepily opening both lids this time, he looked up...and

up, remembering her tirade, to meet a pair of cinnamon-coloured eyes framed by coffee lashes. He wanted to taste them.

"I fell asleep," he mumbled instead.

"Oh. Well, the ball is quite dull."

A bark of rusty laughter escaped him. "Yes, it is. And what are you doing in here?"

She fiddled with her reticule. "I don't really like balls. All the" – she twirled her gloved fingers in the air – "fopping around. I'm not even sure that's a word."

"I do agree. And the Wilshire's are the worst."

Now that the girl stood close, he carefully surveyed her pretty features, drinking in her deep autumn-coloured hair and sweet face. Inhaling deeply, the scent of harvest assaulted his senses, making him wish for hot days and cool cider atop a freshly cut haystack. He should have got to his feet in the company of a lady but he couldn't seem to move.

"Have you seen the bird cage?"

Bram shook his head; he hadn't even seen the ballroom.

"They have all these exotic birds in it. It's so old-fashioned and they look so frightened by all the chatter and heat. The only highlight was when a smaller bird escaped through the bars and left a deposit on the refreshments table. I...I want to set them all free."

"They wouldn't survive in our climate."

"Then they shouldn't have been removed from theirs."

She'd stood there, harshly biting her lip, and Bram had just stared, wanting nothing more than to scoop the girl up and disappear into the night.

Instead, he'd escorted her back to the ballroom, sought an introduction and begun courting Miss Sophie Beckford the very next day.

Meeting her that evening had reminded him of every single thing he'd ever wanted, every solitary dream he'd ever had as a youngster, and although some might say he led an exciting life, there was not one hour of his current existence he'd dreamed about in the same way.

He wanted a loving wife. He wanted to work on his estate, to translate ancient texts, to tend his villagers and to raise children, pigs and wheat – in any damn order.

The last of the port was gone, and Bram wearily sat forward. He'd be in no fit state if he fell asleep here, waking to a painful back and numb arm. Hellfire, he only had four and thirty years, yet it felt double at times.

Glancing at his inept painting, he recalled Sophie's words to her own bosom. He needed that humour, that lack of artifice, that utter goodness.

When your whole life was based on falsehood and fabrication, one craved artlessness like an opium smoker craved their pipe.

8

BREAKFAST: THE MOST IMPORTANT MEAL OF THE DAY.

"Y ou look an absolute delight, Miss Beckford. Like a lettuce – all crisp and fresh."

"Thank you, Lord Winterbourne, such compliments can go to a girl's head."

The marquess strutted ahead to open the carriage door whilst Sophie ignored the sharp prod in her side. She'd chuckle if she peeked at Aideen.

"Lettuce?" the lilting whisper came anyway. "I thought he was a seducing rogue. He just called you a salad and me a cherry. What's wrong with the man – no breakfast?"

Struggling to suppress a snort, Sophie took the marquess's hand to ascend the carriage. It looked to be a spanking new landau and as the day was fine and dry, the hood had been set back. Today, her mother had declared a headache, and so the maid was also squashed in. More likely, Mama wished to admire Bram's mechanical swan and show it to her friends.

Gunter's establishment was situated a few short streets

away in Berkeley Square so it was hardly worth the carriage, but it gave work to the two footmen, coachman and young lad who clung precariously to the back, and the company was jovial with her cousin in fine looks.

The wind drifted wild curls across Aideen's face and Sophie couldn't help but notice Winterbourne's admiring glance. Did he have an interest in Aideen? Was that the reason for today's invitation?

Her cousin's bold beauty and temperament appealed to many men, although they seemed to divide into two factions: those who wished to tame her – a strategy steeped in failure – or those who considered themselves similarly wild and hence thought they could be wild and wicked together. She had to acknowledge a third faction also existed: one that ran scared.

What none of them saw was Aideen's steadfast loyalty, her staunch honour, albeit a little skewed on occasion, and that deep within, she was a hopeless romantic – slimy seaweed indeed.

"Here we are, ladies. I can foresee that sweet indulgences await me."

The Marquess of Winterbourne winked before dashing from his seat, emerald-green coattails whipping their skirts in his haste. Sophie took his immaculately gloved hand to alight from the carriage, and with a deep breath and firm resolve, she headed for the tea shop.

"IF YOU KEEP STARING at Miss Quinlan in that way, I'll be forced to trot out Jack's rule twenty-six."

"I am only in attendance, Kelmarsh, to ensure you don't

mess it all up again and not for any other pretty reason."
Rakecombe shot him a scowl as they stood beneath a leafy
plane tree, watching the threesome plus maid enter the
confectioners. "And besides, I do not stare. I survey and
scrutinise. If I am to consume ices, I need to know the
layout of the establishment, the individuals present and the
options available for escape."

"It's ices at Gunter's, not Paris in '08," Bram chided. He
and Rakecombe went back years, although lately they had
seen less of each other, their paths having veered.

Rakecombe raised a brow, however, and Bram was
forced to concur. "Very well, it could be considered similar
to that ambush in Tortoni's, but hopefully without the
swordplay. Although with you and Jack, one never knows."

"Don't tell him, but I have a slight fondness for
Winterbourne. His principles are solidly unwavering, if a
tad dubious, and he grows on you...not unlike a wart."

That admission was most unlike Rakecombe. Was age
softening him? "Really? Next you'll be telling me that you
plan on courting and marrying one day... Not Jack
obviously," he added, just to clear up any misunderstanding
while he pulled down his cuffs, which had caught further up
his too-tight sleeves.

Silence ensued except for Rakecombe's cane, tapping on
the patchy bark of the tree. "No," he replied. "You can rest
assured that won't ever happen."

Deciding that was enough male confidences for one day,
Bram hastened across the street to the confectioners. A few
barouches dotted the square, with Gunter's waiters rushing
to them, supplies of their famous goods in hand.

Once inside, they both sauntered languidly, pointing out

various delicacies, sidling past waiters and nodding at several acquaintances, until happening to come upon the very table where Jack and the ladies sat, perusing the list of ices.

"Winterbourne, is that you? Ladies? What a pleasant surprise."

For Bram's nonchalant greeting, he received a quirk of the lips from Sophie and a rolling of eyes from Miss Quinlan. Perhaps it was a good thing retirement neared – he was losing his touch.

"*Quelle coincidence!*" Jack replied theatrically. "Do join us, Kelmarsh. And is that the genial Rakecombe hiding behind your tailcoat?"

They all sat, shuffling the fragile chairs, with Bram managing to place himself next to Sophie, the duke on her other side. Hopefully that meant nosy Miss Quinlan would not be able to interrupt.

The elegant red-clothed table felt notably petite for them all, but he could hardly complain about being so closely pressed against Sophie.

She wore a deep-moss velvet pelisse over a mint-green day dress and looked as natural as spring. Thankfully, she'd forsaken those huge goddamn ugly bonnets for a small cap-like structure and he had a clear view of her glossy hair and fine profile.

Unfortunately, sitting this close also meant he felt every brush of her skirt against his leg and every graze of her arm against his. Torture. Her very nearness provoked every inch of skin to leap with desire and here he was surrounded by bloody cakes.

"I think the cinnamon ice, please," requested Sophie of

the smartly aproned waiter. The chap scribbled away before raising haughty Mediterranean eyebrows at the rest of them.

Bram concentrated on the list. "For me..."

"Coffee," both he and Sophie said simultaneously. And that soul-searing craving clawed at his gut again. To have this woman *know* him...

"What will you be having, Your Grace?" Miss Quinlan asked.

A glowering look was bestowed upon her. "Cherry," he finally barked.

"What is it with you gentlemen and cherries today?" the cousin grumbled. "I'll try the champagne ice."

They all waited for their delights with Jack and Miss Quinlan providing most of the chatter. Rakecombe solemnly lounged, arms crossed as usual.

Their small party had created quite a stir in the tea shop and he felt a hundred curious eyes upon them: matrons gossiped behind gloved hands and young maidens smiled coyly at Jack whilst sipping China's finest brew. Desperately, Bram tried to think of an appropriate conversation to have with Sophie, but everything felt trite.

"I'm sorry about the poem," he finally whispered. "Moore didn't say it had a second verse. I supposed it original." The room buzzed with the chatter of elegant patrons as startled nutmeg eyes collided with his.

"You never said you met the man," she replied, equally hushed.

"Yes. Before the rout. I don't usually apportion blame but...it was all Rakecombe's idea."

"Truly? I never would have taken him for the poetic sort."

"Rakecombe's... People are never as they seem, Sophie."

She nodded and toyed with her reticule for a moment before delving inside. A small handkerchief was produced and, after unravelling it, she brought forth his spectacles, laying them on the table, her fingers on the lenses.

"You left these on the bench that night. I knew you'd have a spare pair."

Dread knotted his throat. Had she noticed they were plain glass? He could explain it with some untruth, but his promise to always be honest kept him silent.

"I read half my book whilst wearing them."

Damn.

"I can imagine you in my spectacles. Very prim... Sophie...soon..."

Those coffee curls quivered as she shook her head. "Is it all a pretence, Bram? Is anything real?"

Leaning forward, he placed his fingers over her hand, which still held the lenses. "My need of you, my feelings for you, are no pretence. They are real. You're the only one who sees the real me. And you do, don't you, Sophie?"

She worried her lip, and he brought a hand from beneath the table to raise a finger to her mouth but a sharp elbow in his side halted him.

Gunter's. Respectability. Tea shop.

"Ices, everyone," Jack bellowed.

The delicacies within the silver goblets were exquisite, despite the questionable colours. For as long as he could remember, he'd adored coffee and this ice was obviously made from the choicest of beans. In fact, the whole shop was imbued with the scent of sugar, coffee and chocolate, and he speculated as to whether a young boy was hired to fan the smells of baking into the shop in order to boost revenue.

"How is your ice, Lord Winterbourne?" asked Miss Quinlan.

"Revolting. The menu said it was parmesan flavour and it was right. Shouldn't be allowed. And yours?"

"I prefer actual champagne. This is a little diluted but delightful nonetheless. Are you enjoying the cherry, Your Grace?" she queried, licking the spoon slowly and fluttering her lashes.

Bram observed him tense, those ducal eyes narrowing on the cousin. Was the girl playing with fire on purpose? She seemed to suppose, as most did, that Rakecombe needed his aloofness...prodding somewhat.

What she didn't know was that Bram had once seen the duke's temper unleashed – it hadn't been pretty, with few men left standing. If Rakecombe chose to vent that same temper in carnal passion, he doubted this woman would be left on her feet either.

"It is...tolerable," the duke finally replied.

Sophie and her cousin raised hands to lips, unable to withhold their laughter.

"Did I utter something amusing?" the duke enquired, unamused.

"It appears, Sophie, that like the detestable Mr Darcy, His Grace is in no humour at present to give consequence to flavoured ices."

A teasing smile crossed Rakecombe's lips and Sophie's own mouth gaped slightly. Without his cold detached expression, he appeared younger, relaxed, green eyes gleaming with mirth.

"'My faults, according to this calculation, are heavy indeed,' Miss Quinlan," he replied.

Sophie applauded the adroit retort but her cousin's brow creased.

"Is that a quote? I haven't read past Mr Collins's proposal yet," Aideen said with a rueful glance at the duke. "We'll have to wait a few days to continue this exchange, though I never would have taken you for a reader of novels, Your Grace. Especially not that novel."

Sophie marvelled further as a burgundy hue rippled across Rakecombe's sharp cheekbones.

"I do read prodigiously, in fact."

The duke seemed to have hidden depths. "Including Thomas Moore?" Sophie enquired.

"Some, yes. Did Kelmarsh tell you we met him? Pleasant fellow, if a bit…flighty."

Bram grimaced and not just because he'd finished his coffee ice. "Modern poetry really isn't to my taste."

"Yes, of course," agreed Rakecombe. "You like the old works, do you not? Invariably had a volume of Catullus or some other fusty tome tucked in your coat."

With the duke's words, memories wrapped themselves around Sophie. Memories she'd tried to forget. Of Bram whispering ancient poetry in her ear. If he'd quoted one of those at the rout, it was likely she would have melted into a puddle.

"Kelmarsh, give us something decent to outdo Thomas Moore," Jack requested.

Reaching up, Bram removed his spectacles and placed them on the table. Today, without them, he appeared tired. Dusky shadows darkened his features and as he focused that startling blue upon her, she saw a deeper tiredness, a weariness of the soul.

"*Differtur numquam tollitur ullus amor,*" he said gently.

Sophie returned her spoon to the empty goblet. "Love may be delayed but not destroyed. The poet Propertius, I believe."

"You remembered."

Of course she did. The memories may be buried deep, but Bram's closeness, the sweet smell of coffee and the scorching directness of his eyes – they unearthed them all. She curtly nodded and ignored the smile that crossed his face.

Ancient words were all very well but they could never erase the ones she had overheard just last year.

"And do you remember this?" he asked, clearing his throat.

"Qvaeris, quot mihi basiationes
tuae, Sophie, sint satis superque.
quam magnus numerus Libyssae harenae
lasarpiciferis iacet Cyrenis."

A heated blush rose to her cheeks, her mouth drying. This poem spoke of desire. It asked how many kisses could satisfy a man: as many as the sand crystals that covered Libya? As many as the stars in the sky? This poem conveyed hunger and longing and it echoed down the centuries – as true in this year of 1814 as for the poet who'd written it all those years ago.

It inflamed her, and he was quoting it in this crowded tea shop, this ordinary establishment full of innocent cake and frozen ices.

Words no one else knew.

"Sophie, are you well?" Bram whispered. "You're flushed."

Twisting to face him, she saw that same smouldering heat in his ocean-coloured irises. Dark lashes framed the raging blue, and she suddenly understood why he wore spectacles. His eyes revealed all. They were real and alive and so very, very distracting. They shone with truth and emotion. But also, they revealed he'd known exactly what he was doing when he'd spoken those words, known precisely how they would make her feel.

It was romantic but underhand, passionate yet calculated, and it jumbled her emotions into a higgledy-piggledy ball of confusion and muddle.

She should feign ignorance but honesty was a characteristic she'd never quite been able to shake off. "You know I adore those verses, my lord. 'Tis most unfair to bestow them here."

A smile crinkled his eyes, dispelling the world-weary expression. "I will use any means to regain your faith in me, Sophie."

Would he? But her faith had been inextricably abused less than one year ago and she had yet to hear an explanation.

"Why not truth then?"

Silence was his reply and Sophie quashed the self-hatred that overcame her as the curve to his lips waned and he replaced the silver spectacles upon his nose, turning back to the table and its conversation.

She forced herself to remember last year – the pain of hearing him denounce her as an unexciting broodmare, but as he smiled at one of Winterbourne's sallies, she noted the slump of his shoulders, the clench of his gloved hand upon the table, the tightness of his jaw, the anguish.

Yet how could she relent? Her heart may speak its pleasure, but her instinct screamed louder: how could she ever trust him again?

9

A PLAY IN TWO PARTS. PART I – DESIRE AND MADNESS.

"*D*on't gape, daughter dear. Or you, Aideen."

Sophie snapped her mouth shut, although they really weren't to blame. It was the first time they'd visited the new Theatre Royal in Drury Lane after the previous one had burned down and the sight was truly magnificent. The grand entrance gave way to a spacious hall, with doors leading off into a beautiful rotunda, and thereafter passages led to lavish and spacious stairs. Two huge Corinthian columns loomed, with ten pilasters on each side, the whole effect being of opulence and splendour.

"Where are we sitting, Mama? Have we hired a box or–"

"Oh, did I forget to mention? We have been invited to use His Grace's box for the evening. Such a pleasing, amiable gentleman. I happened upon him in New Bond Street yesterday whilst shopping for ribbons. You two had your noses in that book, so I didn't ask you along."

"Do you know a lot of dukes, Mrs Beckford?" came a strangled voice.

"You must call me Edwina as I've told you before, Aideen dear. And no, just the one."

"And will this duke be here tonight?"

Sophie noticed Aideen clutch her lucky pendant – it was of a clover and as far as she could tell not very lucky, although to be truthful, she was unsure of the answer Aideen wished for.

"Oh, I doubt it. A duke must have so many…dukely duties. And yet he maintains such a polite manner."

Aideen snorted. "It can't be the same one then." And they dashed after Mama, who was asking an attendant the way.

The box they found themselves in was most generous in space and situation. It could easily hold eight and was decked in green and gold. The whole theatre gleamed with sumptuousness as the crimson relief on the front of surrounding boxes caught the candlelight.

Being a quarter after the hour of six, she and Aideen made use of their time gawking at the assembling audience and magnificent stage. The theatre, she always felt, held such appeal: innocent debutantes mixed with women of rather dubious reputation and dress, adding to an atmosphere already excited and heightened by the lavish decor. The place was packed to the rafters, even though Edmund Kean wasn't to play Hamlet tonight because of a chill to the chest.

With the official performance time nearing, a rustle of their box curtain compelled them to turn as Stanton appeared, bowing to her mother.

Sophie did not dislike the fellow as he was amusing in his own way, but she forever felt the need to raise his chin with one hand and point instead to her eyes. A year ago, such *admiration* had made her uncomfortable, but now she merely felt vague irritation at his total lack of decorum.

"Ah, two lovely Ophelias to entertain. Your mother has invited me to keep you company during this tedious play. I shall endeavour to amuse with my own poetry." He made a leg, his eyes unwaveringly low.

"We were quite looking forward to the play, Mr Stanton," Sophie answered, stamping on Aideen's foot to halt the snigger.

"Oh." He looked most disappointed. "You're aware Kean's not playing?"

"Nevertheless, we were hoping to listen and watch."

"Very well, if you must. I shall explain salient points to you then. Hamlet is not the easiest to understand."

Choking back laughter, Sophie sat as the orchestra struck up to announce Act I, Scene I.

ACT I, Scene IV and she'd had quite enough.

"Note the tragic expression on Hamlet's face. I believe he may–"

"Mr Stanton, I am more than capable of following the play without any type of com–"

A fracas with the curtain interrupted her before Lord Winterbourne drifted in. Holding a finger to his lips, he glared at Stanton who was obliged to give up his chair to the peer, relegating him to the rear of the box.

Sophie smiled her gratitude, and now the irritation had been dealt with, she leaned forward, resolving to listen to the play.

However, it seemed that without the masterful acting of Kean, the audience had simply come to chatter, wander around and…and some bucks in the pit were even playing cards. The cacophony half-drowned out the ghost wailing of revenge.

Not a moment later, there was another disturbance of the curtain and Sophie snapped her fan. It was bad enough endeavouring to hear the tragedy unfolding on stage above the general din of the theatre without people traipsing into the box late.

Twisting, she was about to scowl at the newcomer when a tall dark figure draped itself over the chair directly behind Aideen. Her cousin, oblivious it seemed to the noise and disturbance, continued to bite her lip and watch enthralled as Hamlet insanely expounded upon heaven and earth.

His Grace, the Duke of Rakecombe, also put a finger to lip and smiled benignly at Mama, who fluttered her feather fan in salutation. There followed a scrape of chair feet and creak of wood as he shuffled closer to the front of the box. Sophie assumed he required a clear view, but it was a wonder Aideen didn't feel his breath on her bare nape. The loose tendrils of her cousin's hair stirred with his exhalations yet she remained oblivious, watching the play with rapt attention.

The auditorium quietened somewhat as though the appearance of His Grace had silenced them all, although that was ludicrous really.

Lord Winterbourne slumped in his chair, not feeling the need to comment on the actor's facial expressions or methods, and the duke sat as though he'd stared into Medusa's eyes.

Finally Sophie could relax.

Another swish ensued as the curtain was fumbled with again.

"Sit down whoever you are and be quiet," Sophie snarled in a whisper.

"Shush," said five mouths, including Bram's, whom she could now see entering the box in the intimate glow of the candlelight.

Throwing hands up in disgust, Sophie swivelled back to the stage and tried to ignore the raucous jostling for chair space. Considering the size of the duke's box, the front row was jammed absurdly tight, but now certain there could be no more latecomers, Sophie hoped to enjoy the play without further distraction.

How erroneous.

It appeared Lord Kelmarsh had not come to watch the performance either; indeed, she hadn't noticed his face directed towards the stage once.

He watched only her.

Commencing at Sophie's satin lilac slippers, his gaze caressed its way up her skirts, to her waist and then onto her bosom. Why did it feel different when Bram stared? Stanton produced a sensation of queasy dismay but with Bram's esteem, her breath became heavy and rapid.

Desperately, she tried to concentrate on Hamlet's soliloquy, but she could sense those eyes resting on her hair, mouth and throat. A gloved hand suddenly reached out and she gasped as Bram grabbed the long end of the violet ribbon tied beneath her bosom, his movements hidden by the crush of chairs. It was double knotted and unlikely to come loose, but from the corner of her eye, she noted him caressing the end, his thumb brushing over the velvet, occasionally tugging to haul her closer.

Hamlet bellowed, startling her and she peered around the box in appeal but Aideen remained engrossed, almost tumbling over the cushioned front in her eagerness to hear the words.

The Duke of Rakecombe declined to watch the play at all. Like Bram, his focus was elsewhere. His eyes raking, for want of a better word, Aideen's neck and shoulder. Winterbourne was miming something with his hands to a stunning lady in the adjoining box, Mama dozed, and Stanton was unravelling a seam on his embroidered waistcoat.

Gulping, she felt that tug on her ribbon again.

"Sophie." Her name was whispered, low and imploring, and she turned to the plea.

He'd removed his spectacles and that gaze almost made her weep. Fatigue cloaked his eyes, and he looked...lost, which was preposterous as he was a fully grown man of thirty something years.

"Sophie, I need you."

BRAM DIDN'T KNOW what else to say.

Last night, he'd realised that love had never been mentioned. A year ago, their affection had newly begun and it hadn't seemed right. Now he knew the emotion he felt, but grasped that Sophie would only view it as a toadying platitude.

And certainly, the time to reveal his love was not in a theatre surrounded by family, libertines and a deadly duke.

Sophie made no reply, just gazed at him, and he ached to lean close, to kiss her, to feel her breath, that sweetness on his tongue. Finally, she opened her lips to speak.

"By the goats in Gorey, where did all you come from?"

It took several moments to realise it was the cousin

speaking, and that the play had paused for an interval. Jack endeavoured to disentangle the chair legs whilst Miss Quinlan accidently slammed her chair onto Rakecombe's foot. To his credit, he didn't flinch, merely glowering at the girl as she smiled wickedly.

Sophie was already rising to step through the gap that Jack had created. "If you will excuse me, Lord Kelmarsh, I am in need of some refreshment." The gawking Stanton held out his hand.

And she accepted it.

Bram sprung to his feet, but Rakecombe got in the damn way, standing like a granite sculpture and forcing Miss Quinlan to either sidle around the back or brave the front. She chose the back, sensible girl, but as she disappeared behind his tall frame, Rakecombe's body abruptly stiffened and his eyes widened.

Now the theatre box had some breathing room, he made to follow Sophie. That coxcomb could never protect her from the crush of the refreshments table – it would be like feeding time for the hounds.

Just as he grabbed at the curtain, now sagging considerably lower at one end, a sharp pain seared his gut.

A stiletto dagger?

A poison dart?

Had his career finally caught up with him when he was so near to giving it all up?

Flicking his gaze downward, he observed an innocent feather fan pressed into his gizzards. It was only when one looked closely that one noticed, hidden behind the white feathers, a bone decoration in the shape of a pineapple – complete with pointed top.

He followed the line of the fan up a slender arm and

then on to meet a shoulder veiled in pink. Upwards, his gaze finally encountered a pretty face full of distrust and a fair amount of irritation.

Mrs Beckford.

"My husband," she whispered harshly, "tells me I should forgive you." The weapon dug deeper. "But if you harm my daughter's heart once more, I will hunt you down, cut off your tallywags and feed them to my cat... He'll eat anything. Are we quite clear, Kelmarsh?" The weapon twisted – she'd be drawing blood soon.

"Quite clear, Mrs Beckford. I..." He stopped, unable to declare his ardent affection before he'd even told Sophie, but the lady merely studied him for a moment and then nodded, retracting her formidable armament, his skin refusing to return to its former shape.

"Go after my daughter. I don't trust Stanton to find a trollop in a brothel let alone lemonade at a refreshments table." She fanned herself. "And put those spectacles back on – your eyes are a mirror to your emotions."

10

A PLAY IN TWO PARTS. PART II – THEY'VE ALL DIED.

To locate Sophie and the rest of their party took some while. The throng of bodies was immense, with ladies swirling to gaze at the ceilings and gentlemen swarming in search of champagne. Rakecombe scythed a path through the melee, his ebony cane tapping ominously on the floor if anyone dared to step across.

Bram picked out the marquess's broad back protecting the ladies, all standing by a statue of Janus, but he and Rakecombe solely observed for a while, until that conceited puppy Stanton whispered something improperly close to Sophie's ear and then headed for the gentlemen's retiring room.

Silent as shadows, they both followed.

A blue door off the upper hall indicated a room for gentlemen to perform any necessary ablutions and the sound of hilarity within could clearly be heard above the hubbub of the theatre. Rakecombe remained outside, loitering with intent.

Upon entering, he saw Stanton in the corner, relieving

himself in an ornate porcelain piss pot – not a pleasant sight: his aim as loose as his cravat.

A trio of men also stood in the room and Bram held three fingers around the door. He waited for them to fiddle with their cuffs, knowing no more would be incoming whilst Rakecombe guarded the entrance.

Relieved, the trio jovially departed whilst Stanton still preened himself in the mirror, straightening his atrocious loopy neckcloth and tousling his ridiculous hair.

Bram stepped behind, silent as Hamlet's father, until finally the coxcomb saw him and turned.

"Isn't it a wonderful play?" Aideen said with a whimsical tone.

"I'm amazed you could hear any of it with all the disturbances."

"What disturbances?"

Sophie eyed her cousin suspiciously, unsure if she was dissembling or not. Certainly she wasn't playing with her curls, but that would have been difficult holding a glass of champagne and slice of cherry cake.

"I'm surprised you didn't feel that breath shiver your neck."

"Was someone behind me?"

It was asked far too innocently for Sophie to believe her, and she couldn't help the peals of laughter that emerged.

A jostle of shoulder from behind pushed her towards Lord Winterbourne, who turned a menacing frown on the ruffian before bustling them closer to the protection of the statue. It seemed all and sundry had escaped their seats and were intent on shouting, gossiping and refilling their glasses for the next act.

"You *did* know the duke was there then?" Sophie whispered in her cousin's ear.

"Thatch, thistle, thunder and thump, I could detect his cologne as soon as he entered the box."

"I've never noticed his scent."

"Hmm. Subtle, not like Stanton's. Kind of...leather and chocolate."

"And do you like it?" Sophie asked innocuously.

Her cousin's dark eyes flashed. "Too starched for me."

"Who would that be?" interrupted Lord Winterbourne with a refill of champagne for them both. "Shall I guess? Begins with R and ends with– Hellfire! My foot."

Sophie glanced down to see an ebony walking cane digging into his evening shoes. All eyes trailed upward to find Rakecombe standing behind like the Grim Reaper, his black attire a solemn contrast to the light-blue satin jacket and striped waistcoat of the marquess.

"That's a lethal cane you have there, Your Grace," Aideen ventured.

The duke's eyes snapped to hers, suspicion tightening his features, but he shook his head as she sipped champagne, and slowly, with a deliberate twisting motion, he removed the pressure from poor Lord Winterbourne's foot.

"I think you've broken my toe, Rakehell."

"*Rakecombe* is an ancient Viking name." The duke sniffed. "Not some prattling insult."

It seemed the devil had gotten into her cousin tonight, and Sophie noticed a gleam in her eye as she insinuated herself between the two men glaring daggers at each other.

"Perhaps," Aideen purred, "His Grace would like some cake to ease his ill humour. It's cherry." And so saying, she took the fresh fruit from the top of the laden cake and immersed it in her champagne before nibbling at the edges, the cherry staining her lips an even deeper shade. "It's delicious, Your Grace. You should indulge yourself every now and again."

The duke's expression transfixed Sophie. Those spinach eyes altogether charred her cousin, who didn't seem to feel the incineration at all. He opened his mouth as if to speak, when abruptly all fire, all fervency, drained from him. His back straightened, eyes briefly closed, and then his expression turned cold and remote as an Irish windswept moor.

"Cherries have such a short season," he drawled flatly. "Sweet and ripe for a month, before they disappear into obscurity once more. Where they belong."

Aideen leaned forward, an angry red hue dusting her cheekbones. "Who got your starched cravat in a tangle? And to think I was beginning to deem you half-nice."

"Oh no, my little cherry," Rakecombe hissed. "I'm nowhere near nice. I'm a stiff, pedantic, priggish bas–" He caught himself in the nick of time. "*Duke*. And you had best remember that before you open your sweet mouth."

A stunned silence fell amid the clatter of other patrons around them. Aideen fumed, but Sophie could also see a wet sheen to those obsidian eyes, her hand slightly shaking on the champagne glass.

Sophie wanted to smash the Duke of Rakecombe's cane over his blasted head. How dare he upset Aideen in such a way? Yes, she'd been teasing him but it had been harmlessly done and not deserved such a vehement set down.

What was wrong with the man? He seemed to be both attracted to and yet troubled by her cousin in equal measure.

"Your Grace," Sophie found herself saying, "I believe your apology is due." Those ducal lichen eyes slammed onto her, but Sophie refused to look away and held her ground, unflinching. "If you cannot stand to be gently ragged, why attend a social gathering? We will depart this instant if our company is too vexing for you."

The duke continued to glare for some moments, until all of a sudden, his eyes softened and the tautness leached from his body.

"You remind me of my sister, Miss Beckford. She was also adept at making me feel like the veriest toad."

He twisted to Aideen, snatched the plate from her hands and placed it at Janus' marble feet. Sophie could not take her eyes from them as the duke raised her cousin's fingers to his lips and gently kissed the gloved tips.

"My behaviour to you merits the severest reproof. It was unpardonable. I cannot think of it without abhorrence... In more or less the words of that Mr D."

Aideen curtsied. "I am also at fault, Your Grace, and request your pardon. It seems I may have been dipped in the Shannon once too often."

All Sophie could manage was an astonished gawk: she'd never heard Aideen apologise either.

Catching the eye of a portly gentleman gazing over, it occurred to Sophie that their little scene had been witnessed by others too. She took a deep breath: had they really just remonstrated with a duke?

A touch of her waist and she spun to find Bram standing by her side. He wore his spectacles but she was close enough to see his earnest eyes. A raucous group of bloods bustled past, propelling him closer – lips met her ear with a whisper of words.

It sounded like...

Her cousin turned. "Sophie, do you wish to visit the retiring room with me before the next act of the play?"

"Erm..." She could only stare at Bram. Surely, he hadn't said... He couldn't have... "Erm, yes, thank you, that would be a splendid idea."

Aideen tugged her away from the gentlemen, their heads bowing for the ladies' departure.

It was a good thing Aideen gripped her close as Sophie's legs may surely have followed but her tumbling thoughts remained with Bram and his words, utter turmoil pounding at her resolve.

JACK PARTED his lips to speak.

"Not a warble out of you, Winterbourne," the duke warned before wheeling to Bram. "I like your Miss Beckford. Thought she was a bit shy at first but she's got some gumption. Reminds me of Gwen. Softly spoken until riled. Loyal."

Bram nodded. After taking leave of Stanton, he'd been caught by Lady Wittlesome and her five daughters, only arriving to hear Rakecombe's sour rebuke. He had thought to interfere when Sophie had spoken up.

Never had he felt such pride, such overwhelming admiration. It was no mean feat to stand up to Rakecombe – he made even the most hardened spies quiver, and yet she'd done it for Miss Quinlan. She had more bravery in her little toe than Stanton had in his entire trembling body.

But then...bugger.

Having been so full of emotion, he'd just blurted out those precious words. A shove in his side and abruptly there was Sophie's ear, her soft skin, the fragrance of lavender fields...of home, and he'd whispered it...

Damn, I love you.

Her stunned expression disclosed she'd vaguely heard him but–

"Do you think you're gaining ground in this pursuit?" asked Jack. "I wouldn't take any more advice from Rakeshame after that little performance."

Bram grinned and raised a quizzical eyebrow at the duke. "You and Miss Quinlan are like cat and dog. What's wrong with you? A pretty girl with a few impertinent lines doesn't usually get you so riled."

"I said sorry, goddammit."

"Not entirely," Jack corrected. "You just quoted the chap from that book and Miss Quinlan forgave you. I'll have to read it myself if he has such an effect on the ladies."

"She provoked me with her...words."

"Hardly blame the girl. You look at her like a stag on rut."

"I most certainly do n–"

"Well maybe you should. Indeed, how long is it since you've had a woman? Maybe that's why you snapped. We'll go to Covent Garden tonight. It might unbend that poker up your ars–"

"Let's return to the box, or we'll miss the play." Bram had a feeling these two could go on all night and he now suspected the duke purposely piqued Jack for the banter.

"No loss. It's not the same without Kean," grumbled Rakecombe.

. . .

ACT IV of the tragedy was more or less audible as the noisiest members of the audience had deserted the theatre during the last interval for more diverting entertainment. Bram sat quietly beside Sophie, now wishing he'd kept his trap shut. What a thoughtless time to garble those words.

On stage, Ophelia was slowly going insane, and glancing around, he noticed Miss Quinlan with streams of silent tears pouring down her cheeks. Rakecombe proffered a handkerchief.

He scrutinised Sophie to see if she was similarly affected, but her cheeks were dry. In fact, he could have sworn she wasn't heeding the play at all.

Winterbourne slouched whilst Ophelia drowned in the weeping brook. He appeared to be dozing, eyes tightly shut, but his fingers twitched as he clenched the armrests.

Bram lowered his own lids in concurrence.

Seemingly, a mere instant later, a light touch brushed his hand. "Bram." He almost moaned aloud on hearing his name spoken in such a husky manner. Was Sophie in his arms? He reached out to–

"Get up, Kelmarsh. They've all died and we can hunt some grub. I'm fair gutfoundered." Jack's voice rudely interrupted his sensual stirring and he opened his eyes. Sophie was leaning over him with a concerned expression.

"You should return home and get some rest, not go out for more carousing," she admonished.

"Someone has to keep those two in check. There'd be bloodshed otherwise."

She chuckled but forthwith looked up. "Whatever happened to Stanton? He never came back after the interval." Sophie's nose scrunched, and then she turned those nutmeg eyes on him again. "Did you have anything to do with his disappearance?"

Opening his mouth, he realised he was about to lie but he'd foolishly promised that would never happen again. He could do it regardless, but what if Stanton blabbed? She'd never forgive him.

"I told him that if he didn't stop looking at your...beauty, I would...see to him." More or less. In fact, it had involved the threat of breaking legs and been expressed a fraction more coarsely, but that was the general gist.

"You warned away my suitor?" She glowered. "You... you...carbuncle."

He laughed, unable to help himself, as a vague memory returned of her calling him that before she'd kneed him in the cods at Almack's.

The glare she unleashed could have frozen hell. "If you find my insults so amusing, I'll recite an Aideen curse. There's a nice one about a nettle patch." She stood, looking extremely displeased. "Have you warned away anyone else in London?"

Bram thanked God she'd said London, as he recalled the suitors he'd bought off in Ireland. The immorality of that endeavour was slowly sinking in...and Sophie's anger if she ever found out.

"No. But equally I stand by my actions tonight. He's a skulking jackanapes who leers at you."

"And you aren't?"

"No. I'm the man who's going to be your husband."

Silence swathed them, and he suddenly comprehended that everyone else in the box had been listening too.

"Daughter, dear," Mrs Beckford called stridently. "We will depart now. I believe the *gentlemen* need some time to themselves. They've had rather too much excitement at the theatre, one feels."

His beloved scowled and swanned through the curtain, followed closely by her family.

Taking off his spectacles, he rubbed at his aching eyes. He'd well and truly cocked that up.

11

WE'RE DOOMED...

"*Y*ou should try rule fifteen."

"Dare I ask?" garbled Bram into his jug of ale. What a damn disaster this evening had been... again. *I'm the man who's going to be your husband* – how condescendingly arrogant. Sophie must believe him to have windmills in his head.

"Seduction."

"I don't want Sophie in that way."

No response was forthcoming and he peered up to find his two companions gawping at him, confusion writ large across their features.

Rakecombe broke the awkward silence. "I may be somewhat puritan but I believe it would help in the marital bed if you lust after the girl."

"No, no, of course, I do. I mean I don't want to seduce her into marriage. It would be the last resort. I want her to...love me."

"Oh God," wailed Jack, "we're doomed."

The once plush but now threadbare red-cushioned seat

absorbed Bram as he settled back and drank more ale. After the theatre, they had made it as far as this alehouse opposite. The Lamb was actually quite pleasant – shabby but welcoming – and he recognised some of the actors laughing in a corner.

"There is no 'we' any more. After all your appalling advice, I'm better off going it alone."

"You don't want to do that. Remember Chadwick?"

"The poor chap's ambushed and dead," said Jack. "What more could have happened to him?"

"The reason he's in both of those states is because he decided to *go it alone*. Thought he didn't need his fellow comrades and never told anyone what he was up to."

"Rakecombe, it's hardly the same thing," Bram argued. "Besides, there's nothing more to try until I'm given clearance to tell her the truth. Although there's no guarantee Asher will do so," he added dismally. "And even then, Sophie may be repelled by our line of work."

"After today, I think she'll understand. Got some backbone, hasn't she? Just like Gwen."

"Who's Gwen?" piped up Jack. "I'll eat my cravat if she's an old paramour of yours."

The duke remained silent but his lips tightened, and Bram saw the old pain haunting his friend's eyes so replied for him. "She was Rakecombe's sister."

"I didn't know you had a... Was?"

"She died with eighteen years. I was but twenty-two. Long time ago now," Rakecombe replied, but even Jack must have heard the sorrow in his voice.

"My sympathies, Rakecombe." Jack placed a hand on the duke's tense shoulder. "I had an elder brother who died when I was at Eton. I still miss him after all this time." He drained his jug. "Do you have any siblings, Kelmarsh?"

Bram shook his head. "My parents didn't stay in one place long enough to procreate further."

"They liked to travel?"

This time it was the duke who straightened in his seat and answered for Bram. "The Kelmarshs have always been in the Crown's service. I vaguely remember Lord and Lady Kelmarsh. Both involved, were they not?"

"Yes. My mother as well. They dedicated their lives to it."

"But the latest Kelmarsh is retiring," said Jack.

Sprawling in his seat, Bram relished the word. "Indeed, I no longer have the determination. And men who no longer have determination in this profession..."

"End up like Chadwick?"

"He's learning," approved Rakecombe.

"But to have the happy retirement, you need the woman. Have you considered gifts?"

"I've sent Sophie a handpicked present every twenty-second of the month for the past ten months. The day we were due to be married."

That quietened them...for a moment.

"Miss Beckford is more stubborn than I first perceived," Rakecombe mused. "Must be the cousin's influence. Cockish wench."

A sniggering Jack refilled his jug. "I rather like her. She takes you down a peg."

"Bah! Girl had the gall to pull my coattails tonight."

Bram was about to ask if that was all she'd done when a commotion at the entrance distracted him. A small, dark, shabby-looking fellow fell through the door to be greeted with cheers and slaps on the back. He collapsed in a corner

111

seat, growled at the barmaid and then hid behind a jug of ale.

"Bloody hell," said Rakecombe. "Do you know who that is?"

Twisting, Bram gave the man a second look. "Arsenic Archie? Stiletto Sancho?"

"No, you fool. That's Edmund Kean, the actor."

He scrutinised more closely. Previously, he'd never had much interest in the theatre, there being enough artifice in his life as it was without paying to see more, but even he had read the acclaimed reports of the celebrated actor, who'd seemingly come from nowhere at the beginning of the year. "He's much smaller than one would imagine from the playbills."

"More than makes up for it on stage. I was invited to attend his first performance of Shylock in January."

Jack cleared his throat. "I heard that was only for a select few."

The usual scathing expression creased Rakecombe's face. "I *am* a duke. And moreover, I donate to that theatre."

"So do I actually. I have a little opera dancer tha–"

"That's it," said Rakecombe suddenly.

"At last!" bellowed Jack. "A little opera dancer is exactly what you need. I'll introduce you to Millie. She's bound to have a friend with the gypsy look and deep-red lips."

"What are you gabbling about, Winterbourne, you bottle-headed cock-bawd?"

"I say, that's a bit harsh. Just trying to resolve your cherry itch."

The duke stood, his mien particularly forbidding. "We are here to fix Kelmarsh's problem but this does kill two birds with one stone. Sluice your gobs and come meet Kean."

"So, how would one act the wicked seducer then?" Rakecombe was enquiring.

"Wouldn't it be better if I played him?" Jack argued. "I *do* have a reputation."

"But everybody knows you don't debauch innocents, and furthermore you are amusing, affable and wouldn't harm a fly. Whereas I, on the other hand, am already in disgrace with Miss Beckford. I'm hostile, pitiless and–"

"A strait-laced prude! It's too out of character."

"Excuse me, gentlemen," a strident but raspy voice interjected, "with proper acting, anything is possible. You can make people believe *anything*."

Rakecombe sat upright, looking pleased with himself. "Listen to Master Kean here. I may even enhance my ruthless reputation. Perfect. Miss Quinlan deemed me half-nice tonight and that simply won't do."

"We are not, I repeat, *not* doing this," Bram growled. Their garrets were unfurnished if they thought this would work.

Three swarthy faces scowled at him.

"If I may," Kean said. "The plan can do no harm and you will look like the chit's saviour. What is the worst that might happen? That the duke gets a slapped face?"

"I don't want his bony hands on my Sophie. And what if they are seen? Rakecombe will have the bride instead of me."

"I'll barely touch the girl. At most cower her into a dark corner and then you can save the day. Look at that Darcy fellow. He saves the lady's sister and then she's all over him like crows at the gibbet."

Having never read the book, Bram could hardly argue but thought the analogy slightly overplayed.

"We could do it at Vauxhall Gardens," Rakecombe continued.

"No, too public," reasoned Jack. "What about Lady Cooper's ball next week. Always dull affairs and plenty of room for the staging."

"Perfect. I'll make sure the Beckfords receive an invite," agreed Rakecombe. "Now, Kean, any other advice."

"You must..." All the men drew near. Even though Bram had no intention whatsoever of going through with this ludicrous plan, he could see the appeal of Edmund Kean. Even with a hacking cough and snuffles, the actor commanded attention. "You must focus all feeling into the performance. Not just a single emotion, but all of them together – lust, frenzy and ruthlessness."

"I'm excellent at the last one. I'll practise the first two."

"And for you, Lord Kelmarsh, my advice is–"

"I doubt I need any, Mr Kean." After all, he'd been acting the majority of his life.

The man looked rather offended and scowled darkly. "I have higher-placed nobles than yourself desiring my company, *Lord* Kelmarsh. Everyone wishes for my acting advice, even the prince."

"Take no notice of him, Edmund," Jack beguiled. "He's not only lovesick and in need of blowing off the loose corns, but smarting because he didn't think of this plan. Got to have some sympathy for him."

The three conspirators huddled together, discussing acting techniques, whilst Bram finished his ale and wished he'd taken Sophie's advice to go home and get some kip. He needed it as well because Asher had sent a message earlier requesting a meeting on the morrow.

If he received clearance to speak, then this whole absurd proposal could be forgotten about.

As long as Sophie believed him.

There was always the chance she'd think it all a joke, but after the spectacles debacle, she must know there was an odd kick in his gallop.

For so very long he had wanted to tell her all, and sometimes the words had been on the tip of his tongue. He would trust Sophie with his life but whispers could be heard by a hundred ears and a little knowledge used, twisted, tortured. Tonight, the reminder of Rakecombe's sister had solidified his silence. Innocents could so easily become embroiled in a spy's life...

Sir Asher Rainham had always been honest and unwavering in his loyalty to his men and the Crown. So, if he finally deemed it safe to tell Sophie, then Bram would believe it likewise.

A thorough cough brought him back to the table as the great actor seemed to hack up half his gizzards.

"Not going to be back on the stage too soon, are you, Kean?" commiserated Rakecombe. "Get some rest for that great throat of yours."

Toadying arse, thought Bram. He never knew Rakecombe was such a patron of the arts – kept that close to his chest.

They all rose, leaving Kean with more jugs of ale and a plate of pie.

. . .

THE STREETS QUIETENED as the three of them left Drury Lane for The Strand, until nothing but their own footsteps and a tapping cane could be heard. Each lost in their own thoughts.

"That was a fortuitous encounter." Jack cut the silence. "Jolly nice fellow that Kean, if a bit...moody. Always the same with these artistic types. Millie once threw a tantrum for no apparent reason other than I sent some purple hyacinths. Cost a pretty penny too."

"That's because they signify sorrow in the language of flowers," Bram proffered distractedly.

"Oh. Is there a book I can buy on that sort of thing? I mean, where does one learn this knowledge?"

"Did your mother never teach you?"

"Drowned herself when I was thirteen, old chap."

Both he and Rakecombe stopped stone-dead on the cobbles whilst Jack continued sauntering on.

"Bloody hell. I'm so sorry. I didn't know."

Jack turned, his face caught in the soft light of a gas lamp, and although he still appeared congenial, Bram noted a tightness around his eyes, hands fisted, the yellow glow above his head casting deep shadows.

"Long time ago now," Jack replied, echoing the duke's earlier words, and he swivelled back to stroll on.

They trailed behind, Bram's mood sombre as he followed the marquess through the solitary streets. Another pool of darkness submerged them until the next lamp appeared on the corner, its dim light hardly worth the effort. Abruptly, a thought occurred to him, and he looked to Rakecombe.

"Why did you say your acting idea kills two birds with one stone. Who's the other?"

"Miss Quinlan."

"But why?"

"The way she looks at me… I feel…" His eyes shifted away. "She stirs something in me, makes me…want. I like overmuch her bold challenges and spirited goading." He lifted his gaze to the moonless sky. "I have never known such emotion and I cannot allow it. I have tried my very best to be loathsome but… It has to be more, as it appears I am too weak to stay away from her. I need her to hate me. To be repulsed by me." Rakecombe halted his stride to lean on the cane. "Attempting to kiss her best friend and cousin should do the trick, do you not think?"

"But, there's no need." Bram's voice was loud in the cheerless night.

"There is *every* need. You are retiring, but this is my life. I cannot afford to make any more…mistakes and you know very well why I say this."

"I once thought the same, but I am changing my life, changing it for a woman. I was as deeply entrenched as you, but over the last year I have slowly extricated myself. For Sophie."

Bram's old friend merely continued walking, his overwhelming pain palpable, cloak darkening as he stepped from the lamplight's sickly glow.

"So," boomed a jovial Jack over his shoulder, waking the night watchmen. "Better go with the plan then, yes?"

'NO LEGACY IS SO RICH AS HONESTY.'
(W. SHAKESPEARE)

$\mathcal{P}$ ropped up in bed, Sophie flicked through the last chapter and wondered if she should re-read the whole scene again. Her mind kept wandering and yet her unbidden hands still turned the pages. At least Bram had no relatives like Mr Darcy's disapproving aunt. In fact, Bram hardly had any family except for a few ageing uncles in the countryside, so there'd been no judgemental kin to disrupt the courtship between an earl and an untitled miss.

Of course, her father was a gentleman, being the younger grandson of a viscount, and they kept a small estate in Devon, but she knew he'd worked for the navy in his bachelor days and he had quite a few investments wrapped up in shipping, which one could almost class as the dreaded *trade*. Bram didn't seem to care about her lowly status; in truth, it had never been mentioned.

She forced her tired eyes back to the book – these musings were the reason she still hadn't finished it.

There came a light tap on the door, and she squinted at the mantel clock barely visible in the weak flame of her lantern – a quarter before the hour of twelve so it could only be Aideen or Mama.

"Yes, come in."

A candle curved its way around the door, accompanied by black curls and a smiling face. "Have you finished it yet?"

"No. It's like the theatre. Too many interruptions."

"Who else has come to visit?" Aideen questioned, meandering over and making herself cosy on the end of the bed.

"No one. More like thoughts, remembrances, emotions."

"Eugh! I know how you feel. I can't believe Kelmarsh said that to you tonight, about being your husband. How damn presumptuous."

Yes, it was, but whenever Sophie thought on those words, hand in hand with the irritation at his overbearing arrogance was a small uncontrollable thrill. He'd been so certain, so insistent, so very passionate. If all he wanted was a broodmare for a wife, surely he would have looked elsewhere by now? For an earl, and a handsome one at that, there were easier fish to catch in the Almack's sea.

"Earlier, during the interval, I also thought he said…"

"Yes?" Aideen sat nearer, yanking half the blanket away to cover her naked toes.

"No, it doesn't matter. I'm sure it was all the noise. I must have misunderstood." Her and Aideen shared most things, but strangely, Sophie didn't want to disclose what she may…or may not have heard. And after all, it could prove to be embarrassing; he might have said, *Damn, I love that bit about Yorick…*

"When you look at Kelmarsh, what do you feel?" Aideen was picking at the corner of the green blanket, her eyes lowered.

Sophie smiled, having a fair clue as to the reasoning behind her question. "Is this about the duke?"

Grumbling, her cousin gazed up with a rueful smile. "Can't get the damn bug out of my mind. And I don't know why. He's so rude and condescending and arrogant and–"

"Handsome and spinach-eyed?" That earned her a glare. "There is something about Rakecombe, I agree. It's that cold yet burning look he sets upon you. But cousin..." She took Aideen's hand in hers, rubbing the chilled fingers. "Be careful. I sense a danger in him. There are reasons for his reputation and when he attacks, it appears he can be quite ruthless."

Indeed, Aideen's baiting of the duke was rather like the children's game of taking turns to prod a sleeping dog with a stick – except Aideen had sole use of the stick.

"I know. And yet I can't seem to help it. I goad purely for his reaction. I can't stop myself. He may give me a burning look, but then he opens his mouth, says something awful and I do it all over again. We appear to bring out the worst in each other."

Sophie nodded, although she wasn't too sure about that, remembering their mutual apologies at the theatre and the way they beheld each other when they thought the other was unaware.

"And what are you going to do about Kelmarsh? I see the way you look at him, Sophie."

"Until he explains his actions, I cannot accept his suit again. There are too many odd things about him. I thought I knew him a year ago and although he has not changed in some ways, there is a part of him I feel is a stranger to me. I will not put my heart back in his hands...yet."

"And what about your lips? Your–"

"Aideen!" A faint smile appeared. "I admit his touch is difficult to stay away from. When he kisses me, it's like…"

"Hmm?" Aideen leaned forward avidly, eyes bright with curiosity.

"Like he is starving for me. That he cannot get enough. That he'll never be sated. My body responds and my mind forgets the past, only feeling the sensation he creates within. It's most annoying."

"Saint Patrick's bones, that sounds thrilling."

"Have you been kissed, Aideen?"

She laughed. "Of course. The gentlemen in Waterford can be very forward." Aideen twirled a curl around her finger. "But your kiss does sound very…ardent. And I didn't expect that of Kelmarsh. From your telling of him, he sounded quiet and calm…slightly dull if truth be told."

"I know. It is as if he is two different people. He plays at being the Lazy Lord whilst his true character is quite different – earnest, passionate, watchful."

The two of them fell silent for a moment.

"You don't suppose…" they both said together, before bursting into giggles.

"A…spy?" Sophie ventured quietly. "No. I refuse to believe it. Bram is mild and kind. He likes reading Greek poetry and… No, he wouldn't harm a fly."

And yet a slight churning in her stomach refused to settle.

Bram himself had suggested there were secrets he could not tell. She recalled his new-found alertness, the surprising air of danger he'd worn at Almack's, the unexpected strength of his body. There were so many peculiar things. Things she'd ignored last year when lost in love. Things she refused to think on now because, well, what did it matter?

"I'm sure you're right." It was Aideen's turn to pat Sophie's arm, although a worried frown marred her forehead too. "I doubt spies marry. Always abroad and, well…spying on people, and Kelmarsh hasn't set foot outside the country for how long?"

"He mentioned it had been four years."

But tonight nothing made sense; it all felt wrong and his excuses ludicrous.

"And anyway," Aideen continued, "if he was involved in those escapades, he would have followed you to Ireland. For a man with contacts, it would have been easy." Sophie nodded whilst Aideen tucked the blanket up and kissed her forehead. "We're talking blarney. Get some rest, cousin. It will all be clearer in the morning."

Aideen padded out, softly closing the door, but sleep did not come swiftly to Sophie. Unease slithered down her spine and she wished her cousin hadn't tellingly fiddled with her curls whilst dismissing it all as blarney.

"Sir Asher Rainham will see you now."

A rough shake of his shoulder, accompanied by the bellowing words, woke Bram from a fitful doze.

Last night, after the theatre and alehouse, all three of them had converged on the Winterbourne townhouse which, it had to be said, held an impressively stocked drinks cabinet. Some damn fine whiskies had been quaffed and rated whilst they'd discussed Rakecombe's strategy for *La Chauve-Souris*, before staggering home gone four.

Up at the hour of nine this morning in order to send

Sophie some ox-eye daisies and forget-me-nots, he now felt abysmal.

At Asher's nod of greeting, Bram sat, watching his superior neaten documents on his desk. In his mid-forties, the man's demeanour always remained so calm, yet decisive, and Bram enjoyed his company. He never talked over anyone but listened and then put forward his own interpretations in a considered way, even taking advice from underlings, which for an intelligence commander was unusual. But Asher always seemed to know where people's talents lay and hence trusted their views.

"Too late a night at the theatre?"

And then of course, he knew *everything*. "Theatre no. Afterwards yes. Rakecombe and I went to Winterbourne's hovel for a nightcap."

"Do you like Winterbourne?"

About to flippantly reply he was a pain in the arse, he realised the question, it being from Asher, was serious. "Yes, very much. An affable fellow, obviously intelligent and...compassionate."

"Good. I was ninety-six per cent sure, but you never quite know. People can be odd sometimes."

Trying to suppress a smile, Bram asked, "Any more information on *La Chauve-Souris*?"

"No. And I have worse news. I suspect we have a traitor in our midst. Some information has fallen into French hands. Information that was only known to a select few. Rakecombe, Penbury and Stafford. And a few secretaries. No need for you to do anything, but keep an ear open and don't tell the others for now."

"Certainly." Bram responded with a frown, unsure why Rakecombe was on the "don't tell" list as he'd worked for the Crown many years. "We're all attending Vauxhall Gardens tomorrow so we'll listen for any gossip concerning *La Chauve-Souris*. We decided last night that Rakecombe should broaden his search to Whitechapel, and Winterbourne's doing the usual..." Which, as Jack put it, meant pumping Lady Falkirk for more information.

"And will Miss Beckford be at the Gardens by coincidence?"

"Her family have been invited by Rakecombe to attend supper in his box." He shifted in his seat. "I am not overly welcome at present."

"Might be opportune to reveal your past profession then."

Asher lifted his head, eyes glinting with mirth as shock caused Bram's mouth to gape.

"I didn't think..."

"Did you know Miss Beckford's father was quite high up in the admiralty in his salad days? Not in the field, you understand, but he did some sort of cryptography. If you'd told us that previously, the wheels might have turned quicker."

"I didn't know."

"Well, I spoke to him two days ago. Nice fellow, easily beatable at piquet, but then everybody is. I explained your situation and informed him of your occupation. He said he won't interfere with your courting, but it is Miss Beckford you will have to convince. The decision is ultimately hers." Asher reached down to close a slightly misaligned drawer. "No mission information, obviously. But you can explain your career...choice and the incident last year with Celeste."

Bram slumped back, stunned. It was more than he'd hoped for, always imagining that, though Sophie might be told, her family would have to remain unaware and hence disapproving of the match in their ignorance. With sudden clarity, he understood why Mrs Beckford had stabbed a fan in his ribs. It had been both warning and clemency.

"Thank you, Asher. I am speechless."

"You deserve it, Bram. I'm aware this profession was not something you asked for and the last few years have been difficult. But I could not lose you with the country how it was. You were too good. With peace declared, however, and a more efficient network, I can now afford to release you."

"The Kelmarsh family has always been in service of the Crown...until death. It feels strange to break with tradition."

An odd glance was thrown his way. "The Rainham clan have traditionally always been valets...until death, and my mother couldn't write or even count past fifty. And yet here I sit, ordering people about and babbling on about statistics."

"I didn't know that." Bram was filled with yet more respect for this man who'd worked his way up from valet to spy master. It was well known that Asher had once been an exceptional tracker, and he wondered how it had all come to pass.

"Well, it's not something one can tell every proud nobleman who sits in your chair – that my father very probably polished their boots. We all have different talents and mine was definitely not cravat tying. We need not follow in our ancestors' footsteps."

"How did you end up here?"

"I'll bore you another day." Asher straightened his quills. "I live and breathe for this job, but you need more. You've done excellent work and you can be proud of it, but as soon as you told me about the girl last year, I knew it was time."

"Have you yourself never considered marriage?" He knew Asher was a confirmed bachelor although it couldn't be from lack of attention. Female colleagues all seemed to hold a tendre for their superior: tall and good-looking...he supposed, and retaining a trim physique.

A quirk of the lips accompanied a shake of his head. "I do not believe I am marriage material. I'm good at knowing people but also myself, and I'd drive a woman mad after one day."

They shared rueful smiles.

"My thanks again, Asher."

"Good luck. It may still be difficult. Based on what her father said, I think there's only a two in ten chance of forgiveness at the first attempt."

They shook hands firmly, and Bram marched to the door, tiredness forgotten.

"Kelmarsh?" The questioning tone obliged him to turn. "One more thing before you go." Asher rubbed his stubbled chin. "What's it like? This feeling for Miss Beckford."

It was an unusually personal question from his superior and looking into those enquiring eyes, Bram discerned a perplexed glint, as though Asher couldn't fathom or quantify this strange emotion.

"She makes me complete and without her I feel...lost."

A frown crumpled Asher's brow. "And that's good? To find someone you cannot live without?"

"Personally, it is all I have ever dreamed of."

I HAVE A NOT-VERY IMPORTANT JOB.

"*S*ophie, I am an Intelligence Officer in service of the Crown."

No, hopeless, Bram thought, staring into the mirror. Too serious.

"You'll never guess what, Soph? I'm a spy," he tried, hand on hip.

Horrendous, flippantly declared as though it was all a lark.

"I have a very important job." He frowned at his reflection with lips tight.

No, a pompous declaration with a Rakecombe-like expression.

"I have a not-very important job."

Hell no, if Prinny heard that, he'd have him up for treason.

"I have an unusual job," Bram continued, with a sideways grin through gritted teeth.

Sounded like he owned a brothel.

"I have a vital job concerning international security which you cannot tell anyone abo–"

"Lud, Kelmarsh," came an amused voice from the curtains. "You should have paid more attention to Kean's acting advice."

"I need to be me. No acting... How the bloody hell did you get in here?"

Winterbourne stepped from behind the green velvet drapes where the French doors were hidden...and locked, sat himself in Bram's favourite leather chair by the desk, crossed his hessian-booted feet and appeared set to stay for dinner.

"I spent an hour with Jim Toggins. Just practising what he taught me. Amazing what you can do with a cravat pin and sixpence."

"God forbid, is he still alive? Taught me the black art when I was but a cub."

"Can't have taught you how to lock up your study. That latch is a doddle."

Bram crossed to the decanters and poured two hefty glasses. "This is my false study. Nothing but playbills and gaming vowels here. They'd be too bored to look elsewhere."

"Clever," said Jack, saluting him with the glass. "So, you're allowed to tell Miss Beckford. Congratulations but you're doing an awful job of it." The brandy was sipped whilst he settled in, lifting his pristine boots to the desk. "Can't you just throw her over your shoulder and be done with it?"

"I do believe she'd grab me by the nutmegs and bite my arse."

Jack's eyes widened. "Sounds like the culmination of a fun night out to me," he mused. "Why don't you go back to the very beginning then. What age did you start? After Oxford? After the Tour?"

"I was spying when you first gawped up a dairymaid's petticoats."

"Still am. What age?"

"Thirteen."

Jack clanked the glass to his teeth. "That's a bit young, is it not?"

"You forget," Bram said, getting comfy in his second-favourite chair. "My parents were also in this profession. I was learning how to write code in the nursery."

"So, what was your first mission, if you can say?"

"Since it all came to nothing, I can. A peer of the realm was suspected of selling secrets, and my parents asked me if I could ingratiate myself with the son of the house, whom I was at Eton with. Get invited for the summer and snoop around."

An appalled expression decorated Jack's features. "Lud, and I thought my upbringing was awful. You do know that's not normal?"

"I was assisting the Crown."

"You were a child being used by your own kinsfolk. It's shameful." He grimaced. "No offence."

Bram savoured the brandy and shrugged. Yes, that thought had niggled him many a night but the past was the past, and he would learn from it. Any future child of his could be a gravedigger if he or she so desired.

"So he wasn't guilty? This peer?"

"No. And he caught me riffling through his study. They

thought me a thief and ejected me from the house." Bram wouldn't elucidate on the embarrassment and humiliation, or the palpable sense of disappointment that had emanated from his parents at his lack of success. They'd considered him a failure and he'd subsequently re-doubled his efforts to gain their approval.

"Bloody hell. And your schoolfriend? I presume you were never allowed to explain to him?"

"It taught me not to get caught, if anything, and in that I have been inordinately successful. But I couldn't explain to my friend no, not for eight years."

"Eight years?"

"Rakecombe was the son."

Jack choked on his brandy. "Devil take it," he spluttered. "I would have loved to have seen his face."

"I was unamused," came a voice from the shadows.

"Damnation," growled Bram. "Would anyone else like to walk in unannounced? Is Miss Quinlan hiding in the alcove with you?"

A suppressed glare was all he received, before Rakecombe helped himself to a glass. "Sir Asher gave you clearance then?"

"Yes. So, we can bid farewell to your ridiculous acting plan. I will tell her all at Vauxhall Gardens."

"I have no doubt, of course, that she will accept your explanations," he replied, raising the glass to sniff at it warily. "But on the off-chance that telling her goes badly, we could still enact our seduction and rescue plan at Lady Cooper's ball."

"If I may," Jack butted in. "Having heard Bram's attempted declaration of career, I can confidently say it's going to be a disaster."

"Hmm. What are you going for, Kelmarsh? Directness? Innocence? That you were coerced?"

"I thought I'd just be myself."

Two appalled expressions turned his way.

"Good God, man, you can't do that."

"Yes," agreed Jack, "look what happened to Chadwick."

Scowling countenances now turned on the marquess and he raised his hands in apology.

Leaning forward, Bram pointed a finger. "All I need from you two at Vauxhall Gardens is to keep her parents and Miss Quinlan occupied. There should be plenty of opportunities to get Sophie alone."

"Stroll down one of the dark walks with her. The women love it – the danger of the night, the menace of a stolen kiss, the peril of a cares–"

"This is the woman he wants to marry, Winterbourne. Not some blowsabella he wishes to tup."

Bram furrowed his brow. "Do you know, Jack might actually be right. Although I've never wanted to resort to rule fifteen, it might at least start things off." He only hoped he'd be able to focus on his words. Generally, as soon as he felt Sophie's soft skin and smelled the lavender, instinct had a propensity for taking over.

Rakecombe hovered, tapping that cane against his booted leg. "Of course, you might have to reveal why you didn't follow her to Ireland."

Bugger. He'd forgotten about that. "She might forget. In the surprise."

"Women never forget," said Jack. "A blessing and a curse. Anyhow, why didn't you follow? You got to that Milford place, didn't you?"

Bram's eyes met Rakecombe's, whose lips quirked.

"I have a slight problem with Ireland."

"Oh. Mission related, is it?"

"In a roundabout way, yes."

"Well, in that case, I can predict with certainty that we will be enacting our plan regardless. And you, Rakehell, will get the chance to act like one."

14

OF COURSE, MY CUSTARD TART.

"*I*t's... It's..."

"I agree," said Sophie, gazing around in wonder.

Previously, her parents had always considered Vauxhall Gardens to be rather indecent for their virtuous daughter – a den of iniquity had been the actual words used – but an invitation to dine at the Duke of Rakecombe's supper box was not one to ignore.

The evening felt warm with the air sweetly perfumed by the fragrant flowers that bloomed rampantly in the enclosed areas. After the bustle and dirt of town, it appeared a fairy-tale land, complete with music and sculptures. The Beckford household had arrived early in order to appreciate the gardens before joining the duke, and even Sophie's father stood in wonder, having not visited for years.

"There's no balloon flight this evening," Aideen bemoaned. "They've burst it."

"But there are fireworks," Sophie consoled, clasping her cousin around the waist. "And music and the cascade and–"

"And the dark paths to get lost in."

"Certainly not, girls," came Mama's imperious voice. "Stick together and to the lit walkways. There are always rogues about waiting to take advantage of wandering maidens."

An Irish voice whispered close, "I do hope so."

Laughing, they trailed her parents along the avenues and admired the many paintings on display. A woman in a low-cut red gown purred in delight as a town buck in a violet waistcoat presented her with flowers – the clientele as interesting as the entertainments.

Dusk had yet to settle so they meandered the Grand Walk, marvelling at the imposing elm trees that flanked the path. Slowly and with military precision, a brigade of men embarked upon lighting the many glass lanterns that hung amongst the branches, their tapers restless in the benign breeze.

Having convinced her father it was much more romantic to arrive via the river than by carriage, the whole evening had taken on a fantastical aura. At one corner, a juggler threw numerous pieces of fruit in the air, every so often taking a bite, and on another stood a burly fellow swallowing a sword.

Aideen tapped Sophie's shoulder as she gasped at this amazing feat. "Uncle Seamus makes those. The blade collapses into the hilt."

"It's not real?" Sophie lamented, as the man spread his broad arms to receive the applause.

"No. But does it matter? 'Tis quite difficult to make. He designs all sorts of things like that."

They strolled on, pausing again to listen to the musicians in the pavilion.

"Time for supper, girls," Mama called, and Aideen's fingers tightened their grip on Sophie's arm.

"You're not worried about seeing the duke, are you?"

"Of course not. And besides, I hear they serve the finest of puddings, so it would take more than a surly shabbaroon to lessen my appetite. I'll think of custard tarts if he annoys me."

As they neared the duke's box, which appeared large enough to accommodate at least ten, Sophie could see two gentlemen and a lady already seated. Immediately, she discerned that one of them was Bram, who searched the crowds with an eager eye until his gaze lit upon their party. His posture swiftly relaxed to an indolent pose.

The other gentleman had his rigid spine to them. Draped in black, his dark hair gleamed under the candlelight. Sultry laughter rang out from the lady in response to the duke's intimate whisper, and Sophie could feel her cousin tense.

"Remember, he's rude, condescending and arrogant but is also in control of the puddings."

"You're right. When I look at him – custard tarts."

On arriving, her parents made their bows and curtseys, and Sophie frowned as they greeted Bram with...not quite cordiality but nevertheless a discernible thawing of their previous frostiness. What was going on?

Sophie had intended to stay close to Aideen, for both their sakes, but Bram whisked her to the side and bringing her fingers up, he kissed the very tips of her gloves, his hand pressing firmly. The strength of that touch sent quivers all the way down to her, not so inconsequential, feet.

"You look so beautiful tonight, Sophie."

"Thank you, my lord. And you are very..." She trailed

off. This evening, Bram had not worn his ubiquitous grey, but a coal-black coat and buff breeches, matched with a fine pair of top boots. A midnight-blue waistcoat adorned his torso, complemented by an unsullied cravat.

For some reason, he was gloveless and she stared at his bare hands. They were calloused with a slight scar over the right knuckles, its silvery line begging to be traced. A dusting of hair graced the backs before being swallowed by his white cuffs.

She'd seen her father with sleeves rolled up, and certainly having lived in the country most of her life had noticed the field workers baring their necks and arms in the summer heat of harvesting. But staring at Bram, she suddenly felt an indecent desire to fling off his jacket and push up his sleeves. To run her fingers up his wrists, caress those strong forearms. To undo that extremely neat cravat and kiss his bared throat.

"Sophie." Her name was huskily whispered. "If you continue to look at me like that, I will not be responsible for my actions."

Ashamed and annoyed he could read her so well, she said the first thing that came to mind in way of excuse, "I was picturing you as a custard tart."

A broad smile broke his smouldering features. "You can partake of me any time you wish, Sophie." He leaned forward, his breath misting her cheek with a fennel fragrance. "Just ask."

This close, she could see the twinkling of his eyes behind the spectacles, but in the twilight they appeared as dark as his waistcoat. A bottomless sea waiting to catch and drown the unsuspecting...Sophie.

His grip tightened. "My beloved swan, I need to speak

with you tonight. Privately. It's very important. Can we perhaps meet after supper? Maybe when everyone is occupied by the cascade."

"I hoped to see the cascade myself." Indeed, she had heard wonderful things about the illuminated scene that came to life at the end of the first concert act.

"We will return to see it every single night from now 'till eternity, as long as you listen to what I have to say...please."

And it was because of that earnest tone that she found herself nodding.

Taking their seats, Sophie was aware of her parents watching guardedly, but she smiled and they resumed their conversation with Lord Winterbourne, who seemed to have appeared from nowhere as was customary.

Servants scurried around the tables, depositing hams, salads and cheeses. Across the piles of food, she peered at Aideen, who was balefully glaring at a piece of bread – nothing tasted quite like Irish bread apparently. She was seated between Lord Winterbourne and the duke, but the latter man's body still curved towards his other beautiful companion.

"Who's the lady, Lord Kelmarsh?"

"Please, Sophie. It's Bram. And that is Lady Falkirk. Forgive me for stealing you away before the introductions."

"A friend of the duke's?"

He frowned whilst placing a piece of cold meat pie onto her plate and then refilling her punch glass. "No, Winterbourne's actually, but..." Bram trailed off as purring laughter came from the lady, contradicting his words. "I believe Rakecombe is acting the blaggard tonight."

From the corner of her eye, she noticed Lord

Winterbourne entertaining Aideen with a story, but although her cousin was chuckling, it sounded strained.

"Why?" she asked as a rumble of deep laughter now broke from the duke.

"Well, it's... Oh hell, Sophie. I won't lie to you. He's trying to deny an attraction to your cousin. Surely the best way is to pretend an interest in someone else."

She scowled and took a large gulp of the fruity punch. "Everywhere I look there are shams and fakes and people telling clangers, pretending to be something they aren't. Does no one say and do as they mean in London?"

Bram's eyes dropped, and she guessed those words had struck deep. When he raised his head, however, Sophie did not expect to see such hurt shining in those ocean depths.

"Sometimes, there is no choice."

A bout of raucous giggles broke their gaze.

"Most gratified I could amuse, Miss Quinlan," the Marquess of Winterbourne was saying. "That tale of my Great-Aunt, the highwayman and Roger the dog is usually well received."

"Trotted it out for all your ladies, haven't you?" The low snarl of words drawled from the duke, his tone silencing Aideen with the dart of criticism that she was merely the latest of many.

"At least I amuse, Rakebore. I'm not saintly but thank God I'm not a dull dog."

"Well," Mama said almost too desperately, "we are very grateful for the opportunity to dine with you all. Such good company. Thank you, Your Grace, for the invitation."

The servants bustled in with puddings and her father thankfully claimed the conversation. "I must say, Lord

Kelmarsh, that silver swan you bought Sophie is a stunning object. I hope she thanked you for it."

Bewildered, Sophie glugged more punch. What had happened to the piercing looks and wintry silences?

"She did, I thank you, sir."

"And the swan and eagle inkstand," added Mama. "French, isn't it? The rendition of the swans in bronze is most lifelike."

Sophie sat most un-lifelike as her parents and Bram *chatted* about the gifts. Had all past grievances been erased upon entering the gates tonight?

"Didn't Napoleon have an inkstand like that?" asked Jack. "I remember reading an article about it. Cost a pretty penny. Went missing a while ago."

Silence fell upon the table and her parents looked rather stunned. Surely, they didn't think…

"Probably a vast amount of copies about," suggested the duke. "Much the same with fashion. Prinny gets a new waistcoat and every nobleman in town follows suit."

"Except you," said Aideen, looking pointedly at his black attire. "Do you follow any fashion?"

A spluttering from Mother, a smirk from Father, a chuckle from Winterbourne, an astounded gawp from Lady Falkirk, and Bram… He was biting back the laughter. Honestly, Sophie thought, could this evening become any more bizarre.

"Fashion," the duke said, eyeing Aideen's sky-blue dress with silver gauze, "is for fools."

"And yet your cane with its ebony length and silver-topped head of a dog with jade eyes is the very epitome of *la mode*. Understated, I grant you, but expensive and of the prevailing taste. Do you need a cane to walk?"

Sophie watched the duke's eyes narrow. "Every gentleman needs some defence on the streets of London. And how do you know they are jade?"

"Ah," interrupted Sophie's father. "Is it a Seamus cane? No wonder you recognise it, Aideen dear."

"Who," growled the duke slowly and sternly, twisting to Aideen, "is Seamus?"

"My uncle. He designs swords, walking sticks and unusual...weaponry. Receives orders from London all the time. I help him out occasionally. Terrible with the paperwork."

Silence.

The duke's nostrils flared as he took a deep inhalation of breath, but Sophie wasn't sure if it was because Aideen had admitted to having a relative who worked for a living or something to do with this silly stick.

It was like watching a Greek play.

"Those two exhaust me," whispered Bram from the corner of his mouth.

"Do you not like to argue?" she asked, knowing the answer already.

"Life is too short." He shifted his seat nearer. "If that were us, we would have kissed by now and resolved the situation far more agreeably."

"Oh." It was all she could think to say, and as she licked her lips, Bram's eyes followed the movement so she hastily spun back to the Greek tragedy – or comedy, she wasn't quite sure – being performed across the table.

"I am certain," the duke was saying, "this cane is not the same one."

"Are you sure?" replied Aideen. "Doesn't it have a–"

Her words abruptly ceased and a flaming crimson

deepened Aideen's already heated cheeks. Sophie noticed one of the duke's hands was…missing. Surely he wasn't doing anything inappropriate?

"Perhaps we can discuss this later." The duke glowered and the air positively crackled with tension.

Aideen drew in another short breath and stared up at him. "Of course, custard tarts."

"I beg your pardon?" he barked as Sophie stifled her mirth.

"There's a waiter behind you with custard tarts."

The duke peered around and her cousin looked over beseechingly.

"Lord Kelmarsh," Sophie began loudly, "did you enjoy Hamlet the other night?"

Bram winked. "I did but we happened to meet Kean afterwards and I have to say, the performance might have been improved with his presence. He does seem a masterful actor, even with the snuffles."

With the new topic introduced, the company fell into a discussion of the theatre. Aideen mouthed a *thank you* between spoonfuls of custard tart, and Bram filled her glass *again*, shuffling his chair until their thighs met beneath the table, the sensation rousing a heady thrill.

"Oh, it's time for the cascade," her cousin exclaimed, after the plates had been cleared and the music had ended.

Bram brusquely stood, offering Sophie his arm.

"We will stay here, my dears," Mama said, "but don't wander too far."

"I'll see they come to no harm," Lady Falkirk promised, taking Lord Winterbourne's arm and leaving Rakecombe to reluctantly offer his to Aideen. She glared at his black superfine coat as though it was a viper ready to bite.

"Hmm," Mama replied. "It depends what you view as harm."

The dash to the cascade was wholly uncivilised, but the three peers managed to divert most intrusions with Rakecombe and his cane leading the way.

"Bram, can we not at least see some of the cascade?" Sophie implored, but a strong arm clasped around her waist and pulled her in the direction of a small, indeed dark, path that curved its way innocently behind a large elm.

Just as she was about to protest, gruff words whispered urgently in her ear, "Come with me, Sophie. I've something to tell you."

15

SIMPLICITY IS BEST.

*B*ram didn't mean to hurry his beloved down the shadowy path with quite such haste, but he was aware his afforded opportunity was finite if her reputation was to be kept intact.

As luck would have it, Jack had a far too intimate knowledge of the Vauxhall Gardens outlay, including the more hitherto unknown, and hence unpopulated, winding tracks. The marquess even had a season ticket and had merely flashed his metal medallion at the gatekeeper – a picture of Hades carrying off Persephone embossed on the surface.

This path was only sporadically lit, and any other time he might have enjoyed the romanticism, but worry churned in his vitals. How would Sophie take the news? She didn't seem to have noticed but he'd kept refilling her supper glass with punch, hoping her reactions would be slower and hence his ballocks safer.

Finally they came upon a wooden bench set under a large ash, its delicate leaves creating an arbour of seclusion.

He unbuttoned and stripped off his tailcoat, placing it on the damp seat for her. Sophie's eyes widened and he hoped he hadn't offended her with his state of undress, but he'd never come across an English bench that wasn't imbued with moisture.

"Please sit, Sophie."

Perching on the very edge, her eyes wandered over his shirt sleeves so he checked for stains. The billowing white linen looked to be clean, if a bit creased, having been roughly shoved up his jacket by the valet. He ruffled his hair, marched the area in front of her, and then took off his spectacles, placing them in a waistcoat pocket.

In the end, he had decided not to come up with any pre-planned words and had instead chosen to rely on divine inspiration. But God seemed otherwise engaged.

This moment called for the most important words of his life and yet none were forthcoming. Sophie still gazed at his wrists as he cleared his throat to begin.

"May I see your arms?"

Bram closed his wordless mouth, halted his pacing. What? Had he heard correctly? "I beg your pardon?"

Even in the dim light of the lantern, softly swaying above Sophie's head, he could see the delicate blush that stippled her cheeks. Those slender fingers lifted to her mouth as if to stuff the words back in.

"Sorry. Please remove that request from your memory. I think I may have had too much punch."

No, he could not remove that request. Sophie wished, for some reason, to see his arms and he was more than happy to comply. Sitting on the bench next to her, he began to unfasten the emerald cufflinks.

Her eyes widened.

"Honestly, no," she said breathlessly. "I didn't mean…"

Bram pocketed the links and started to roll up his left sleeve. "Then why ask, Sophie? Liquor can often free our tongues to say what we really desire." Her eyes tracked his fingers, until he tucked the material just above the elbow. Slowly, he did the same with his right but then paused mid-forearm.

Oh. He'd forgotten about that.

Too late now, and he continued drawing up the endless material, revealing a long, jagged scar. It alone would terrify most maidens but it was, perhaps, what covered it that would provoke further questioning.

Eight years previous, he and Rakecombe had gotten into a skirmish in Spain, where they'd both ended up with knife wounds. Two years later, they had met again reconnoitring in the then Kingdom of Holland and, becoming inordinately bosky, had deemed it a capital idea to visit Huang Mei, a fellow who drew wonderful images on skin.

Bram looked down, following Sophie's eyes to the elaborate W that twisted around his arm covering some of the rough silvery gash.

At three in the morning and full of bad Dutch gin and potatoes, it had seemed ingenious to place their alias initial over the scars. As luck would have it, his surname was Walcott, so questions were rare. He didn't know how Rakecombe explained his away – if, indeed, anyone ever saw it.

"What is that?" she asked, her fingers hovering over the inscription. She didn't seem disgusted, thank blazes, but…curious.

"It's a tattoo. They use a fine needle to place ink just under the skin. You can touch it."

Expecting her to reach out one gloved finger, he was thus surprised when she pinched the ends of her satin glove one by one and tugged it off, the movement so erotic he could envisage her gown slipping free in the same manner.

Slowly, her hand descended, until soft fingers traced the W. It was the lightest of touches and yet sent darts of pure pleasure straight to his nether regions.

"Does it hurt?"

My groin, yes. "My tattoo, no," he said, "although at the time, I do remember some pain." He brought his other arm forward. "Do you like what you see?"

She raised eyes to his, and he nearly groaned at the mixture of curiosity and desire that was exhibited within them. Her gaze dropped, and Sophie brushed a delicate hand down the forearm to his wrist.

"If I said yes, does that make me wanton?"

"No. And as long as it's only for my arms, it makes me..."

"Makes you what?" she asked, now starting on the other wrist, gently pulling the chestnut hairs.

He couldn't contain his ardour as she tried to encircle his arm with her small hand. It was ridiculous to be thus aroused by the smallest of movements, but he'd waited for Sophie so long, desired her for so long, loved her for so long.

Raising his scarred limb, he tipped her chin up and stared into that expressive face. Vaguely, Bram was aware he should be getting on with his explanations, but Sophie's lips were parted, those light-brown eyes slightly glazed, whilst that hand still stroked his arm...and now she added fingernails to the sensation.

Overwhelming desire punched him in the gut, words

146

scattered, and he lowered his head, capturing that rose-pink mouth.

This time he *did* keep the kiss gentle, bringing a hand around to cup her cheek, dropping soft touches of lips upon hers. But then he felt sharp nails dig into his arm and he pressed harder, slanting his mouth over her provocative gasp.

She softened against him and so, despite the restraints on time, he brought his other hand to draw Sophie closer, breasts grazing his chest. As he invaded with his tongue, to better taste that beguiling sweetness, there was a touch of bare fingers at his neck, grasping hair.

A feminine sigh declared its pleasure as the fragrance of meadows overwhelmed his senses, and he realised his own fingers had descended to her soft neck, the slope of her breasts. Bram followed the trail with his lips, pressing open-mouthed kisses upon her.

Soon, his hand reached its goal and he brushed over the heavy mound, fingers grazing the fullness that pushed against the satin. A guttural groan left his chest as he smothered kisses down, still further down to the edge of her dress. But his lips were not to be denied access to her skin, and he tugged at the sleeve, savouring her bare shoulder – only fair after his own undressing.

He tasted lavender and licked at the smoothness but the bodice was tight, too tight for his meandering fingers, so he simply kissed his way across the silk until meeting her tight nipple beneath, grazing it with his teeth.

Her body bucked, and for a mad moment, he considered laying her down on the bench and…

Sophie would be his. No more denial.

But even as he turned his attentions to her other breast,

guilt began to roil in his belly. Sophie deserved more. And for himself, he could not deny that to have all the misunderstanding and fakery revealed would be a release – from his past, from his deceptions.

A new start.

Ever so reluctantly, and with a last lingering kiss, he pulled away to fuss with her disordered sleeve, to quench the throbbing ache that demanded release and didn't give a damn about words or conscience.

Bram cleared his throat. "Forgive me, Sophie. I couldn't resist. But I…we need to talk."

Her moist, swollen lips parted to reply, and he tried to recall the pain of being tattooed, to tamp down his screaming body, but all he could picture was having an S inscribed alongside it – entwined and complete.

"I probably shouldn't have asked to see your arms, but they are so different from a marble statue's. I like the rough hair and the taut muscles bunching under the skin."

Those words really weren't helping. All he could now imagine was displaying his physique. He was trim for an aristocrat – well trained in riding, fighting and swordsmanship – and although he wasn't a braggart, he wouldn't mind leisurely undressing for Sophie. To uncover his body and have her delicate fingers slowly explore.

Bloody hell.

He stepped away, breathing in the fresh Vauxhall country air. "Sophie," he said without looking at her – he couldn't as his wits would go a wander again. "I have… At last, I am able to explain myself."

The announcement brought a straightness to her spine. "I was thinking earlier," she whispered, "that this place erases old memories. And I did forget all about that night for a moment." Sophie directed her gaze upon him. Desire had been replaced by sadness and a certain weary acceptance. "I'm not sure I want your poor excuses any more."

"They are not poor, I assure you." He reached out a hand and brought her fingers within his grasp, aware time was no longer on his side. "Sophie, I have a profession. My whole family have always had this profession, passed on from father to son...and the occasional daughter." Her brow creased so he hurried on. "The Kelmarshs have forever had a duty to the Crown."

"In what capacity?" she asked, her voice catching.

"As intelligence gatherers."

"Spies, you mean." Her tone did not bode well. It was almost...accusing.

"Yes."

"Please take me back to my family, Lord Kelmarsh."

It was the last response he had expected, so sudden and resolute as she jerked her fingers from his hand. He expected Sophie to be incredulous or to laugh or splutter... but her gaze had turned icy cold and she stood, presenting him with her back.

"You don't believe me," he said, also rising to his feet.

She spun, laughing, bitterness evident, and despite being a spy for nigh on twenty years, despite having faced a multitude of situations with fortitude...he stepped back.

"Oh, I believe you, my lord. Tell me more, then. How do you *gather* your information? Seduction?"

"God, no, Sophie, that's not my method. I spent much time in France as a tracker, but four years ago I returned. It was decided my talents could be useful here, in England." He paced, willing her to understand. "No one notices an indolent, lazy nobleman and therefore I act that part."

"So all the falling asleep and idleness is pure subterfuge?"

"To a certain extent, yes. I have always been good at listening and watching, and consequently I have cultivated that persona yet more so. It has been extremely useful to the Crown, even uncovering a plot to assassinate the Prince Regent two years previous."

Sophie did not look impressed. In fact, she looked even more furious. "And to think I sought to help you. At one point, I thought you had an illness!" she shouted.

"Now wait a goddamn moment. Are you saying you allowed my attentions through *pity*?"

She growled, it was the only word, and then stalked closer. "I adored that languid, kind, thoughtful man."

Both elated and jealous of the fictional creature, he grabbed hold of her shoulders. "Is that really all you saw in me? Did you not see anything deeper, Sophie Beckford?"

Silence fell and he knew he was right. "You saw deeper, Sophie. I know you did. Not everything was fakery. My devotion to you, my desire to return to the countryside and raise pigs and wheat whilst reading Propertius to you. None of that was a lie. My need...my want for you is not a sham."

Her eyes raised to meet his. "I always thought you were...hiding something. Your intelligence, your strength. Always falling asleep yet with an innate alertness. I deceived myself last year that it was your nature... I am a fool," she said, her head dropping. "Take me back, Lord Kelmarsh."

"Sophie, I need to explain Celeste. Why I never told you."

"And will it be the truth? How will I know? Are you acting even now?"

Frustration pounded through his body. "There is no

more trickery. In two weeks, I will no longer be part of the intelligence office. I have left it all, Sophie. For you."

Rather than looking pleased, her expression fell to aghast. "And when you miss the thrill of the chase? Who will you blame?"

"No, I don–" He tightened his grip, but she shrugged him off.

"None of this matters, Bram. I am sure you could answer all my questions and convince me of your devotion, but there is one thing I cannot let go."

He waited. That he hadn't followed her to Ireland? Or the debacle with Celeste? If only she let him explain.

"We were nearly betrothed last year. If I had not heard you with Celeste, would you have ever told me? One month and we were to be married. *I* was to be married...to a stranger, a fake, a man I didn't know. Did you think me that pathetic and stupid? That I wouldn't notice? Or was I nothing but a dull little bird you could bamboozle?"

"No, I thought..." He paused. What *had* he thought?

Last year, he'd supposed himself clever. That he could slowly extricate himself from spying whilst starting a new life with Sophie. She need never know about his activities. After all, what woman wanted to know their husband had been a sneaking eavesdropper? Even if it was for the country's protection.

Yes, it was true, he had thought to keep Sophie ignorant of his past, but purely to keep her far from danger. In hindsight, he could see that attitude had been in turn arrogant, dishonest and supremely wrong.

Sir Asher's odds of two in ten that she would understand were wretchedly optimistic.

He had no answer.

"Exactly, Lord Kelmarsh. You thought you could hoodwink *humdrum* little Sophie. And you very nearly did. But that is my shame and–"

"No! You want the truth," he almost shouted, grabbing hold of her hand and pulling her flush with his body. "I didn't think past making you mine. That first time we met. As soon as I heard you in that room, I knew…"

He stared into her startled features and lowered his voice. "I had never felt such a ferocious need as when I opened my eyes that day. Nothing mattered but courting you – my family profession, the current mission, nothing. Always I have followed a path I did not choose, and tradition and loyalty has ruled my life. You were the first thing I have ever wanted just for myself."

Pressing his forehead to hers, he whispered, "I apologise, Sophie, but that need, that want, made me run roughshod over your feelings. A spy's life can be nasty…low. A life so full of deceit and treachery you can almost taste it – bitter and thick. I didn't want it to touch you. It wasn't only a matter of not telling you because of the danger… I didn't want to lose you either. My past does not provide much to recommend me but I'm starting afresh… I hope with you."

Breath stuttered against his cheek in heaving pants but Sophie didn't struggle within his tight grip. Finally, a soft hand pressed and he lifted his head.

"Thank you for telling me, Bram, but I need time. I appreciate your suffering but it still stands that you were willing to let me live a lie. To involve me in your trickery and to allow me to marry a man that plainly didn't exist. Please, Bram, I wish to return to my parents."

Even though every nerve in his body screamed *no, never*

release her, he did so. Her dress appeared crumpled and tears glinted in her eyes, but he kept silent.

Time. He would give her time. He'd already waited a year after all.

Holding out his arm, he heard a resigned sigh before she gently placed hers atop. They drifted back, subdued, their feet out of step on the gravel path as chatter and laughter met their ears, music tinkling louder as the lanterns grew more numerous. Vauxhall gardens, which had previously seemed so fresh and blithe, now appeared gaudy and full of noise, and Bram hankered to reveal the island in a large bottle of brandy.

The Grand Walk neared but as it did so, there came a shout from the darkness. An Irish tongue yelled its anger, underpinned with a sob.

"May savage dogs eat your feet and the devil damn you to the stones of dirges. And…and all my calamity, harm and misfortune for a year on you!" A resounding slap echoed down the murky trail followed by the crunch of slippers on gravel.

Miss Quinlan careered around the corner and seeing the two of them, flung herself into Sophie's arms. "Rag mannered devils! They were in collusion to separate us so Kelmarsh could speak to you. I want to go home and I'm not sure I mean the townhouse."

Panic gripped Bram. Hell, please not Ireland again.

"Now, cousin, what are you always telling me? 'A high and windy gallows to the lot of them.' We are in London to have fun. And fun we shall have."

Miss Quinlan raised a tear-stained face – bloody Rakecombe, Bram thought, what had he done?

"You're absolutely right. May they be mangled by cows and have their gizzards ravaged by crows."

Hoping the curses didn't hold too much sway with the Almighty, Bram stepped in. "Shall I escort you ladies back?"

"No," they both yelled.

He hesitated but decided to follow Wellington's advice on strategic retreats. It didn't mean you had lost, simply that regrouping would be advisable.

Bowing, he clasped Sophie's hand. "I will call on you soon, Sophie. But *please* think on my words."

A MAN ONLY GETS SPLOTCHIER WITH TIME.

"*I* don't think Elizabeth should have married Mr Darcy. A leopard doesn't change its spots. If anything, they just become less defined...splotchier."

Sophie gazed over as Aideen let the leather-bound book fall into her lap. "Splotchier?"

"You do know what I mean. Can men actually amend such personality defects?"

"Whose are we talking about?"

A wry smile graced Aideen's tired features. "What a disaster the Gardens turned out to be. I've never seen your parents so angry."

Neither had Sophie, although she felt their anger had been directed more at the gentlemen than herself and Aideen. They'd both arrived back at the supper box slightly creased and woebegone. Mama had taken charge, bustling them home before the fireworks, and muttering under her breath about Lady Falkirk, Sodom and Gomorrah, and the conduct of noblemen in this day and age.

Today they had both slept late, until Sophie had awoken

to Aideen bringing her a cup of chocolate. A musical evening had been planned for tonight, but no one had the energy or heart, so they'd cancelled, citing illness.

Bram had sent a bunch of white lilies interspersed with field lilacs, and her mother had asked where she wanted them, her tone so disapproving it was obvious the kitchens were considered too good for the gigantic blooms.

Instead they sat on Sophie's writing desk, their sweet fragrance filling the room. She herself wasn't angry at Bram but somewhat saddened. It all seemed an illusion – his courting and proposal – but at least she could now relate the two contradictory sides of him. The languid attitude but intense kisses. The disinterested manner yet intelligent eyes. His spectacles and that perfect vision.

Stupid.

Overall, that was how she felt. A self-pitying emotion, maybe, but so it was. How could she have not seen it? Or rather, how could she not have listened to her instinct more closely?

After kicking off her slippers and stretching her toes, Sophie meandered over to Aideen, who was lolling on the chaise with her feet up, a mint-green silk shawl slung around her neck and shoulders.

"You haven't spoken about the Duke of Rakecombe," she said, sitting on the edge and playing with the fringe tassels.

"And you haven't mentioned what Kelmarsh revealed, although I can hazard a guess."

She shook her head, glancing up. "I doubt you could. It is too ridiculous."

Aideen raised a brow and took one hand in hers, the shawl falling. "Could it be similar to our conversation the other night?"

Frowning, Sophie didn't answer. Not because she didn't want to, but because something had distracted her. Reaching out with her other hand, she turned Aideen's chin. "Was that Rakecombe?"

A cherry-red hue swiftly traversed Aideen's cheekbones as she gathered the shawl around herself again, cursing under her breath.

"Aideen Quinlan," Sophie said, gasping, "you will tell me everything this instant. I thought you merely argued, but he kissed you? And nibbl–"

A hand slammed over her mouth. "Don't say it out loud! If your parents hear you, I'll be in the parson's mousetrap with the odious man."

Sophie smirked behind the cold palm before pulling her cousin's arm away.

It may now be hidden by the shawl, but on Aideen's neck had been a ragged dark-red smudge. A year ago, Sophie might have innocently thought it an insect bite, but the day Bram had proposed, he'd also left his own mark on her. As though 'twas yesterday, she remembered his teeth grazing her throat, fingers twisting in her hair.

"Is that why you slapped him?"

"You heard that?"

"Hmm. And the cursing. That one is usually reserved for the veriest of rogues."

The rosy shade abruptly drained from Aideen's cheeks, leaving them wan, a glitter of tears lighting her eyes.

"I lost you…during the rush to the cascade. Rakecombe said he knew where you were, so I followed. 'Twas a dark path but this was the strait-laced duke so I thought…" Her eyes dropped. "I tripped on a tree root or something and he held me to stop my ignoble descent. Then, I don't know, he seemed…flustered. Without warning, he was kissing me and…"

"And?" It was Sophie's turn to grasp her cousin.

"Then his lips were at my neck and his hands were… And he kept growling 'cherry' as he… That blasted cane clattered to the ground and he stopped." Aideen's lip slightly trembled. "He stood back and wiped his sleeve across his mouth as though…as though disgusted. And his expression – he looked horrified."

"What did you say?"

"I told him he was a stiff-rumped bore and that he kissed like a wet fish, and he retorted I was a vain, capricious saucebox."

"You told a duke he kissed like a fish?"

"A cod to be exact. And then he snapped that I was a cockish jade and he'd only touched me to prevent my finding you and that I kissed like a shrew." Aideen covered her eyes, tears seeping from behind the clenched hands.

Never had Sophie seen her cousin even remotely shed a tear, and she felt an unladylike urge to bash Rakecombe senseless…if she had a chair to stand on. Did he not see that Aideen's fierceness covered a soft, easily hurt interior? She may act bold but her personality was complex, shaped by her life, father and experiences.

And so too, she promptly thought, was Bram's. She'd fretted over not knowing the real him, but maybe all his personas were him – the quiet, the sly, the idle, the clever and the indolent. No man had a singular trait – we were all full of contradictions.

"You two do seem…"

"I know," Aideen wailed. "I shouldn't have called him a cod fish."

"If it's any consolation, a man doesn't do that to your throat if he thinks you kiss like a shrew."

"Really?" Aideen peeped through her fingers. "Not that it concerns me, at all."

Laughing, they collapsed into each other's embrace, until Aideen propped herself up on an elbow. "What are you planning to do about Kelmarsh?"

What indeed?

Sophie slid from the chaise and sat on the floor, leaning her head back against the well-worn furniture. "I asked for time. He explained certain things, but I still do not know if I can trust him."

Aideen leaned forward, her lips close to Sophie's ear. "Is he a"– she glanced over each shoulder – "S. P. Y.?" she spelled.

"How did you guess?" Sophie whispered back.

"Rakescum's cane," the whispering continued. "I know it was made for an agent at Whitehall. Uncle Seamus designs special pieces for them. That cane was a singular commission. Never knew the name, but I polished those jade eyes. All three of them must be involved. Explains a lot."

"Even Winterbourne? He seems so…"

"Has a reputation for being an excellent lover. Many women would gladly confide in him for a quick tup…or slow one."

"Aideen!" Sophie shrieked.

"What?" Her eyes widened with fake innocence.

"I didn't let Bram explain about Celeste. I was too furious at being misled."

"It's a dangerous vocation, Sophie. He can't tell people willy-nilly."

"Are you on his side?"

"No, of course not, but I can imagine it's hard to reconcile that profession with love. Always abroad and up to no good."

"He says he's giving it all up...for me."

Aideen's eyes broadened yet more. "You might have to give the English bug a chance then."

"YOU'VE NOT A CHANCE IN HELL."

Bram shot a bleary-eyed glare at Jack. Last night, he'd escaped from the lot of them and retired to his false study where he'd proceeded to drink his real self to oblivion. Even that hadn't worked. Dreams of Sophie had plagued him. She'd kept asking who he really was and yet he'd been unable to speak, gagged by some mystical spell.

"Sophie says she needs time."

"Faugh! I know the tortoise supposedly wins the race but I'd rather be the frisky hare. Besides, I've heard Stanton means to ask for her hand so a little urgency wouldn't go amiss."

"What? I threatened to break his bloody legs. Have I become that ineffective?" Bram stomped to the decanters.

"Love does seem to soften people, I've noticed," Jack said, wrinkling his nose. "What a horrible thing to happen. One must avoid it."

"I once tracked Henri Du Pont across Paris for three days and the man pissed his lemon satin breeches when I caught him. What's changed?"

"Well, your threats did send Stanton into hiding, but he's

wooing from afar with poems and whatnot. He's got IOUs up to his ears and your girl has a tidy dowry. Broken legs from you or similar from his creditors probably makes no difference."

"Damn the coxcomb. I knew I should have strangled him with his own cravat at Almack's."

"You know the only recourse now, don't you?" Jack said idly, twiddling his gold signet ring.

"No. And no again. Sophie doesn't want any more acting. That is her main source of displeasure with me."

"*You* wouldn't be acting. *We* would. You'd be saving the girl from the clutches of an evil scoundrel...well, Rakecombe. And anyhow, I believe he too needs some help as he's in such a lather over that Quinlan chit. Did you see his face last night? That red handprint? I've never laughed so hard."

Bram couldn't keep the grin from his lips either. Most sincerely, he hoped Sophie's cousin hadn't been too upset, but it was amusing nonetheless to see his upright friend in such a state.

"I still say this acting plan is flawed. Can you honestly see Rakecombe playing the...well, Rake? Sophie would know something was awry." Dumping himself in his study chair, he plunged impatient fingers through his hair.

"In that case," Jack proceeded, "you have until the Cooper's ball to think of something else. Otherwise, Rakecombe and I will continue unassisted." He slouched back, looking satisfied with this ultimatum.

"Why is my happiness so important to you both?"

"Hmm." Jack paused. "I think 'tis because we all hope to end up the same way: retired, a beautiful wife in the country and a finely stocked cellar," he said, shifting in his seat. "Not *yet* obviously, but what's the alternative? Chadwick's untimely demise? A knife in the back?"

"I thought love was anathema to Jack Winterbourne?"

"Indeed, I do not hope for love as I don't believe 'tis within me. My interest never lingers but one cannot endure my lifestyle forever. Many years from now I hope to marry, but while I have the...energy, I shall continue to unselfishly give myself over to the service of my country."

Jack gazed into his brandy, a smirk on his lips, but Bram, ever the sharp observer, saw the slight downturn of the brows and tightness around his eyes.

Topping up both their glasses, Bram changed the subject. "By the by, have you spoken to Rakecombe today?"

"No, but he sent a note. A similarly described Frenchman has been seen at Tattersall's, so he's viewing horseflesh today. And I'm off to the gaming hells tonight. What about you?"

"I'll be at the clubs, listening."

As per Asher's orders, he kept quiet about the disclosure of sensitive information to the French. He felt sure Jack wasn't being blackmailed, but one never knew. What would Bram do if Sophie was ever taken? Her life threatened if he refused to betray secrets? Nausea churned in his guts. The duke was right: emotional attachment and this profession were not good bedfellows.

"Ever the wolf, patiently waiting to pounce, eh?" Jack pulled a face. "And I get *Moth*. I ask you, is that fair? Mind you, I still don't know Rakecombe's code name, so it must be bloody awful as well."

Bram smiled. "Don't look to me for it. His Grace can be a stubborn cur when he wants to be."

THE FEARSOME THREESOME ENACT A PLAN.

*L*ondon smelled.

After a few unseasonably hot days, the weather had turned sultry, and Sophie wrinkled her nose at the odious whiff emanating from the streets.

Horse manure, chamber pots, rancid fish and rotting rubbish could all be discerned on the breeze that wafted into the carriage. In fact, the faster the horses trotted, the worse it became. Her mother held a lavender-scented handkerchief to her nose, but Sophie almost wanted to smell the decay of the city – it reminded her why she longed for the country.

Pastoral areas had their own fair share of problems but at least the air was sweet.

"That stinks worse than Da's stockings," complained Aideen.

Mama raised her face from the fragrant cotton. "Please, dear, do refrain from commenting on the aromas tonight. Lady Cooper's balls are only for the crème de la crème. I imagine our invite must be the duke's doing, such a courteous young man. I'm sure whatever happened at Vauxhall Gardens was simply a misunderstanding."

Aideen stifled a snort.

"Is the duke involving himself for Kelmarsh's benefit?" Papa asked. "Or has the gentleman an interest in one of you as well?"

Silence met his question as her cousin pretended to be taken with the scenery of London, despite the putrid fragrance.

"I have no idea, Papa."

"Hmm. And what do you intend to do about Kelmarsh? If you truly do not wish the man's attentions, you should tell him straight, Sophie. Do not lead him a merry dance."

She gazed at her father, stunned. Is that what she was doing? Over the past few days, Bram had showered her with flowers but hadn't called. As requested, he was giving her time but she felt no closer to a decision.

Her heart belonged to Bram, of that there was no doubt, but trust still lay just out of reach.

"You have altered your opinion somewhat," Sophie retorted tartly. "Would you welcome him as a son?"

Wise brandy-coloured eyes, the same hue as her own, stared back.

And then her father winked.

Her mouth fell open – he knew. Somehow, he knew about Bram's occupation and reasoning.

"Sophie, my love. You are an intelligent girl. Always have been, but you hide your light under a bushel. That gooseberry-eyed windbag Stanton doesn't even see it."

"Mr Stanton is a fine man," Mama interrupted.

"Wife of mine," he said, stroking her hand, "that *fine* man is so mired in debt it's no wonder he can't tie his cravat properly. Prefer to see Sophie become a spinster than marry such a sorry fellow. As for Kelmarsh... I shall leave the decision to you, daughter, but you will find no refusal from...us."

She looked to Mama, who gripped her fan with white knuckles, but her silver-blonde head gave the slightest of dips.

Gosh. Bram must have friends in high places indeed.

"Now, let us get this ordeal over with." Papa sighed. "The stench of London affects my piquet skills."

"IT'S GOING TO RAIN," Jack lamented as they all stood in Lady Cooper's rather stifling ballroom. "That could untwist the whole plan."

Low thunder rumbled through the open French doors, and Bram could only pray the rain arrived soon: even Jack couldn't argue with divine intervention.

Perhaps if he was more certain of Sophie's feelings, he would demand they stop this ridiculous plan, but a small, very small, part of him did wonder if it might work. He should have told Sophie he'd wait forever – that would've been romantic, but it would also have been a lie. Impatience and fear of losing her now compelled him to act. And besides, he'd come up with nothing else...

Over the years, he and Rakecombe had oft created faux scenes: a bar brawl as a distraction, playing a wounded man for sympathy, acting the part of brigands in Spain. All of them had worked superbly so why not this?

And even if she kneed Rakecombe in the cods, what

harm could come of it? The man deserved it for the farcical plot.

"If you touch one hair on her head, Rakecombe," Bram warned, "I shall take that dog-headed, ebony toothpick of yours and ram it up–"

"Now, now," interrupted Jack. "I'm sure he will play the unconscionable villain with perfect propriety."

The duke merely held his own counsel, looking ruthless. Obviously, the other two emotions Kean had mentioned of lust and frenzy were still beyond his acting capabilities.

Rolling his eyes, Bram gazed across the ballroom floor. Sophie skipped around with a sapscull lord who'd already trodden on her foot twice, and he remembered the perfect harmony they always found together when dancing. Once, they'd waltzed at a private ball and her body had curved to his, that lush softness unresisting against his tight grip.

"It shouldn't be too hard a job for Rakehell. She's looking delightful."

Undoubtedly, she was. A lilac gossamer net shimmered over a white satin gown, fringy bits at the feet. Slashed sleeves of a deeper violet were embellished with bands of silver, and ribbons of that same colour caught her hair in a Grecian knot. Ephemeral. She looked ready to disappear in a flash of amethyst if she so chose.

"Thus, I will distract Miss Quinlan," Jack blathered on, "and Rakehell, you will suggest a walk on the terrace with Bram's beloved. When you are at the dark column, you will twirl her around, give a nefarious grin and say?"

"Kiss mine arse," the duke hissed.

"No, no, that won't do, she's a maiden. I told Kean I should have done it. Have you nothing else?" Jack questioned. "You can't just make it up there and then.

Preposterous. Rule eleven: plan all seduction lines in advance."

"Never tried a bit of spontaneity?" asked Bram. "Doesn't it get a bit tedious?"

"Difference of a night betwixt cold sheets or a shag up aga–"

"Witterbore." The duke fixed a cold, narrow-eyed scowl upon the marquess. "The day I take your licentious advice, I shall be ten feet under." He slicked back his hair with a sweeping hand. "Bram. I expect to see you on the terrace precisely on the hour of ten to rescue your lady from my evil clutches. Don't crease my cravat and try not to rip the jacket: it's my best black."

He strode off, his gait stiff.

Jack leaned over. "Not exactly Edmund Kean, is he? Perhaps you were right to be cautious."

"Psst."

"Yes?"

"Shush. Pretend you aren't listening to me."

Sophie swivelled to her cousin who was hiding behind an ornate marble indoor fountain. "And why would I do that?"

"They might see me."

"Who? The leprechauns?"

A bad-tempered frown was thrown her way through the water cascade. "Why does everyone in London always go on about leprechauns? I've never seen one, although Da swears they raid his whiskey stocks every week." Aideen peered left, then right. "No, it's so the trifling threesome don't see me."

"The trif… Oh them. They do seem rather close tonight, don't they?"

"Hmm. After what I heard a moment ago, thick as damn thieves."

Sophie decided to join Aideen around the back of the gushing fountain. The ball, despite all her expectations, was dreary. The so-called crème de la crème consisted of lots of dowagers and elderly lords, quizzing glasses at the ready. Sophie had been eyed and dismissed with a sniff at least a half-dozen times.

Her father had wandered around with a bemused expression before abandoning them for the card room, and her mother was finding solace in the company of Lady Ardenbury, discussing face creams. Herself and Aideen had been left to their own devices, her parents obviously presuming the uppermost nobility would not deign to bother with such lowly misses.

At least there were no caged birds at this affair, she thought, recalling the ball at which she'd first met Bram. After that particular evening, an acquaintance had revealed how all those exotic species had been purchased by a peer and taken to a special zoological park, their cage to be the size of a house which could only be an improvement. She had often meant to ask Bram about it.

"Sophie, I have just heard of the most deceitful plan ever conceived."

That caught her attention and gazing at her cousin, she noticed the disgruntled expression. "Whatever do you mean?"

"I was circling the ballroom, a wee bit bored, when I saw the cloven-hoofed threesome, all looking very serious, so I crept up behind them and–"

"You earwigged?"

A canny smile curved her cousin's deep-red lips. "I did and I have no excuses or regrets. They have a wicked plan to throw you and Kelmarsh together. It's devious, sly and fiendishly clever, to be sure. I mean, I do admire the bug for his persistence, if nothing else."

Sophie also had to admit that being pursued in such a manner – by Bram, anyhow – did bring a certain fervent beat to the heart and a slight giddiness to the mind. After her awful Seasons of despondency and then Bram's betrayal, she'd considered spinsterhood to be a safer life, but his ardent pursuit could not be denied.

Annoyance should be her prevailing emotion – annoyance that he refused to be rejected – but instead her pulse beat fast with excitement.

"Tell me of their plan, Aideen. And we will see if we can be as equally wicked and devious as the *gentlemen*."

LIGHTNING CRACKLED against the black night but the skies refused to douse the muggy air. The ballroom was now insufferably hot, yet no one circled the terrace, no doubt afraid to brave the imminent storm.

Bram slid a finger inside his tight cravat; the bloody thing was near strangling him in the oppressive heat and he couldn't wait to throw it off. By his fob watch, it was nigh on ten, yet Sophie seemed to be leading the duke a merry dance.

Sent off like a puppy to procure champagne, the duke had then, not an instant later, been observed fetching cake, both of which Sophie had consumed rather slowly. He watched Rakecombe furtively glance at the longcase clock with a resentful expression.

Equally failing was their eminent rogue Jack Winterbourne. Totally immune to all his rakish smiles and practised requests for a dance, Miss Quinlan was last seen scooting in the direction of the orchestra, Jack trailing hastily. The whole scene would have been hysterical if he himself wasn't so inextricably bound up in it.

Finally, he spied Rakecombe leading Sophie to the terrace and so grabbing a flute of champagne from a passing tray, he quaffed the contents in one and cracked his knuckles. The duke had better not lay a fingernail on her or he'd find himself on his graceless arse.

Skirting the ballroom proved trickier than expected. Lady Cooper appeared from nowhere and asked if he felt the heat. "Yes." Lord Banload sauntered up and enquired whether he desired to sell his gelding. "No." Miss Lootingham queried if he liked blond women. "I beg your pardon?"

A panting Jack appeared as the French doors lay just ahead. "I lost her. One moment she was... Oh damn." And he tore off again in the direction of the supper room. Hell, and they considered themselves shrewd spies – the women were running bloody rings around them.

The air was no better outside. Sticky and clammy, it clung like buckskin breeches after a rainstorm.

Pausing, he glimpsed his beloved promenading. Thank God! The duke must have realised he'd been detained and not begun the seduction yet. A snap of lightning lit the sky and Rakecombe looked up, catching his eye. The couple continued to the edge of the terrace, the rake steering them both to where the shadows clung like lovers, lanterns unable to brighten the very edges.

Bram frowned: surely his beloved shouldn't be allowing another man to guide her to the shadows?

Skulking nearer, he saw the duke finally twirl Sophie around until she was hidden from view by his tall dark frame. Kean had said it was important to enact all emotions, but only one coursed through his own body – horn-mad jealousy.

It's no more than a plan, he berated himself; Rakecombe is temporarily acting a part, but as he stepped closer, a breathy voice halted his step and heartbeat as one.

"Oh, Your Grace," Sophie purred, "you're so strong. So very, very…masculine."

"What?" said the would-be seducer.

"I've always admired your merciless looks."

"You have?"

"Oh yes. Those scowling frowns, that menacing walk and…as for the way you wield that cane." She sighed. "Oh, do that again!"

"What? I haven't–"

"Mmm. More. Your touch makes me so…mad. And to think you feel the same. Kiss me agai–"

Bram seized the Duke of Rakecombe by the collar, hauling him away, rage searing through his body as he noticed Sophie's wet lips, her dishevelled ringlets. He fisted his hand, slamming it into the rascal's jaw without a thought.

Rakecombe fell, sprawling onto his backside, and Bram stood over him, quite ready to repeat the process, when another voice filtered through the dark.

"Oh, Lord Winterbourne," came an Irish purr, "those hands of yours are just *sooo* masterful."

The duke moved so fast, Bram was unable to get in another strike as he leaped to his feet and sped to the other side of the terrace from whence the soft lilt had emerged. A harsh smack of knuckle on cheek was followed by another as the two gentlemen audibly involved themselves in fisticuffs.

Miss Quinlan strolled out from the shadowed melee and, straightening her skirts, winked at Sophie before sauntering back inside, far away from the uncouth din of male grunts and curses.

Twisting, Bram spied a smirk on Sophie's glistening mouth and stalked up to her, feeling more like the wolf of his alias than ever before. "Did you enjoy your little ruse, Miss Sophie Beckford?"

A smile that could only be described as roguish played around her lips before she licked them.

The final straw.

Grabbing hold of her wrist, she gasped as he hauled her across the terrace, down the steps and along the path, the lanterns becoming infrequent, the garden lit fleetingly by the occasional jagged strike of lightning. Ahead, a broad oak loomed and Bram darted toward it. Spinning Sophie around, he pressed her against the tree.

"Enough, Sophie." He slammed his palms to the bark either side of her. "I am going to kiss you until you forget the duke ever laid a hand on you." Leaning close, he let his breath rasp in her ear. "I've played by the rules – flowers, presents, bloody poetry but no more. Now you will have me. The real me. Isn't that what you wanted?"

18

A HEROINE MUST CONSIDER THE CONSEQUENCES...

a decision needed to be made.

Should Sophie indignantly recoil against the bark and shriek her displeasure? Or should she fling herself forward into his furious arms, pressing hard enough to feel the buttons of his tailcoat digging at her breast?

The choice should be obvious, she thought. In books, any heroine worth her salt would be attempting to escape a scoundrel's sinful clutches and yet she didn't feel at all saline – she felt sweetly wicked.

When she and Aideen had discussed their devious counterplan, they had failed to ponder on the consequences, but she'd vaguely assumed it would involve them smirking over more champagne, not being pushed up against a tree by an irate earl.

In no way was she fearful. In fact, Bram looked quite delicious in his scariness, his face tight, body taut.

She decided on an admission. "The duke did not kiss me."

One of his hands removed itself from the large oak and stroked a finger over her lips, arousing a shudder, before caging her again, an arm either side.

"Your lips were wet."

"I licked them so you would think he had."

"To make me jealous?" He tilted his head.

"Rather to mock your little plan."

"With you, Sophie, plans are futile. I've followed a rogue's advice on how to woo a lady and you kneed me in the groin. I've taken words from a poet and had a second verse thrown back at me. I've tried to explain the situation but find myself pacing with worry at giving you time...time to hate me. Tonight, all the plan achieved was to make me insane with jealousy." He leaned closer, his lips almost touching hers. "What will it take, Sophie Beckford?"

Reaching up, she unhooked the spectacles from his ears and pulled them off.

"What would *you* do, Bram?"

A crack of thunder tore the sky but he didn't even flinch his gaze unwavering in the faint light from the distant lanterns.

In the end, she didn't need to press her body back or forward because Bram bent close, slowly squashing her between two unyielding surfaces – rough bark and firm physique.

Lightning silhouetted the garden and his face was briefly lit in its alabaster glow – Bram didn't look irate any more his expression more fervid, eyes gleaming. A painting in her father's study depicted a satyr capturing a winsome nymph – his countenance was very similar, and Sophie only hoped her expression didn't replicate the nymph's, whom she'd always considered to have a pathetic but ultimately hopeful visage.

"Wh–" She tried again, "What are you going to do, Bram?"

A wicked smile curved his mouth and he dipped his head. She watched his lips float closer, slightly parted, the faint smell of champagne and coffee leading her nostrils to twitch their partiality. He teased, his face so close but not touching, movement so slow she wanted to scream.

Instead, she licked her now dry lips and with a growl, Bram slanted his mouth over hers, not bothering with softness or care but devouring with unashamed hunger.

Sensation, pure and opulent, thudded through her body, every nerve and hair alight with feeling. The air sizzled with humid heat, prickly anticipation, and Sophie dropped the spectacles to the ground, flinging her arms around Bram's neck.

A thrusting of his hips made her gasp against the kiss, his tongue taking the opportunity to push inside once more and tangle with her own. With palms still braced against the tree, Bram ravished with mouth and body, rocking against her with harsh groans.

At long last, his hands left the bark, one finding its way to her nape, the other firmly caressing down her shoulder, the side of her breast until it rested at her hip. His nipping mouth slid to her delicate throat and a moan escaped as breath caught in her ear. "If you knew what you did to me, Sophie, you would never have teased me so."

If it was anything like the sensation Bram was eliciting from her own body, she was beginning to comprehend the dire but not unpleasant consequences of her actions.

"It was *your* plan," she managed to rasp.

A slam of pelvis was his answer, a broad press of something only vaguely known, her sole education coming from a motley array of marble statues and a book of so-so drawings that Aideen had found at her godfather's house. They'd laughed over the inept pencilwork – she wasn't laughing now.

"Would you have enjoyed the duke touching you in this way?" he murmured, voice hoarse. "His hands on your body?"

She shook her head. Of course not. It had all been a ruse, but Sophie realised she'd exposed a part of Bram previously unseen – possessive and ever so slightly dangerous.

Light breeze raised a goose skin on her arms despite the stifling air. "I've never wanted anyone but you, Bram."

This time, he replied with a nip of teeth through the satin bodice and she tried plunging hands through his hair to keep him grazing her breast, but Bram raised his head.

"I'm sorry for the absurd subterfuge," he said, panting, his lips brushing her eyelids shut. "I shouldn't have listened to anyone or anything, only my own mind and heart. But if a man offers you a rope when drowning, you take it. And I *am* drowning without you, Sophie. I kept seeing you slip away and I grasped at anything to prevent it, however foolish."

How was she supposed to remain hard-hearted when he spoke thus? It was easy when he parroted poetry but she could tell these words were no one else's – genuine and heartfelt.

"Bram, the problem is... I think... I feel..." Drowning was an apt adjective. Those large hands fixed on her hips, eyes dropping to watch his body rock against hers as he compelled her to match the rhythm, their clothes rustling as the combined satin attire slid and slipped. "I feel as though I don't know you."

His long lashes swept up. "We always danced so well together, didn't we, Sophie?"

She nodded, unsure what that had to do with anything.

"It's because you do know me." Fingers crept up, tugging at her sleeve until they revealed a bare shoulder. A kiss was deposited on the exposed skin. "Who's my favourite poet?"

Bram's wet touch caused words to fail her and a nipping prompt on the same patch of skin did little to help. Why was he asking such questions?

"Erm, Propertius," she murmured.

Attention shifted to the other sleeve and an open-mouthed kiss brushed her naked shoulder. "And colour? What do I like?"

She was about to say grey, as surely a man wore the colours he liked, but she recalled a carriage ride they'd taken a year past. The day had been fresh, a morning downpour having coaxed everything to bloom. Vigorous growth had graced the highways, from the palest jade to the deepest moss, and Bram had remarked how he loved the verdancy.

"Green."

A sigh emanated from deep within his chest. "You remember," he rumbled into the curve of her neck.

Nodding, Sophie touched a hand to his cheek, felt the rasp of stubble beneath her fingers.

"And what do I want, Sophie?" he asked, nibbling on her earlobe, his fingers busy at her breast. She gasped as his nails raked the tight crests and thought the answer rather obvious.

"At this moment?"

A husky laugh tickled her ear. "Too easy. Although I'll want that as well...lots. I mean in a year? Where would I like to be?"

She gulped, and her legs started to feel quite wobbly so she concentrated on the actual question. Last year, the answer would have been easy. Was Bram saying he hadn't changed? That he had always told her the truth? When it mattered.

"You want goats. To live on your estate and grow more wheat, to plunge your hands in the soil and feel the gritty earth. You want to grow old watching the harvests every year. You want to see the whole life cycle of an apple... You didn't mention if you would eat it th–"

The words were halted by a hard mouth that smothered hers, and she responded to the almost violent pressure, pushing herself to her toes and biting at his lip.

Finally, he tore himself away. "You know the true me. With those three answers, you see me better than anyone ever has in my entire life – even my parents. But there is something else. Something missing." He paused, cupping her face in his broad palms. "None of that would be worth a damn without you, Sophie."

"Bram..." A flare of lightning again threw his features into relief – a look of utter yearning frozen in a blink of white. Without any reserve, she responded to his passionate words and flung herself at him, struggling to get closer, dragging his mouth to hers.

"Yes, Sophie. Say you'll be mine forever." Fevered kisses peppered her face. "Be mine here and now." His body strained, and Sophie tore at the jacket buttons, pushing the garment from his shoulders. She only had the vaguest inkling as to what he meant but she didn't care.

A shiver quaked her as Bram's fingers tugged at the satin skirts, sliding them up, over ankles, then knees. He skimmed a hand under, a hot palm caressing its way up her thigh, the material rippling over his hand like water.

His breath stirred. "I love you so very much."

Qualms melted with his declaration and she let him part her legs with gentle but urgent hands, her gasp muffled as his mouth swallowed the sound.

"Sophie." Her name was merely a groan as he lightly stroked with earnest fingers.

Aching need sung through Sophie's body, and she instinctively pushed against the touch, to feel more of the white-hot ecstasy that flooded her.

Bram buried his head in her bosom, pulling the material low with his teeth. "You may hate them, but these make every thought in my head disappear." He nipped at the slope, his fingers still circling, exploring, torrid pleasure coursing through her body.

Then she felt it.

A light drip of water landed on her chest, tracking its way down the slope. Bram licked it up, seemingly unaware of its portent.

Another fell to be caught with greedy lips, but the breeze gathered speed, swirling her skirts. She tried to recapture the sensation, the desire, but one more drop of rain trickled onto her breast, the satin darkening to violet.

Glancing upwards, a sudden flash of lightning lit the thick oak branches that loomed overhead, the thin covering of spring leaves trembling on their boughs. Tracing a path were grey splashes that clung to them before plummeting as sullied drops.

One fell in her eye, inducing a blink and a splutter. "Bram, I think—"

With a final cannonade of thunder, the heavens opened, casting down with all their might a deluge of liquid. The oak offered protection, a haven against the curtain of rain that surrounded them, but now the raging wind whipped twigs from the branches and finally...finally he lifted his head.

THE ENORMITY of what he had been about to do slapped Bram in the face as heavily as the sudden squall.

Hell, he had nearly taken his beloved Sophie up against a tree. One hand was still intimately pressed against her, his other on her buttocks, and recriminations could not come fast enough.

She was an innocent. Anyone could have wandered by. Standing up wasn't ideal for a maiden. Against a tree even worse. They weren't married. Devil take it, not even betrothed again. He'd yet to fully explain everything. Unforgivable.

Nevertheless, his body screamed its contempt as he gently removed his hands, allowing the skirt to slip back down.

The shelter of the oak was waning, the soft early leaves no barrier to the relentless onslaught. Water crept through the canopy with gathering power to sluice Sophie's gown, plastering the satin to her lush body. He tried not to gawk, but then noticed Sophie doing similar to his chest. The waistcoat had become unbuttoned in their heated encounter and the shirt now clung to his torso, displaying dark chest hair and delineating the muscles.

She reached out to place her palm on the wet linen at his stomach, and all his recriminations turned tail and ran. Covering her hand with his, he moved it...up, over his chest to his lips, where he kissed the fingers.

"Sophie, I... To have you so near, I lost control."

She smiled, the sight almost lost in the sweet rain. "I am as much to blame and it was a most agreeable consequence of my ruse. One I didn't foresee. But what now? I'm drenched."

Thankful she wasn't angry, Bram could only hope his *friends* had returned to their lookout posts instead of killing each other.

The wind picked up again, coating them in an additional flurry of water, and Sophie shivered. Although the night was warm, the rain brought freshness, and grabbing the soaked jacket from the floor, he attempted to cover Sophie with it.

"I doubt anyone is on the terrace in this storm to see our return but wait by the steps. I will ask Rakecombe or Jack to fetch your cousin and see if anyone has noted our disappearance." He paused. "My love, I would not wish you to lie, but...it might be better, until we are–"

"Bram." Fingers stopped his words. "I'm not about to tell anyone of this night. It is our affair. And as to our future, we do still need to talk."

He bowed his head in acknowledgement.

The clouds shimmered with opalescent lightning, and Sophie yelped with laughter, unafraid of the heaven's anger, as they sprinted towards the house. He stopped to thrust hands into her drenched hair and kiss her giggling lips, not caring if anyone saw, more aroused and emotional than ever by her fearlessness. Sophie Beckford would never bemoan the cold or wet – she looked like she could waltz the night away in this pounding rain.

Soon, they reached the steps to see the curtains had been closed behind the tall French doors. No doubt Rakecombe had complained about the sight of the dreary weather and the hosts had obeyed – it did pay to have a duke on your side.

As Sophie sheltered by a column, Bram searched for a crack in the curtain to peer through, but a door at one end opened and a bruised Jack squinted around. "Bram? Is that you?" A dry woollen cloak was thrust in his direction. "Sophie's parents believe she's in the retiring room comforting Miss Quinlan whilst the duke is keeping them busy with a story about a ruffian accosting us in the garden. Apparently, *we* fought him off and now we're being lauded as heroes. We've had propositions from four ladies but Rakeprude has gone all–"

"We're wet through, Jack."

"No doubt," he replied with a muffled snigger. "Rakeprude has offered his coach so the two *frightened* girls can return home quickly. The parents will follow in their own carriage with him, so if you're hasty, she can change before they get back… I'm sure he'll arrange a delay to their journey. Anyhow, the coach is waiting in the mews – can't miss it. I'll round up Miss Q."

"Thank you, Jack."

A somewhat swollen eye winked. "Least I could do. What a bloody disaster! Should never listen to actors."

Bram agreed with the latter but not the former: the evening had not been an utter disaster. Sophie would never have responded if she didn't hold affection for him. Tonight had shown that at least.

Turning, he hurried back to enfold her shivering form in the cloak.

"I heard," she muttered, "but I'll wager the silver swan my parents don't believe that fiddle-faddle."

19

A NEW DAY, A NEW LONDON.

"Sophie, dear, do stay close. We don't want you to go *missing* again."

The strident tone caused a wince and left Sophie in absolutely no doubt that her mother knew exactly what she had been doing at the Cooper's ball, two evenings previous.

A ribbon was held close to Sophie's ashen cheek. "What do you think, Aideen? Surely there is *one* shade of pink that suits my daughter."

Also being in the suds, Aideen decided to be diplomatic. "That paler shade is quite becoming." However, the subtle shake of her head and terrified widening of eyes belied the truth.

"Hmm," Mama mumbled, pottering over to the darker rose ribbons stashed away in the corner of the Mayfair haberdashery.

"Was it that bad?" whispered Sophie.

"I love your mother, you know that, but her taste in colour is rather confined to pink and you don't suit it."

"I can't believe I let her choose all my previous Seasons'

gowns, but when your mother says you look pretty in pink, you believe her. And besides, they are paying for them."

"You aren't a doll though and it makes you look sallow, unlike your fair-haired mother. When you're married, you'll be able to wear the most wonderful of colours – emerald green and vivid blues." Aideen looked a little envious as she fingered a turquoise velvet ribbon.

"And you as well."

"Hah," she said, dropping the ribbon. "Who is going to marry me? I know how those English lords look at me – more as mistress material." Her lips drooped.

"Aideen!"

"'Tis true. The duke may like to dally but wedlock? To an Irish bog trotter?"

Sophie took a firm grasp of her cousin's shoulders. "You are not a bog trotter. I will not let you belittle yourself. The duke would be a lucky man to kiss your toes."

A distasteful frown wrinkled her face. "Eugh! For me and the duke. I'd prefer he kissed my–"

Fortunately, Aideen didn't get to the where, as Mama called over and bustled everybody onto the street.

London felt fresh and new after the storm's soaking and the continued downpours of yesterday. The hideous odours and rotting rubbish had been washed into the river, leaving the streets glistening and appreciably empty. A carriage barrelled by, spraying the pavements with water and all three of them hurriedly leaped back, their hems raised.

Sturdy boots encased Sophie's feet, but she suspected water had made an ingress into her stockings so she wiggled her toes – they squelched as they had done running back through the gardens at the ball.

Her mother and Aideen chatted happily as they

promenaded down Bond Street, and she followed, musing on that night. She could still feel the imprint of Bram's hands on her skin, the caress of his tongue lapping the rainwater at her breast.

Exhaling heavily, she skipped to avoid another large puddle. After their return to the house, he'd hustled her to the duke's carriage, a cloak covering her from head to toe, promising to call the very next day.

But he hadn't – flowers had been sent along with profuse apologies and a note explaining that business had called him away. That worried her – business? Or *business*?

Even though Bram had said he was leaving the intelligence service, it would surely be difficult to disentangle himself fully. His head must be full of important information. Was he in danger even now?

Despite desperately trying to let go of last year's events, a faint irritation erupted at his past silence. If they had married, would he have furtively left their bed late at night? Left to go hunting traitors without letting her know of his activities?

Ahead, Mama and Aideen turned into the drapery shop, followed by the maid, and Sophie hurried her step, aware her guts would be garters if she dawdled.

Herself and Bram needed to talk properly – without kisses and touches. She wanted to know if he enjoyed the life of a spy. Would he miss it when he gave it up? Would he come to resent her for that? Why hadn't he trusted her? Had he made love to that Frenchwoman on the eve of their betrothal...for the Crown? Why hadn't he followed her to Ireland – to explain in person?

Grimacing as her foot landed in another deep puddle,

she raised her hem and stomped on when suddenly a hand grabbed her wrist.

"*Non*, Mademoiselle, you come with me..."

About to clout whoever it was with her reticule, a firm arm swiftly snaked around her waist and began dragging her down the alleyway to one side of the shop. She opened her mouth to let out an almighty scream but a moist pudgy hand pressed to her lips as he hauled her down the darkening alley and flung her against the damp brick wall. The main thoroughfare now appeared a strip of cheerful light, near yet far from the muddy tunnel she found herself trapped in.

"Not a sound, Mademoiselle," said a deep, exotic voice. His face was hardly discernible, covered as it was by lots of black hair and a large pulled-down hat. Surely she could successfully knee him in his gentleman's area – Sophie was becoming quite practised at it after all – but a sharp pain to her ribs stilled her leg. Did he want her reticule? She only carried a few pence and certainly wore no jewels.

He leaned close, and she shuddered as sultry breath reached her ear, his body pressed, the wall grating her back, the alley barely a horse's width.

"This is warning. To your lover."

Sophie gasped behind the clammy palm. Where was Bram? What was happening to him? Was he safe?

"Tell the duke to stop asking questions."

Frowning, Sophie shook her head. *The duke?*

The pain in her rib sharpened, causing what little breath she had to catch.

"*Mais oui*, I see you on the terrace with him. He invites you everywhere."

His body pushed again, his cologne redolent of

frankincense. Why did a perfidious fiend have to smell so nice?

"Tell him no more hunting," he growled. "This time a warning. To show how easy for me to catch what I want, when I want. Tell him I could kill you here." The sharp thing prodded again and Sophie flinched. "But today, *ma chérie*... I am merciful."

Revulsion and terror shuddered their way through Sophie's body but she wouldn't let this odious villain know how scared she was. Instead, she nodded, but as soon as the sharp thing moved away, she stamped down heavily with her foot and bit hard on his palm, tasting blood on her tongue.

Twisting, she hurtled for the street, but the Frenchman was fast and caught her wrist to haul her back against him. One arm formed a strong band around her waist, and the other came around her front, clutching an ornate dagger that pressed upon her stomach and then slowly inched its way higher. It stroked her ribs, digging into the woollen pelisse, and up, brushing her bosom, her décolletage.

Stupid.

Why did she fight? But it had seemed so innate, not to be subdued by the rat.

Bond Street lay yards ahead, a narrow crack of light and safety, and as he dragged the knife up to her neck, a man and young boy meandered across the opening. But they didn't even pause to peer down the murky alley, oblivious to the nefarious deeds being committed.

The scoundrel chuckled and gripped her closer, whispering in her ear from behind. "They do not *want* to see. Your Englishmen, so effeminate – dandies. But the women..." He pulled her tight to his body and it sickened her to feel that male part of him press. Cruel fingers wandered leisurely up her body and then squeezed her breast hard, bruising. "You are tough. Strong. My bride is English but I have not yet claimed her. She waits for me. My silent one."

Sophie refused to whimper as the blade caressed her cheek, declined to cry out when the edge dug at her bare throat. But the wet touch of the man's tongue licking her ear brought forth a low sob.

"See that your duke receives my message, *ma petite.*"

Abruptly, she was thrown forward, falling to her knees, scraping hands in the gritty mud. The flutter of a cloak brushed her face as he ran past to the street ahead.

"You hellbound oaf! You nearly knocked me over. Curses to... Sophie!"

A dash of footsteps and Sophie was enveloped in the scent of violets, Aideen kneeling on the ground beside her, blue gown darkening as it draped in the puddles of water.

"Oh, Aideen."

"What happened? Did you fall? We only noticed you missing but a moment ago. Your mother wants pink curtains in the library."

A chuckled sob escaped. "We need to speak to the duke at once."

IN THE EVENT, it took three hours to locate the duke and a further hour to be interrogated by him – as Aideen put it. To be more truthful, Sophie thought his questioning sensitive. He had paused when she'd needed to gather herself, but prodded if she'd been reticent.

As he'd left, Rakecombe had even kissed her forehead, whispering she was incredibly brave and comparing her to his sister again. She knew he had no living siblings and felt a rush of sympathy and warmth towards him that he treated her as such. Apologies had been adamantly professed for the danger brought upon her, guilt clouding his features.

Aideen sat in the corner, cursing him. "He could have waited till you'd taken a nap."

"I needed to speak with him. This villain must be caught."

"Bejabbers, 'tis all their fault, especially *his*, that you attracted the Frenchman's attention in the first place."

Sophie nodded reluctantly. "True, but if my description helps catch the man, then it was worth it."

"Argh," Aideen cried out, standing and throwing her arms about. "Why do you have to be so...so reasonable. I would be clouting the bug for getting me into such a mess."

"I'll let you bash him for me. I think he'd enjoy it more." Sophie smiled but still shuddered. Her mind told her the ordeal was over, that she was now safe, but her body made its own complaints apparent, with trembling hands and a bone-deep chill within. She pulled the pale-pink blanket closer, huddling into the chaise.

"And where's Kelmarsh? A fine time to disappear."

"Apparently, he went to his estate on business, but the duke has sent him an urgent message. I said I was perfectly well but–"

The door opened and her father stalked in, both concern and anger written on his face. Leaning down, he bussed Sophie's cheek. "The Duke of Rakecombe has stationed a few sturdy footmen about the place, so if you see new fellows, don't be alarmed."

"I am quite well, Papa."

He put a hand up, worry deepening the creases on his brow. "Not another word, Sophie. You will go nowhere alone, not even the retiring room, until this villain is caught. All those gentlemen should never have come near you if they suspected this would happen."

"It's not Bram's fault," she found herself saying.

"I'll be having serious words with the young buck. I was promised he was leaving all that behind."

"You were? By whom?"

"Never you mind." He scowled. "Although the fellow who gave me that promise left me short by five pounds at piquet so I hope he can be trusted." He clucked her chin. "I presume you *are* marrying the earl? Put him out of his misery soon, won't you? He looked like a drowned rat at the Cooper's ball."

Smiling, he sauntered from the room, and Sophie pulled a wry face. "He knows."

"Your father is much cannier than he portrays." Aideen put a finger to her lips, tapping them. "Who does that remind me of?" Sophie threw a cushion but it bounced harmlessly off her cousin's iron bonce. A sudden shiver took her and Aideen came to sit close. "Are you sure you are well?" she asked, tucking the blanket around until Sophie couldn't move.

"Yes, I just..."

What could she say? It was gratifying to have all her family close and churlish to wish for any more, but she yearned for Bram's strong arms to hold her tight, for his hands to smooth away that revolting man's touch.

"I know," Aideen replied quietly. "I expect you want

Kelmarsh here as well. I… I was so frightened earlier, but on the duke's arrival… I just wanted to hug him."

"Pah! When he walked in, you said, and I quote, 'About time too, you wretched English bug.'"

She clasped Sophie close. "In Ireland, that's considered flirtation."

20

OF MICE AND MEN.

A clicking sound woke Sophie from her slumber. It came from outside the balcony doors to her bedchamber and the unusual clatter would cease but then continue after a certain length of time.

For a while, she lay still on the bed, debating whether to call one of the brawny footmen. But what if it were nothing more than an owl? Or a mouse? She would look extremely pudding-headed.

The clicking stopped. And then…a footstep. Light to be sure, but distinctively footfall on the balcony.

Rising quietly but swiftly, Sophie grabbed hold of the large pristine silver candlestick, which sat atop her mantelpiece. Hefty and solid, it would make quite a dent in anyone's head – even if it did turn out to be a heavy-footed mouse.

Voluminous blush-pink curtains easily hid her by the door. Tonight, she'd forsaken the shutters so as not to be left in total darkness but now that seemed foolish. Perhaps even more foolish was not calling a footman, but today in Bond

193

Street helplessness had overwhelmed her; now she was armed and had the element of surprise. She would not be cowed again – by mouse or man.

The scrolled brass handle slowly turned and Sophie's heart thumped rather too loudly.

Mice couldn't open doors.

A sweet breeze filtered into the room and a shadow stepped through.

Sophie kept completely still until the figure stood just the other side of the curtain and then, with an utterly silent swing, she bludgeoned the intruder with the candlestick.

It made not a sound, merely sinking to the ground in a crumpled heap.

Without any hurry to her stride, Sophie made her way back to the mantelpiece to feel for the tinder box and then fiddle with the contents. The lump on the floor wouldn't be going anywhere for a while, although she did hope no lasting damage had been inflicted – what if it was someone who had mistaken her room for Mrs Layton's two houses down? A woman well known for her male late-night visitors.

Shrugging, she finally lit the candle and made her way back to the large form crowding her floor. She poked it with a bare toe but it didn't move. Indeed, a horrible tightness suddenly clawed at her throat – had she killed it? Her arm strength wasn't that fierce but the weapon had been quite weighty.

Candlelight quivered in the room, both from her own hand and the breeze. She bent down and the tightness in her throat grew to suffocating as a pleasant aroma assaulted her nostrils.

Leather. Horses... Coffee.

Desperate speed harried her limbs as she kneeled on the floor and attempted to push the figure over onto its back. Damn hulking men – he was a blasted deadweight. The word *dead* reverberated in her brain and she bit back a sob, shoving with all her might.

With a last massive heave, he rolled onto his back and Sophie collapsed across his chest, sprawled inelegantly in a heap.

A THUMPING ACHE seared Bram's shoulders and neck, but he also felt swathed by a soft squidgy object.

It was rather pleasant.

The squidgy thing moved around and it seemed to be sobbing about murder, death and...candlesticks? Surreptitiously, he opened one eye to be confronted by a luscious female form draped across his chest; honeyed locks tickled his nose and a delicious warmth emanated from her skin.

Sophie, of course.

And then all the other occurrences rushed in. The scribbled note from Rakecombe telling him to get his arse back to London. The attack on Sophie. Riding for six hours straight and arriving at a city cloaked in darkness.

Yes, he could have waited until morning, but he needed to see Sophie with his own eyes. To hold her in his arms, tight.

Stretching out a hand, he caressed the soft head of curls, loving the feel of silk sliding under his palm. But why did his shoulders hurt so much? He'd used his cravat pin on the lock, a shoddy affair he'd talk to Mr Beckford about, but aware of frightening Sophie, he'd tried to be as quiet as possible. As soon as he'd opened the door, however something or someone had belted him. Any higher and they'd have taken his head off.

"Bram, have I killed you?" a sobbing voice sobbed some more.

Ah. His attacker would also be Sophie then.

"Shush, my love," he muttered, bringing his other hand up to calm her quaking body. "I'm alive." He pulled her tight "I want to know about you. Tell me that whoreson did you no harm."

Sophie pushed up from his chest, hair in wild disarray cheeks wet with tears.

"I didn't kill you," she cried.

"Was that your intention?" he asked, suddenly concerned. She had a right to be angry, but surely not with murderous intent.

"No. I thought you were...were..."

Oh God. He sat up, his shoulders on fire, and pulled Sophie close, cradling her soft form. What a dolt he was Obviously, she'd thought the Frenchman had returned to finish the deed and he'd given her the scare of a lifetime.

Mind you, if he *had* been the French bastard, Sophie would have saved the day and the country by knocking out one of the most dangerous enemies of England with, he could now see on the floor, a dented silver candlestick.

"I'm so sorry, my love. I rode back today and couldn't wait to see you. I needed to hold you."

"You never mentioned at the ball you would be disappearing to your estate. Why did you go there?" she muttered into his jacket.

Pulling back, he peered into disgruntled features. "Did you think I was on Crown business?"

Sophie picked at a button on his waistcoat. "It crossed my mind."

He tipped her chin up and looked deep into tired eyes, the dim candle chasing shadows across her face. "I know I do not deserve your trust, but I said I would always be honest with you. There are no more missions. I *am* leaving it all behind, Sophie. I don't need it. I never needed it."

Gently, Bram gathered her to his body and raised himself to his knees. He stood with Sophie in his arms, glad his legs were still working after the wallop, and carried her to the bed despite mumbled protests. Placing her in the middle, he plumped the pillows and drew the coverlet up.

The room resembled a pink sugar plum, except for the coverlet which was a luscious mint green. Fresh and innocent, he wanted nothing more than to lay down beside her, pull her close and...sleep.

But words needed to be said, the past discussed, deceptions apologised for.

His satchel had fallen amongst the material of the curtains and he went to gather it up, inspecting the contents to make sure it was still there. Having grabbed the candle from the writing desk, he hastened back to the bed, stripped off his tailcoat and sat at Sophie's side.

"I received some details from Rakecombe who said you were stout-hearted, but tell me all."

"In truth," she said, with a tremulous smile, "it feels like a dream now. And it was such a short time. One moment I was ambling down the street, the next dragged into an alleyway and then... Aideen was there. It happened so quickly. But I am unhurt, Bram. At most a wrenched shoulder and a little shaken."

"And while you were being attacked, I was faffing in the

country," he muttered to himself, shaking his head. Sophie's brow scrunched and so he drew out the flat box from his satchel. "I thought this might help my...cause, so to speak. I know you are not swayed by material fripperies – I have your response to my gifts to show that. But I thought..." He placed the box on her bed and grimaced. "As I have said before, I have little to offer you. A wearied man who brings danger to your door and wants nothing more than to retire to the country, far away from the excitement of the city."

"What a load of fuddle-headed nonsense." She snorted. "Should I list your attributes? Handsome. Considerate. Intellig–"

"Crafty. Sly. A liar... I know how to kill a man with my little finger."

"Have you killed innocents?"

"God no. I'm not a murderer."

"Then how is that different from any soldier who fights for the good of their country? They are one and the same."

He leaned forward and brushed a gentle kiss across her eyes. "I don't know what I would have done if harm had come to you. It *is* my fault. Rakecombe sent you invites at my behest."

Another protest was muttered into his shirt but neither could deny the truth.

"I need to explain about Celeste and Ireland, but I can come back when–"

A finger forestalled his words. "No. I am tired of waiting, of wondering. A year ago, I considered you a miserable, lying toad and now I no longer know what to think. My heart and head are in constant conflict."

Bram dipped his eyes. Maybe he had been putting it all off. Afraid to lose her. Afraid his excuses would not be enough. He prodded the box nearer. "Not that I'm trying to soften you up, but Jack does have a rule..."

THE BOX WAS shallow and covered in a rich black velvet, the letter K so elaborately scrolled in silver thread it was nearly impossible to make out. Sophie didn't need gifts from Bram, but obviously this meant more to him so she reached out a hand to open the case.

"What sort of a rule?" she asked absent-mindedly as the lid hinged.

A clearing of his throat and she glanced up.

"He has these... I probably shouldn't tell you as I'm sure there's some gentlemanly code of non-disclosure involved."

Sophie rolled her eyes. What gentlemen's *rules* could possibly require such secrecy?

"Although to be truthful," Bram continued, "every single one of Jack's rules has been utterly useless. In fact, I believe if I had done the exact opposite, we might have been having this conversation a lot sooner."

The hinge was a tad stiff but the lid finally squeaked open to reveal...

Sophie gasped. Despite only having the flicker of a lone candle, the sapphire gems sparkled with delight at being thus exposed. As though real and alive, their blue hue glinted in freedom – pleading to be released from their velvet home.

"Oh, Bram..."

"These are the Kelmarsh jewels. Mother never liked them, but I vaguely remember my grandmother wearing them. They are yours, Sophie. Along with myself and everything I have."

Sparkling diamonds surrounded rich blue sapphires on every piece. A ring, bracelet, necklace, earbobs and a tiara – they were sublime, magical, overwhelming.

"That's why you went back to your estate," she whispered, pressing a single finger to the vibrant gems.

"Yes. I had a time finding them as they seem to have been forgotten. I first searched the family bank vaults, then the townhouse, but to no avail. They were at my estate, stuffed in the back of a safe." He prodded the box again. "Take one out."

Sophie was very much aware this was bribery. Indeed, Bram had admitted it himself, but she was also mindful it meant much more than mere wealth. He was offering himself, his family, his title, his dreams…

Taking the necklace from its snug protection, she raised it to the candle, blue light splintering in every direction. "They are beautiful." Always his eyes had reminded her of the sea, but now she had a new comparison – both as deep and alive as the other.

"Let me place them on you." He reached over and undid the simple clasp, before draping the necklace around her, hands warm at her nape. "Enchanting. They suit you, Sophie, or you suit them. I know not which."

At that moment, a breeze sprung up, slamming the balcony door. Bram stood to close it, but on his return simply hovered by the bed, tapping his foot and fiddling with his dirt-stained cuff.

A nervous silence descended and she hated this feeling of unsaid words that hung in the air like bitter fog.

She patted the coverlet. "Sit beside me, Bram. Sit and tell me everything."

DO SPECTACLES MAKETH THE MAN?

"*I*'m not entirely sure where to start."

Sophie waited patiently. It wasn't as if she had anywhere to go. She narrowed her eyes as Bram paced to the mantelpiece in the gloom and fiddled with the clock, looking for the winding key.

Why did men find it so difficult to talk about things? Papa was the same – taciturn and silent when it came to certain subjects. Her mother had explained he always needed help, a little prodding in the right direction. It appeared Bram was of a similar disposition.

"Celeste is a–"

"Why did you become a spy, Bram?" That French harlot could wait: she wanted to know him.

His forehead wrinkled and his eyes avoided hers, staring at the empty, cold fireplace.

"I didn't really become one. I was born one. As I said, the Kelmarshs have always been in service of the Crown. It is…expected."

"And if your son did not want to become a spy? What would you do?"

"Be thankful, I believe. The Kelmarsh clan do not have a history of longevity." He turned to look straight into her eyes. "First I want to tell you this. Keeping my profession from you was not because I meant to deceive. Rather, it was to protect you. It was drilled into me from the nursery that you did not tell outsiders. Maybe when you were officially my wife… But no, I cannot promise that either. Selfish, I know, but I did not like my occupation, so why would I bring danger upon you and force you to share that treacherous part of my life."

"Did you want to follow a different path when younger?"

"I wanted, as every son does, to make my parents happy. They told me endlessly that it was important work, that I was one of a select few who would protect the Crown. My country."

"And it is important, Bram."

"I know, which made me feel even more guilty when all I wanted to do was to make the Kelmarsh estate and tenants profitable and content. But the teaching my parents gave me was thorough. I was…am adept at languages and so those skills were utilised in Spain, Holland and France."

He pressed his lips together and came to sit by her. "I will not gripe like a child as there have been exciting times and I've made some good, good friends. I would not say I was…unhappy. But I have been aware in the last few years that a weariness has crept upon me and such weariness causes mistakes, lapses. My days were numbered. I could feel it like a dark shadow watching me. Then you came along."

"Me?"

Bram took her fingers and she allowed him, loving the feel of his calloused skin. She could just imagine him as a little boy, diligently learning the trade of spy.

"You made me long for the life I'd almost forgotten. I remembered the estate I hadn't seen for years. The poetry I wanted to recite and translate. The land I wanted to walk on. I told my superior, after meeting you, that I wanted to retire at some point. We were still at war so I couldn't just leave, but I made ready to slowly remove myself. In retrospect, I should have done that before proposing," he said wryly.

"You could have confided in me. I would have told no one."

He released her hand before running frustrated fingers through his hair. "I know. But I have seen many times the merest word or look end a life. 'What you do not know, you cannot show.' I feel those words burned into me by my parents. And after Rakecombe's sister... Forgive me, Sophie, but I would not risk a single hair on your head." And so saying, he raised a hand to stroke her curls. "I also worried you may dislike my profession, and yes, maybe I thought it best to keep it from you. I have had so many personas over the years..."

Sophie caught his fist tugging once more at his poor hair and brought it to her lips. She could understand his reasoning and acknowledged her own misinterpretations. Silence had been protection not dishonesty. Bram was a loyal and brave servant of the Crown and for that she loved him yet more. She wondered what tragedy had befallen the duke's sister...but another time.

"As soon as I heard you were returning from Ireland," he continued, "I requested permission for a second time to tell

EMILY WINDSOR

you all. A week ago, I finally received my superior's sanction and disclosed to you my profession."

"And I was even more angry with you."

A rueful smile lit his features. "I actually thought you might not believe me."

"I knew something was amiss. I'm not stu—"

"Of course not. Don't even say that word." His grip tightened on her shoulders.

"But, Bram, can you understand that I worried I would have married a stranger? That I didn't know *you*."

"I can see that now. But you saw the true me more than any other person ever did. I tried to always be genuine with you, Sophie. My dreams, hopes and aspirations that I shared with you were all my own. My love for you was my own."

He bent forward and brushed lingering kisses across her mouth. Something glinted at his fob pocket, and she reached down to pull out his spectacles. "Were these for your last persona?"

A slight flush graced his cheeks. "Would you believe me if I said I feel as though I can't see without them?"

She cocked her head.

"My parents gave me spectacles at the age of twelve. Told me my eyes were too expressive for a spy. I wear them out of habit now."

"That's awful!" she cried.

A shrug was his singular response. "I didn't know any better. I wasn't the rebellious sort and when you see most of your family meeting a premature death, it seemed the sensible thing to do."

"Do you know," she said, hooking them over his ears, "I believe I would miss them. I like the fact that only I see your handsome eyes."

"Besides your mother."

"Mother?"

"At the theatre. She caught me for a brief moment without them and threatened me with her deadly fan."

The image made her grin – sugar-coated Mama scolding Bram with a pink feather frippery.

He coughed lightly and gave a tentative smile. "We should discuss Celeste."

Her grin dropped.

BRAM FIDDLED with the ring from the jewellery box. So far it had all gone better than he'd ever expected. He didn't like talking about his family and childhood, but Sophie seemed to have gained some insight from it. But the Celeste debacle?

"Do you remember the conversation I had with Celeste at the Trowbridge ball?" he asked.

Her touch withdrew and instantly he missed the comfort, the heat. Glancing up, he flinched and realised the question had been incredibly bacon-brained. As if she could forget that night.

Returning the sapphire ring to its velvet protection, he spoke again, "Forget I asked. It was a...carbuncle-ish thing to say."

It didn't even raise a smile.

"Celeste was a French spy, but she turned to us when Napoleon's own men killed her brother. Her information as a turncoat has been incredibly useful and saved many lives. I was her main contact when I worked in France."

"Was she also your paramour?"

A pistol could not have fired the question any quicker... or lower.

"Once. A long, long time ago – before I returned to England, before you. There was no love, it was mere..." How to explain it? "It wasn't even lust...just two people stuck in France with death at their door. It didn't mean anything and I soon realised Celeste was not a pleasant person at all."

"I am not averse to hearing how dreadful my rival is," Sophie said honestly.

"No rival, Sophie. Never." He brought his hands back to her shoulders, despite the stiffness that enveloped her at his touch. "From the moment you filled my eyes, there's been no one but you."

"Bram, you arranged a tryst that night at the Clarendon Hotel."

A long breath flowed from him. He'd always wondered how much she had heard – quite a lot apparently.

"I'm sorry to be coarse and I know her information has saved many, but Celeste is a vindictive termagant. She sells information for money and to avenge her brother, not for humanity. As soon as I discovered her true nature, I kept our relationship purely business and since then that is all it's ever been."

"I imagine she wasn't best pleased."

"She'd already moved on – enjoys the conquest and nothing more."

Hell, he was tired. Sophie still sat upright, but he couldn't help himself and collapsed back on the bed, pulling his feet onto the coverlet, head hitting the hay-scented pillow – bliss.

"You still have your boots on," she chided softly.

"Sophie, love, I have ridden for six hours straight. The smell of my feet would knock out Napoleon's army at twenty yards, let alone your sweet nose."

A gurgle of laughter emerged and he turned his head on the pillow, glad to hear that sound. She was propped up on an elbow beside him so he took a lock of hair betwixt his fingers, rubbing the softness.

"Repeat to me the conversation you overheard." He wouldn't make the same mistake of thinking she could forget anything of that night.

"No, I don't–"

"Please. It's important."

She frowned, but mumbled, "Celeste, not now."

Good, that gave him a starting point.

"When I left France, Celeste was given a new contact. Unfortunately, a year ago he was…removed." *In truth, shot in the back.* "She didn't trust anyone else to introduce another contact except a previous comrade. There was no one else but me." *All others were dead.* "I argued against it." *Told Asher to shove it up his arse.* "But my superior promised that in return, he would start to lessen my duties in preparation for my retirement." *The blackmailing bugger.* "I accepted." *Fool.*

A sceptical look crossed her features. "Did it have to be at the announcement of our betrothal?"

"I received the message half an hour previous. No time to change plans and at that point I thought it portentous. This act would signify the beginning of my new life…with you." *Addlepated idiot.* "Whether Celeste realised the importance of the evening to us, I know not. It wouldn't surprise me. As I said, she was a bitc– shrew." *Bitch.* "What else did you hear?"

"Rustling," Sophie said accusingly, and the lock of hair was pulled from his grip.

Instead, he enlaced his fingers behind his head. "I admit Celeste tried to seduce me, tried to undo my cravat, but a lot of the noise was me fending her off. I had no desire for the woman. I remember grabbing hold of her wrists and saying her name."

Sophie huffed. "I'll repeat the next words I heard, '*Bram, mon chou, we du a leettle biiit.*'" It was the most awful but strangely erotic French accent he had ever heard. Celeste's purring hadn't even raised an eyebrow let alone anything else, but Sophie's whispered words did primitive things to his body.

He shifted on the bed. "And then I said I wasn't a cabbage or some such but a betrothed man, did I not?"

"All well and good, Abraham Walcott." He flinched at his full name. It sounded so...old. "But then the harlot insulted me and your next words were not in my defence. Worse, you said my wide childbearing hips were the reason for our marriage."

"Yes." He grabbed hold of her flailing hand, which looked like it may whack him somewhere painful. "But it's rather the things I did not say that you should listen for. As I have said, Celeste was a vengeful woman. My best way to protect you from her was to agree. But even then, I did not lie, just left out...pertinent details."

"I could have held my own against the French cat," she snarled.

"Today I have no doubt, but a year ago I wasn't sure. She could have spread lies to your ear, set others upon you... hurt you. She's a woman with no thought except for maliciousness. Delights in it, in fact."

"Hah." Sophie snorted, pulling her wrist away and leaning over. "So, what *pertinent details* were left out concerning my wide hips."

"I thought, yes, I am marrying you for those...and your delightful bosom. No need to lie." She bared her teeth, so he quickly continued, "And your pretty coffee-coloured eyelashes that I wish to kiss every day. Your walnut hair that wends its way down your back like a path of chocolate. The lips that make me smile and cause my heart to feel so alive."

"Hmm," was the only reply. "And then you said, 'I do not want a wife that craves excitement–'"

"In danger and deceit," he finished. "No, I want a wife that craves excitement in peace and loving, with me."

"Hmm," she murmured again, although he detected slightly more warmth this time. "You said I was 'quiet and humdrum'. Talk your way out of that one, Bram Walcott."

At least he was no longer Abraham. Surely he must be gaining ground.

"I love your kind of quiet, Sophie. Not shy or timid, but thoughtful and caring. You say what you mean and you cannot imagine how that feels to me. Honesty. Innocence." He cupped her shoulders and dragged her face close to his on the pillow, drawing her body to his side. "I want to hold you here and never let go."

"Humdrum," she repeated against his cheek.

"Did I ever say *you* were humdrum?" he barked. "No. I said it suits *me* perfectly. I love humdrum. I crave humdrum. I think humdrum is a state of utter perfection. I desire to be fully humdrum for the rest of my life. I want my tombstone to say *Here lies Lord Kelmarsh, an exceedingly humdrum fellow.* That is what you didn't hear. I can only hope you wish to be most humdrum with me," he said, kissing her forehead.

"And 'smitten as a kitten'?" she mumbled.

"Exactly as it should be because I looked at you the same way. I was besotted. Should I have admitted that to a French harpy who detests anyone that is happy?"

He felt a shake of her curls and then a warm breath in his ear. "Did you meet her for a rendezvous? Later that night?" This was whispered quietly, tentatively.

How could she have ever thought he'd spent the night of his betrothal with another woman? Or indeed any other night once he'd set eyes on Miss Sophie Beckford. But he now realised they had been too unsure of each other's feelings a year ago, their courtship too rushed in his haste not to lose her.

"Yes, of course, but only to introduce the poor bugger who was to be her new contact. I didn't even speak to her as I was in too much of a state after discovering your engagement ring on some statue's pinkie. I left the chap being dragged backwards into her room." He shuddered.

A snort met his ear this time and he twisted his head.

"I am so sorry for the deception. For the pain I caused."

Fingers cradled his face, soft against his rough chin. "In some ways," she said, "I'm glad we've had time apart."

SOPHIE SNUGGLED into Bram's shoulder, wondering what their lives might have been like if she had remained in England to hear him. But she would not regret this past year. Most probably, neither of them were quite ready for marriage last summer: both discovering turbulent new emotions, Bram trying to extricate himself from his profession and her lack of confidence in herself and others.

They had both learned from mistakes, realised what they

wanted and come to know each other and themselves better
– the real them.

"Bram," she whispered.

"Hmm?"

She leaned up to find his eyes closed, a combined look of
utter relaxation and utter weariness branding his face.
"Ireland?"

"Yes," he slurred sleepily, without opening his lids.
"Sorry about that. But did you know Sir Giles slept in the
kennels with his hounds?"

What in heaven's name was he talking about? Sophie
frowned. "Sir Giles? The gentleman who courted me in
Waterford?"

A nod was discernible. "Couldn't let him court you," he
murmured. "Ridiculous fellow. The report said he spent all
the days with his horses and all the nights with his hounds."
He nestled against her breast, mumbling, "You deserve more
than that."

"You had reports commissioned on my suitors in
Ireland?" She didn't know whether to be shocked, outraged
or…flattered.

The nod came again, his nose grazing her nipple. "That's
nice," was all he said.

"You need not have worried. Giles smelled of cheese. I
had no intention of marrying him or anyone else."

"Cost me a breeding stallion to get rid of him."

Sophie peered down in amazement, but Bram merely
covered her night-rail-clad breasts with sleepy open-
mouthed kisses, as much as he could anyway, without
raising his head from the pillow.

"Couldn't lose you," he muttered again. "Love you too
much. Had to try…everything," he said with a long sigh.

"Oh, Bram," she said quietly, stroking his hair. "I should be angry with you for that but find myself delighted at your tremendous efforts. You had no reason to scare anyone away. No one made me happy like you...or could cause me to cry. But why didn't you come and see me? Maybe after a month or two?"

A heavy breath sounded against her breast and she shook him gently.

"Bram?"

A full snore reverberated through her.

Carefully, she unhooked his spectacles and placed them on the bedside table. He didn't stir as much as an inch and snuggling down beside him, she could only hope one of them would awaken before her maid came in the morning; otherwise, they'd both be in the suds.

And as to her question? It didn't matter: they had all the time in the world for answers now.

"I love you, Abraham Walcott," she whispered. "All of you."

22

EVERYONE INCONVENIENTLY GOES OUT.

hrough the open window came a cacophony of noise from Conduit Street. Fruit sellers chanted their wares, carriages grumbled past and sheet music peddlers warbled the latest ditties – rather badly it had to be said.

Yawning at the chaotic scene, Sophie wondered how much longer Aideen would be. There was no sign of her jaunty yellow bonnet, although with the rainless weather, the streets fairly teemed with life and it was difficult to distinguish anyone clearly. Mayfair seemed busier than ever and her father frequently complained that simply crossing the road was a risk to life and limb, the carriages travelling far too fast nowadays.

Yesterday's freshness still lingered, although the faint smell of horse manure also wafted in, accompanied by the aroma of biscuits. She spied a hawker with a delicious-looking cart of sugar-coated delicacies and considered stepping out to buy a box but her instructions had been most definite – do not leave the house.

Straining her neck, she could still not see any sign of Aideen, who had made an early escape to Hatchards bookshop. Sophie had attempted to make the same dash for freedom but despite promising to take four of Rakecombe's burly footmen, she had been outvoted.

Apparently, she was shaken, frail and distressed.

And the family knew all this without her needing to open her own mouth once.

Having spent the night snugly enfolded in Bram's arms, she'd slept like a babe but could hardly thwart their familial fussing with that confession. Aideen, however, seemed to harbour suspicions, noting the aroma of horse and coffee in Sophie's bedchamber this morning. There was also the fact that the frail and distressed Sophie managed to tuck away four rashers of bacon, two eggs and three cups of tea.

Bram made her hungry, in more ways than one.

Somewhere around the early hour of five, she had been sweetly awoken by a soft press of lips. She'd savoured the warmth and comfort until it'd become apparent Bram had been trying to disentangle himself. Unhappy with this turn of events, she'd pulled him closer, wrapping arms and legs around his solid frame. Not unlike a limpet, she now reflected.

A low groan had been the response to her movements – highly gratifying.

But alas, he had continued to unhitch his body. Her thigh had been gripped and removed from his waist, although not without a slow caress. An arm had been unscrambled, along with a languid kiss to the pounding pulse in her wrist. Finally, the heat of his torso had slipped away.

She vaguely remembered muttering his name.

In response, she'd received a delicate brush of lips to the eyes and forehead.

"I have to leave, Sophie," he'd whispered as she'd clutched at thin air. "However much I would love to utterly compromise you, your parents would tear me apart before feeding me to the cat."

She recalled grumping about feeling cold but sleep had indeed claimed her, just as Bram had whispered he'd be calling on her later...and her father.

So here she was, awaiting everybody.

Her mother had ventured to the apothecary to buy Sophie some sleeping powder despite fervent objections it wasn't necessary, and her father had mentioned visiting Whitehall – no one dared ask any more.

Two of Rakecombe's huge footmen remained with her, the rest having been commandeered by her cousin and mother. She glared at the clock as it chimed eleven. Aideen had promised to bring something decent back to read, although a boundless energy coursed through Sophie's veins this morning, and she couldn't seem to sit still.

Bram's explanation of Celeste had reconciled her and knowing more about his upbringing had helped her to understand his loyalty, his judgement, why he had thought to keep secrets. It had been to safeguard the people he loved, including her. His motives for not revealing he was a spy arose from many events in his past, complex and multifaceted like the splendid sapphires he had presented her with.

Which reminded her – she would have to hide the beautiful bracelet she'd found affixed to her wrist on awaking. The brilliant blue had dazzled her eyes, the gems glinting in the fresh morning light – far better than a written *au revoir*.

A commotion at the front door interrupted her thoughts. A clattering din followed by loud sobbing filtered from the hallway to the drawing room. Had Aideen returned? Was she well? Just as Sophie sped to the door, it flew open with a tremendous crash.

The most gigantic of the borrowed footmen entered with a small figure tucked under his arm. He was patting it a little clumsily and had the panicked expression of a man not really knowing how to deal with a weeping female.

"What–" Sophie got no further as the sobbing figure hidden in the burly shoulder squinted up, before darting across the floor to fall into Sophie's arms.

"Oh, miss!"

"Jane! What's happened? Where's Aideen? Are you hurt?"

The poor maid shook from head to toe, and Sophie gently wrapped her in a close embrace, worry coursing through her veins.

"Th-the… I saw… He jus-just… Oh, miss!"

"Jane," she said, cupping the quaking maid's cheeks in her palms and looking directly into her eyes. "Where's my cousin? What's happened?"

"A man took her. Outside the bo-bookshop. Knocked the guard flat and…and… I ran, I ran away. I'm so sorry."

Pulling Jane tightly into her arms, Sophie looked over the girl's shoulder to the footman who was now shifting worriedly from foot to foot. "What's your name?"

"Peter, miss."

"Peter, we need messages sent to the Earl of Kelmarsh and Duke of Rakecombe. Find my mother, somewhere on

Piccadilly, and my father is at Whitehall. Make extreme haste. Also send a man to Hatchards bookshop."

Looking grateful that someone knew what to do, he bobbed his head and ran from the room.

She led Jane to the chaise and sat her down. "Now," Sophie said, sitting beside her and proffering a handkerchief, "tell me exactly what happened."

"Mi-Miss Quinlan had left the bookshop..." The handkerchief was snuffled into as the tears began again.

Sophie patted the maid's hand, impatience and kindness a conflict within. "And?"

"One of the footmen had our purchases whilst the other sat atop the coach, when a curricle careered around the corner. A man, a dark-haired man, jumped down and hit poor George. The other footman went to help, but this man was so quick and he had a knife... I saw our man fall and then Miss Quinlan was grabbed and...and he..."

"Yes?"

"Carried her off. I think he may even have..." Sobbing, she hid her face in trembling hands.

"What, Jane?"

"Miss Quinlan was cursing and I think he clipped her jaw."

Sophie's stomach lurched in fear and anger. Oh God, what would the man do to her?

"I'm so sorry, miss," her maid cried. "I ran. I was such a coward."

Gathering her close, Sophie patted her back. "No, you did exactly right. Now we can get help."

Sophie nodded at the butler who hovered at the entrance with a pot of tea.

"Messages have been sent, miss," he said softly. "With all speed."

"Thank you. Let me know as soon as anyone returns. Why does everyone have to be out this morning?"

"I believe," he began with a grave smile, "they thought you needed rest without the chatter of the household and so sought to make themselves busy."

"It's true, miss," interrupted her maid. "Your mother said you needed peace and quiet to recover. So we all went on errands."

Unsure what to say to that silly fudge, Sophie leaned forward and with shaking fingers poured the tea.

Thoughts assailed her: instinct said she go searching for Aideen, but she had no clue where to look. And what about the poor footmen? She prayed they were not badly injured.

A polite unhurried knock on the front door interrupted them, and the butler scurried away to attend to it, sighing in relief.

Not a moment later and Bram entered, his face wreathed in worry. "Sophie? What's wrong?"

Leaving Jane to quiver on the chaise, she dashed over. "You didn't get my message? No, obviously not. It would be too soon."

"What's happened?"

"It's Aideen, she's been taken by someone. Outside Hatchards."

"Hell." He clasped her hands. "Tell me."

They sat on the chaise whilst Sophie poured more tea, passing a cup to the maid. It felt an irrational thing to do, but it steadied her nerves and the warm brew chased away the cold in her bones. Jane slugged it like brandy.

Bram was better at extracting the full story from her

maid, even obtaining a vague description. He sounded similar to Sophie's own attacker and fear clutched at her heart.

A bustle at the entrance followed by the rapid tapping of a cane on the hall floor tiles compelled them to turn as one to witness Rakecombe striding into the room. His handsome features contorted, mouth tight and grim, eyes narrowed in agony.

What she didn't expect was for him to lower himself on one knee before her as she sat on the chaise, taking her hand and gazing into her eyes with a beseeching expression.

"I am so sorry, Miss Beckford. This is all my fault. But, rest assured, I will find her."

Bram laid a hand on top of theirs, sealing the three together. "*We'll* find Miss Quinlan. Never fear, my friend, it shan't happen again."

23

WHATEVER NEXT...

"*I* am coming with you."

"No," both voices snapped.

Sophie stood, glaring at the two nobles who'd requisitioned her drawing room for the past hour or so. "Aideen will need someone when you find her. And neither of you are very good with...emotions."

"That's not true," Bram protested.

"That's true," the duke said simultaneously. Sophie could sense him wavering.

Her parents were yet to be found: Mother was last sighted at the draper's and Father had apparently gone for a drink with a crony – every tavern in the City of Westminster and every shop in Piccadilly was being searched.

A flurry of messages had been sent out by the duke which had resulted in a rather ragtag collection of errand boys coming and going. Each had been given descriptions of Aideen and her captor, and a location in the City to be searched.

Not one hour later, a small blond lad had returned with news of a sighting at London docks.

"Sophie," Bram said, standing close and giving the duke a not very subtle nod. "I will not have you put in danger. We don't know what we'll find and may need to move quickly." He took her hands, threading his fingers tight. "And as for propriety... You cannot accompany us alone."

"I can take my maid."

"Poor Jane needs to rest. She's too upset."

"I'll take Esther. Her husband's a sailor and she's...well built. Most of our household come from my father's navy friends so Esther's no lily-livered lady."

"It's still no. Likely we won't be travelling by carriage."

"I can ride! And anyway, you need a carriage for Aideen as she could be injured. The cur hit her."

Sophie would not be left behind to worry and fret whilst everybody else risked their lives and *did* something. She could feel him vacillating and so continued her barrage. "There are no more footmen to protect me here, as they are at Hatchards. What if it's a ruse to leave the house empty and myself unguarded?" His shoulders drooped. "And besides, you can always leave me at the docks or send me home if need be. My parents will be found by then. It would be safer to keep me with you."

"Sophie–"

"Surely the safest place in London is with two of its finest...guardians." She noticed the duke raise a brow.

"Flattery will get you...to the docks, but after that I make no promises. And Esther comes with us."

"Thank you. I would go mad sitting here, waiting."

"Yes, I do know the feeling." He kissed her fingertips. "I spent a year like that."

. . .

BRAM ORDERED the coachman to travel at best speed, but even so they were slowed by a fallen flower cart on The Strand and an attempted shortcut turned into an uneven jumbleguts of a lane. Finally, nearing the hour of one, the river came into sight, although the smell of rotting waste had announced its proximity some while back.

He still wasn't sure bringing Sophie with them was the wisest course of action but her arguments had been sound, and quite frankly he couldn't bear the thought of leaving her behind, alone.

Miss Quinlan's kidnap being merely a ruse was possible and not something he'd considered. He was damn glad Asher had never met Sophie: most probably he would've tried to recruit her.

The new maid shifted in her seat, sniffing the air as though sweet nectar had pervaded the carriage.

"Do you know the docks well, Esther?" he enquired. Her bushy eyebrow rose and Bram realised how that question could easily be misconstrued. "I mean because of your husband."

"I do, me lord." Her accent was of the east side of the city, slack and melodic. "My Jim usually drops anchor here. I know some people think Father Thames stinks but it reminds me of hurrying to the docks to welcome him home." Her jolly face then scrunched. "I can ask around, if you like? 'Bout Miss Quinlan. And I know a respectable inn where we can hole up. Beggin' your pardon, but I doubt you swells are looking for the more *genteel* places when you come down 'ere."

Bram felt sure he'd just been insulted but considering

the dire circumstances, he wasn't about to take umbrage. "Thank you, Esther. We would appreciate it."

"Tide's in," she said. "All part of their plan, no doubt. Be able to get a ship out and disappear sharpish."

"Surely," Sophie interrupted, "it would be quicker to take a carriage to Portsmouth if they were headed for France."

"True, but it would also be easier for us to catch them by road," Bram answered. "If they were in a carriage, we could have chased on horseback at greater speed, but if he has a ship at his disposal, he can slip away very easily. And we do not know their destination – it could be eastwards. I only pray they haven't sailed yet, as we will have to hunt out a skipper and ship to take us to sea."

Sophie slumped back in her seat. He hadn't meant to be pessimistic, but every possibility had to be considered.

A stirring from the corner caused them to glance over as Rakecombe stretched out his long legs, brushing Esther's skirts, who hastily pulled them away. He cleared his throat and flexed his gloved fingers. "I happen to have a schooner moored at the docks."

"You do?" Bram asked, a little taken aback. "What for?"

"I like to have every option available nowadays. Luxury carriage. Fine horses. Comfortable boots... Fast ship. When we received news of the sighting, I sent a message to have the *Charon* readied, on the off-chance. It does have three masts."

This dramatic mast revelation elicited a gasp from Esther, who was obviously the only one to comprehend its importance.

Sophie also appeared sprightlier, but Bram felt the duke's stare, assessing and penetrating. He refused to look back, concentrating on watching the sway of Sophie's skirts as the carriage clattered unevenly over the cobbles.

"What I would like to know," came the duke's gravelly voice again, "is why Miss Quinlan? Why was she his chosen target? Why make this sudden move when he threatened you, Miss Beckford, just yesterday? What would he want with an unconnected, lowly Irish girl? I can only suppose he thought she was you."

Rakecombe's assumptions were *mostly* accurate, but there was also the supposed traitor Asher had talked about. Had someone leaked information that they were closing in on *La Chauve-Souris*, leading him to panic?

Bram opened his mouth to correct the inaccurate part of the duke's information but Sophie forestalled him.

"My cousin," she began sternly, "is god-daughter to the Marquess of Waterford. Their mothers were very close and Aideen more or less grew up with his own daughter. She has his full patronage and protection."

The lone sound in the carriage was of Rakecombe swallowing, and despite the desperate situation, Bram couldn't help a small smile play around his lips. Usually his comrade was so thorough, so exhaustive on detail, and yet he'd missed that.

"Did you know this, Kelmarsh?" he grouched.

"I'm afraid I did. As soon as Sophie went to Ireland, I had reports compiled and one of them mentioned Aideen and her family connections." He reached over to hold Sophie's gloved hand, despite a censorious tut from the protective Esther. "I apologise again, my love, but I needed to know you were safe."

Her lips curved slightly and he felt a light pressure on his fingers. "All that seems very inconsequential now."

The carriage brusquely halted, causing them all to lurch somewhat, and Rakecombe charged off without waiting for the steps to be lowered.

As the rest of them descended onto the quay, he saw Sophie gaze around, wide-eyed.

It was quite a sight, he had to agree. A high wall surrounded the London docks and the entire place swarmed with labourers, sack or sail makers, watermen and hawkers. Discordant sound assaulted the ears: the relentless hammering of the coopers, animals bleating their displeasure from departing ships and the yelling of captains and salty tars alike.

Bram sniffed the air as they searched out Esther's respectable inn. Tobacco, rum and the scent of coffee perfumed the docks. Huge warehouses towered over them, as much as four storeys high, their red-brick facades glinting like hell itself in the peeping sunlight.

They took over a private first floor room of the inn, a clank of money falling into the landlord's greedy palm. Rakecombe disappeared whilst Bram sent out more communications. Between them, they had quite a few...he wouldn't call them friends exactly, but men well used to scouting, and lads only too willing to earn a penny by keeping a lookout.

The door burst open and they all peered up, expecting Rakecombe's return, but to Bram's surprise, Sir Asher Rainham strode in, a rusty-brown cloak thrown back over his shoulders, a hatless head displaying thick wind-tousled hair.

"I've brought trustworthy men, enough gunpowder to startle the ravens in the Tower and an experienced midshipman lest they've dared to set sail. Bloody disgrace."

After shaking hands vigorously, Bram signalled the boy to fetch an additional tankard. "Thank you, Asher. None of us expected this."

"'Tis my fault. I should not have asked you to assist Rakecombe this one last time."

"Blame," Sophie interrupted, coming to Bram's side, "is pointless. 'Put your trust in God and keep your powder dry.' My father's advice...or possibly Cromwell's...although as a child with a lost cat, I considered it fairly useless."

"And you must be Miss Beckford." He gave a courtly bow, lips curving. "Enchanted. Sir Asher Rainham, at your service. I can now see why Bram desires to leave us, although you should know I am losing one of my best men. But then three in ten abandon me for a beauteous female."

Bram peered suspiciously at his superior. When did he acquire such a silver tongue?

Sophie curtsied prettily. "I thank you for releasing him. And coming to our aid."

"We *will* find your cousin, my dear. No one quite like Rakecombe for this sort of thing. He's like a dog with a bone."

He and Asher discussed tactics for a while, directing men to search the warehouses, and Sophie disappeared to help the midshipman plot the fastest course to open sea on the current tide, in case they'd already sailed. It was a skill Bram didn't even realise she had, but knowing her father had an interest in maps and had been in the admiralty, Bram guessed he must have taught her.

Not long after, Jack appeared, expression grim. "I'm not sure I can be much help at this end of town, but I couldn't stay at home twiddling my thumbs." He glanced over Bram's shoulder as they shook hands. "Ah, Miss Beckford. A terrible deed, but I have no doubt these fellows will find her."

With arms wide, Sophie dashed forward. "I am *so* glad to see you."

Why did the man always get this reception from females? It was most aggravating. Bram scowled and waited to hear the reason.

"We need you for something, Lord Winterbourne."

"It would be a pleasure and please call me Jack. All my friends do."

"I will, and I thank you." Sophie blushed. Bram glowered. "My maid Esther has come up with a list of ladies that... work around here. Maybe you could ask them if they've seen anything? You're good at charming the ladies, are you not?"

Bram didn't know whether to frown or smirk at that comment.

"Some say I have that talent." Jack smiled broadly at a dazed-looking Esther. "Come sit by me and let's go through this list of ladies and where they can be found."

With the maid distracted in the corner and Asher busy with his men, Bram could finally put an arm around Sophie's waist, pulling her tight.

"I am so scared for Aideen," she whispered, sinking her head into his shoulder as he tenderly caressed her hair, the bonnet having been abandoned long ago. "And what will happen after we find her? She'll be ruined if word spreads."

"Rakecombe will see no gossip is attached to either of you. He's very good at intimidating people."

Her choked laugh was muffled by his coat. "I hope Aideen is yelling at that French cur with her very worst curses."

"I thought she earmarked them for the duke."

"Oh no. He's only earned the nice ones so far."

Bram brushed a curl from her eyes and was about to enquire more when the man himself strode in, cloak flapping about him, cane held so tight it might snap.

"We sail immediately. They weighed anchor on the *Orpheus* a little over an hour ago, but it's a slow lugger so with my three masts, we'll easily catch them – the mouth of the estuary would be my estimate. Any later and…"

He didn't need to expound further: if the lugger made open sea before dusk, they'd never be able to spot it.

"All is prepared, Rakecombe. Good luck," Asher added.

"My thanks." He shifted. "And Winterbourne? Is that you? 'Tis possibly the first time I've ever been glad to see your libidinous self."

"Why thank you, Rakehell," the man replied, firmly gripping the duke's hand in both of his. "Glad to see you're still an arrogant arse even in dire circumstances. It shows all will be well and that the world has not yet upended."

"Excuse me," Sophie interrupted, "but can we skip the pleasantries and leave."

"Sophie." Bram gave her a strained smile. "I… We are not going."

"What? Of course we are."

"No. I shall wait here for news, and you will be going back to the townhouse with Esther."

She crossed her arms, face belligerent. "I don't think so. My cousin will need me. I *am* going, Abraham Walcott."

Oh God, his full name again. "Not without me you're not. And I… I can't…"

"Excuse me," Rakecombe interrupted, "but can we skip the argument and leave."

Bram sat heavily, eyes avoiding...everyone. "I can't. Rakecombe, Sophie. I'm sorry, but I just can't."

Shiny boots appeared on the threadbare rug in front of him, a wicked cane tapping at their side before it was abandoned against a chair.

"I have an idea," Rakecombe said, voice low.

Squinting up, Bram had no time to dodge the fist that met his jaw.

It was a punch designed to last, and the force of it sent him spinning, crashing from the chair to the floor, and although he flung out a hand for Sophie, the blow had been too hard and too well-placed for him to do any more than succumb, vision dimming to black.

24

THERE'S FREEDOM AT SEA.

"*Y*ou hit him too hard."

"My dear, his head is akin to stone, and I *do* have experience in these matters."

The raised voices clattered through Bram's skull, but before he could clearly think or open his eyes, freezing cold water doused his face.

"What the hell?" He shook himself like a wet dog, struggling to sit up as intense sunlight compelled him to squint – everything was so blue and swayed around him. A sinking feeling roiled in his gizzards.

"Wakey, wakey, Bram. The *Orpheus* is in sight. Sorry for the clout but we need your superior swordsmanship, and I know you'll sharpen up when the battle is upon us."

"Fetch him a sea biscuit. He'll be shipshape in no time," bellowed Jack.

"Oh, Bram, my darling. Are you well? They hit you again, the rumrats, when you started to stir. I told them to sling their hooks."

Of the three voices, he much preferred the

compassionate tone of the latter, but not if it meant Sophie was on the bloody schooner...and who in the hell had been teaching her sea cant?

"Rumrats... Sophie?" he rasped. "What are you doing here?"

"I wasn't to be left behind, Bram," she said softly, pressing a tender hand against his forehead. "Especially when the duke explained...about the sea."

Oh, mortification kill him now. He could just imagine Rakecombe's shoddy explanation and he closed his eyes in self-disgust. A renowned spy, afraid of ships? Absurd.

Even now, held in Sophie's arms, tension wound his body taut.

It hadn't always been like this.

The sea had held little fear for him in his youth, although he'd never quite been able to feel the sense of freedom and liberty the sailors talked of. A slight unease had usually slithered down his own spine as they'd weighed anchor but he'd attributed it to the coming days of endless dreary grey.

Then, nigh on four years previous, he'd been captured on a routine dash across the channel by Spanish picaroons. They'd thrown him in the ship's hold and forgotten about him, for which he should have been grateful, but the enclosed space, the lack of anything to drink despite the salty liquid seeping through every joint, and the complete darkness seemed to have heightened his dislike of ships even more.

The *Charon* pitched, creaked, even in these flat estuary waters, and yet it wasn't the motion of the schooner that narrowed his windpipe – it wasn't that at all. It was the concept that he couldn't step off, the enclosed feeling with no means of escape, the wide endless expanse of blue making his head swim, the below-deck rooms with no windows: trapped.

After the Spanish incident, he hadn't boarded a ship until a mission with Rakecombe. And it was there it had first happened, in an utterly calm Portsmouth harbour. As soon as he'd stepped on the frigate, his breathing had become laboured, heat creeping from his toes, burning in his guts, feeling as though his lungs were to explode.

No air. None at all.

Breath had rasped and he'd been absolutely sure he was about to die. His throat had contracted, suffocating, and Rakecombe had held him flat on the deck, believing him choking to death, tearing at his cravat to no avail.

Everything had dimmed.

Dead.

They'd carted his fainted arse off the ship and he'd never set foot on one since, the mere thought of it enough to rekindle the strange sensation.

He hauled in a harsh breath, feeling sweat break on his forehead. It was going to happen again – he'd be useless to the other men, a bloody albatross.

"Bram, look at me. I had an idea when talking to the duke."

Forcing his eyes open, he stared at Sophie, head swirling – he could see the men in the rigging, hauling in sails, ensnared.

"No. Not at the boat. Not at the sails. Only me. Look at me." The fierce command focused him. "Look at my eyelashes. Look at the colour. Concentrate on them. How many are there?"

They were quite curly, he realised, and faintly tipped with gold. Despite thinking her request rather silly, he started to count. The ship pitched again but he ignored it, intent on the coffee lashes.

"Bram? Your breathing has eased. How do you feel?"

Frowning, he switched focus to her cinnamon eyes. The timbers discernibly creaked, a light-headed sensation hitching his breath, but he concentrated on Sophie's pupils contracting as the sun hit her face and the hitch eased.

"Better. As long as I don't think..."

At some point, she had changed her sprigged muslin for a serviceable brown dress, and he single-mindedly focused on the strands of wool keeping her warm against the moist winds. The complicated chignon of this morning was now sensibly braided, colours flashing in the knot: umber, walnut and copper, and as he glanced down, he noticed her pretty feet were bare. They were quite large.

"Sophie, what are you doing here? It's dangerous," he said, breathing slowly, kissing her fingers and counting the buttons on her dress.

"I couldn't bear to be left alone and I can be very... persuasive." She dabbed at his forehead with her petticoat. "The duke believes your problem will diminish in battle, but if you feel this...whatever it is, then try and focus on just one thing. Concen–"

The words were cut by a shrill whistle, and Bram scrambled to his feet, swaying slightly. He grabbed Sophie in a fierce embrace and kissed her wildly. "I love you so goddamn much."

Sophie didn't get to reply; she opened her mouth, but Bram had spun and was already dashing to his comrades at the rail. The duke tossed a sword in the air which Bram caught with a swooping arm and Sophie smiled. Whatever strange fever overtook him on ships, he had managed to shake it off...for now.

Broad-shouldered men hurried hither and thither, carrying pistols and loading shot. Ropes were thrown and shouts echoed in her ears from all sides. She stood, a motionless statue amongst all the organised mayhem. Sailors slid from the masts and Sophie could see the lugger a little way off, gaining in detail as they neared.

"Miss Beckford!"

Esther grabbed her and avoiding the flurry of well-drilled men, they darted to the small door that hid steps leading to the lower deck. Bouncing against the tight sides of the gloomy passageway, Sophie followed the maid to the duke's quarters, which looked more sumptuous than her own bedchamber. Deep burgundy curtains, spine-cracked books and a very large bed dominated the room.

Lurching across the cabin, they both fell to the floor as the boat dipped and noise battered their ears: muffled yells and curses, feet scampering overhead with noisy thumps and the sound of pistol fire. Sophie prayed for them all: her beloved Bram, Rakecombe, Jack, and all the sailors who fought for Aideen.

A harsh scraping sound shivered the backs of her teeth and after it came a huge shuddering crash as though the schooner would break apart.

"Nothing to worry about." Esther smiled gamely. "Always sounds worse below deck. They throw a grappling hook when near enough and then haul the boat closer. That was us colliding with the lugger."

Not feeling terribly reassured, Sophie donned a sturdy

pair of sailor's boots she found under the bed and seized a velvet coverlet, draping it over their shivering selves.

During the chase of almost four hours, the duke's schooner – with its three masts – had seemed to skip over the waves, catching every slight breeze. She'd felt joy at sighting the lugger before they'd reached open sea, although the yawning chasm of deep-grey water in the mouth of the estuary hadn't appeared any more benign. Now fear suffused every part of her as the clash of steel rang out, interspersed with grunts.

"It'll be over soon," comforted Esther. "We seem to have acquired an awful lot of very capable men. Did you see the size of them? Very fine-looking."

About to ask if a married woman was permitted to describe other males as fine, they were disrupted by the door crashing open, lock splintering, and a man staggered through, sword in bloodied hand.

"No frigging surgeon on board," he cursed. "Don't suppose one of you could patch up this scratch. I'm bleeding like a stuck pig and my sword keeps slipping."

Esther immediately jumped to her feet and pushed the man to sitting. "Search the cupboard, miss. I'm sure there must be something."

Feeling at last useful, Sophie hunted around and found rolls of linen and a sharp knife.

"How are our men faring?" she asked tentatively as Esther doused the wound in brandy and words spilled from the man's lips that she'd never heard before.

He took some moments to reply. "Good. The Frenchies weren't expecting anything. There's not many of them and most seem drunk. All be over soon."

Sophie deftly cut the cloth, and Esther wound it around the nasty gash before tying a tight knot.

"Saw one of theirs dead," he continued. "Nothing to be done for the bugger. Shot in the gut, spilling everywhere he was."

Clutching her stomach, Sophie gasped.

"Ladies present, so mind your Billingsgate lingo." Esther nudged him. "You'll do, so get back out there and finish them off. If your sword's as big as your mouth, it shouldn't take long."

The burly sailor stood, poking at the bandage. "Any time you'd like to see what's in my scabbard, lovely, you just say the word."

"Oh, hush your blubber," Esther reprimanded, a rosy blush lighting her plump cheeks. "I'm a happily married woman. Honestly, Miss Beckford, these sailors are such randy coves."

Sophie sat on the bed, hopelessly lost in the linguistics of the conversation as the man left the room muttering about docking somewhere. Where did people learn these terms? And more importantly, where could she acquire an understanding?

Another knock and Esther hurried over to unwedge the door. "Fetch more bandages, miss. We could be in for a busy time."

Turning to rummage in the cupboard more thoroughly, a shriek caused her to spin back in time to see Esther slam against the wall and sink to the floor, a small cut to her cheek, blood seeping. Sophie's horrified stare lifted to the Frenchman, stood smirking, scratches to his face, rope stretched between his hands.

"My pretty Englishwoman, again we meet. I more prefer

you to your cousin – *la harpie*," he taunted, moving forward. "She is *putain chiante*. Cursing in the stupid language."

Sophie shifted right, eyes anchored to him whilst her hands searched behind for the bandage knife, but the boat tilted and in that moment, he dived forward, looping the rope around her neck and pulling taut.

"*Aw, ma chérie.* No struggle or you choke, and I need you for something."

Along the passageway, he pushed her, standing behind at arm's length, one hand on the knot at her nape, the other on the dangling end, ready to tighten the noose. They reached the narrow stairs to deck but clambering up, she stumbled, ramming her knees on the open treads, eyes wet at the suffocating sensation around her neck.

All at once, he seemed to realise he needed his quarry alive as the rope slackened and she breathed in fresh sea air. Bright light caught in Sophie's scrunching eyes as he pushed her out onto deck. Most of the noise came from the other ship, a mad confusion of men, swords and clamour.

"Stop!" the Frenchman roared. "Stop your fighting or *ma belle* is dead."

A few men heard and peered over, arms dropping. She saw Jack through the din, blood staining his fine shirt, terror in his eyes as he looked up.

Then Bram's voice. "Goddamn whoreson. Get your filthy hands off her."

Relief swamped her as he tore over the gangplank between the two ships, followed by Jack and then Rakecombe, who forewent the bridge and leaped the rails instead. They stood poised, watching, but the Frenchman solely chuckled in the abrupt silence.

"And why would I do that, Englishman? She is safe

passage for me. Move aside and get your men off my boat. Or I tighten. Choking is so painful a death, *non?*"

Sophie weighed her options. She knew the men were afraid to attack for fear of her strangulation. The Frenchman's back was now to the rail and if he fell with the rope, her neck would snap. She also knew she had to act quickly, provide a distraction or some such.

Would her heel reach his groin if rammed backwards? He still held her at arm's length and Aideen had demonstrated this was a possible manoeuvre if one's attacker was behind, albeit more difficult to execute than the frontal knee.

Creeping fingertips under the rope to give herself air, she noticed Bram shifting, his muscles tight, sword in hand. And so, with all her strength and a stout leather boot, she kicked her leg back, almost strangling herself with the momentum.

The heel struck hard into something soft and squidgy.

A stifled cry broke from behind and the rope slightly loosened before a pistol shot rang out, only for the noose to be pulled tight once more as the man staggered back. Pain seared her throat, but a whoosh of air and abruptly it slackened again, pitching her forward. She fell to the wooden deck with gasping breaths, a faint splash resounding in the distance.

"Search the water," Rakecombe shouted. "Any man that can swim will receive twenty guineas if they catch the bastard...alive or dead."

There was a mad dash to the rail as sailors threw themselves in with wild abandon, a few nearly trampling Sophie in their haste.

Strong arms engulfed her, tugging the noose free and

hauling her into a savage embrace. "Sophie." Bram's frantic voice. "God, my love." Hands roamed her body, rough and desperate.

"What happened?" she rasped.

"Rakecombe shot him but the whoreson kept hold of the rope. I severed it with a sword."

"Aideen?"

"They've gone to find her." And he covered her face with hard kisses, clasping her tight. "Sophie, my sweet love."

"I need to help them," she garbled into his cheek. "Aideen will be distressed."

"Get your sweaty hands off me," came a loud Irish brogue, "and let me at that French buckeen so I can kick him in the nutmegs till they dangle from his gob, and may the lamb of God stir his hoof through the roof of heaven and kick him down to hell, and..."

"Distressed?"

Sophie laughed, never having heard a sweeter sound than that of her cousin in full curse.

25

AN END. A NEW BEGINNING.

"*H*aul your arse to anchor, and get some lobscouse down yer neck," Jack yelled.

"No time, Witterbore," the duke lobbed back, "and please refrain from the nautical terminology. It's barely been a day. Kelmarsh! Stop playing with the fish and get out the soup – some nasty diseases in there."

Sophie gawked as Bram hauled his wet-self up the rope ladder. As the new tide had cleaned the estuary, so the men had done the same to themselves, washing off the blood and grime in the salty water. She and Aideen had been imprisoned below until they'd finished, but Bram had stubbornly remained in the grey expanse: she suspected to delay his return to the boat.

As he reached the deck, water sluicing down his body, Esther froze for some moments, until finally she shoved stubby fingers over Aideen's eyes, to much Irish squawking.

"And you look away too, Miss Beckford. You're not married yet," she scolded.

Pretending not to hear, Sophie instead stared, never

having been so envious of a shirt. The white linen stuck to every part of his muscular torso, both hiding and revealing at the same time. Wet droplets coursed down his bare throat, and as to his breeches...

A shirt was thrown in front of him, impeding her view.

"Try the Duke of Seadogs's stuff on for size," said Jack. "I raided the wardrobe in his cabin – 'twas most disappointing. An array of black, black and, oh look, another black. Never tried any Pomona green, Rakedog?"

Sophie missed the reply because she was abruptly spun around as Bram tore his shirt off.

"Not for your eyes, miss," Esther chided, her own eyes suspiciously bright. "Don't you worry though. I'll keep watch till he's safely clothed and got some boots on."

Frowning, Sophie nevertheless obeyed, relishing her small glimpse of slender hips and firm stomach as he'd commenced wrenching the wet material over his head.

With both maidens at last permitted to turn, Sophie and Aideen observed all the fellows slap each other on the back with manly thumping whacks.

The duke was to continue sailing on in the lugger, as after *conversing* with some of the Frenchman's compatriots, he had discovered a rendezvous was to take place off the coast and as they had the two boats, it seemed provident for him to hunt down more of the plotters. The rest of the lugger's meagre crew were tied up in the *Charon's* hold, awaiting Sir Asher's welcome.

Aideen clutched Sophie's hand something fierce as they rose to say farewell to the duke. As the sun began to slide behind London in the distance, so his stern visage of the day also seemed to slip away. With starched cravat having been abandoned to battle and his hair tousled, he looked more approachable, ordinary even...if it wasn't for his noble and aristocratic aura, of course.

"Miss Beckford, here we must part." And so saying, he brought her fingers to his lips. "My sincerest regrets, once again, for the danger I brought upon you. I leave Kelmarsh in your capable hands. As he is my brother in kind, so you are now my sister."

"I'm honoured, Your Grace, but there is no need for regrets. We are all safe, and if not for the noose, it would have been most exciting."

"A sister should address me as Alex," he said with a very unduke-like twinkle in his eye. "Mayhap we'll next meet for a wedding, Miss Beckford?"

"Mayhap...Alex, and please, it's Sophie. Godspeed to you."

He nodded his pleasure and she took herself to stand by Bram's side who, it had to be said, looked quite pale again. His breath rasped, eyes rooted to the pitted rail, lips moving without sound. She touched his fingers and he gripped them with a crushing force.

"Miss Quinlan." The duke reached out his arm, and Sophie expected him to take Aideen's hand, but instead he brushed a fingertip along her bruised cheek, remorse writ upon his features. "I am so sorry for all that you have suffered."

"Bah. 'Twas nothing. Did you see his face? I'll be scraping his skin from under my fingernails for a week. Pity you never found the fiend though. I hope he sank to the bottom and was suffocated by the green-haired merrows of the sea. Quite benevolent usually, but I'm sure they'd make an exception."

The duke's lips quirked. "You should not have provoked

the man. He could have seriously hurt you. Rather totty-headed, in fact."

"Totty-headed!" she bawled, hands on hips, temper rising. "Why you, English dog, may the..." She paused and promptly waved a finger at him. "You are deliberately baiting me, are you not, Your Grace?"

He shrugged. "It has been my pleasure to know you, Miss Quinlan. I wish you every happiness in your life." The words had a finality to them, and Sophie saw a fleeting expression of anguish cross her cousin's face.

"May the..." Aideen faltered. "May the Irish hills caress you. May her lakes and rivers bless you. May the luck of the Irish enfold you. May the blessings of Saint Patrick behold you. May the strength of every one of us be in your journey."

Silence cloaked their little group, the beauty of those words lingering to wrap itself around them.

"Goddamn it," said the duke, breaking the peace as he dragged Aideen against him and pressed a fierce kiss upon her mouth, his hand twisted in her hair.

Just as quickly, he let go and jumped the rail to the other boat. "Weigh anchor and release the grappling hook." Glancing back, he bellowed, "Wretchedbourne, look after them all. And I expect my woollen tailcoat cleaned and returned to me."

The *Orpheus* caught the breeze, slowly moving off, and Sophie joined Aideen at the rail, linking arms as stuttering breaths shook her cousin.

Alexander Westhide, the Duke of Rakecombe, did not look back. He merely stood, spine straight, hands on hips, motionless by the wheel. A tangible sense of aloneness encircled him as his tall shadow stretched over the lugger's deck and Sophie prayed they would hear his ebony cane tapping some day soon.

"I can't bear the thought of never setting eyes on the pompous bug ever again," Aideen whispered, and Sophie hugged her close.

"Don't worry, sweet cherry," Jack interrupted. "Fellow's like a bad penny. You'll probably find him in your pocket one day. Well then," he said, standing back in his borrowed black finery and throwing out both arms as though they were to promenade with the king, "can I interest you and Esther in some lobscouse? I think we should take full advantage of Rakecombe's well-stocked larder, wine cellar and silverware. Personally, I couldn't give a tinker's curse about three masts, but the three bottles of champagne I spied do indeed look impressive."

As Jack spoke, the sailors that remained with the *Charon* busied themselves turning the boat about. The plunging sun cast the Thames in a romantic glow, its fading radiance setting the water to fire. It no longer seemed an ugly expanse of grey dreariness but an intimate backdrop of flame and reflection. The glide back up the river would be glorious.

Her cousin took Jack's arm, but Esther hesitated. "Miss Beckford?"

"I will stay with Lord Kelmarsh."

"I'm not sure–"

"Now, now," the Marquess of Winterbourne cajoled, dazzling the woman with his ivories. "I think we can leave off the chaperoning and let the two turtle doves have some time alone, eh? They'll be shut in the parson's pound soon enough, correct, Bram?"

A tight nod greeted his question.

"And anyhow, look at him. He's about to collapse. Doubt the poor fellow could say his own name let alone seduce the girl." He gathered Esther's palm to lay it on his other sleeve. "Sophie, do shout if you need me to clout him. You can have the duke's cabin to rest."

Jack marched them all off, murmuring assurances to Esther, but as they reached the stairs, he glanced back. "Rule thirty-two, remember?" He turned again. "Now, Aideen, have I told you about the time Rakecombe had me thrown out of his dreadfully dull ball?"

As they disappeared below deck, a glassy flat look overcame Bram's sapphire eyes, spectacles lost. A fine sheen of sweat bubbled on his forehead and his breath grated, rapid and shallow.

Everyone seemed to think she knew what to do with him.

Grabbing hold of his hand, she hauled him across the deck to the steep stairs. Along the dark passageway, his breathing grew worse, and once inside the cabin and having dragged a chair to hold the broken door closed, she turned.

Bram swayed, face drained of colour.

What was she to do?

"Call Jack," rasped Bram. "I tried counting the pit marks on the rail – one hundred and fifty-six – but then it stopped working. I can't focus."

Any moment he was going to faint and he refused to utterly humiliate himself in front of his beloved. He tried to inhale more air through his mouth but it only made the sensation worse as his head lightened and thoughts scattered across the dark expanse like stars. Small boat. Tiny cabin. Endless sea. No escape. Captured.

"Bram, my love." His eyes flicked to her. "You once told me my breasts could remove every thought from your head, was that correct?"

"Erm."

"Or were you lying?" she asked whilst undoing a button on her coarse brown gown.

"Erm." His usually agile noggin seemed to have been overtaken by a pigwidgeon. All he could now manage to focus on was Sophie's silky skin above the line of her chemise, which was slowly being revealed, button by button. Bram almost wished for her to slow. To tease him yet more. To tantalise his body until its very limit. The constriction in his gullet eased as he concentrated on Sophie's erotic unveiling.

"Your breathing is still shallow but your colour is better. Is it working?"

Yes, it was working. Every single part of him was functioning perfectly as Sophie reached the final button. He noticed her slender throat moving with the sound of her words. His eyes tracked further down, beholding the rapid rise and fall of her chest above the cotton undergarment. A deep-green ribbon threaded the top of it, tied in a neat bow at the centre, contrasting with the creamy skin.

"No. It's not working, I believe you might have to undo that green ribbon."

Rose-pink lips curved to a smile, as she seemed to realise her control over him. "This ribbon?" she said, toying with the ends and pulling slightly so that the loop of material drew ever smaller, the slightest of knots thwarting his desires.

Stumbling forward as the schooner yawed, he slid a fingertip down the exact same route his eyes had traced. Her neck, the slopes of her breast, that tantalising ribbon on her chemise.

At that moment, the setting sun took its final opportunity to glance at the day. A red lustre streaked through the square leaded windows, setting Sophie's skin aflame, crimson sparks glinting in her loose hair. An aching hunger consumed him, to be scorched and burned by that flame until nothing was left but naked skin and raging passion.

She caught his arm and turned it, gazing at the scar or tattoo, he wasn't sure which. Bending her head, she kissed the silver line and his entire body jolted in response to the soft, wet touch. Her efforts to divert his attentions were unquestionably working. His mind had cleared, but his body demanded.

All the same, something worried him.

"Sophie, my love. I adore your boldness but I do not want you to continue this solely to distract me. I'd rather be punched in the face than have you do something you are not ready for." He lifted her chin. "You've had a distressing few days and although I have wanted, nay loved you for so long, I *can* wait a little longer."

In answer, Sophie tugged the green ribbon and all his protestations became undone with it.

But the loosening didn't disclose as much as he'd expected, the stays keeping everything together, with only the valley between her breasts revealing itself. Deep and voluptuous, he wanted to lick the luscious curve, suck delicate skin between his lips and bite softly into that sweetness.

The sun's red hue abruptly abandoned them, leaving the cabin in opalescent grey.

Night's approach conjured vivid images as he trailed a hand down to rest on the smooth slope exposed. In this leaden light, his hand looked rough and dark against her gleaming breast.

"The only problem, Bram," she said, her breath cooling his heated skin, "is that now my boldness has to end, as I have no idea what to do next. I mean, my mother explained some things before our betrothal, but I got a bit lost on stamens."

"On what?" He glanced up to find Sophie's cheeks darkening with discomfiture.

"Mama thought it prudent to explain everything in flower terms. Hence stigmas and stamens but I really didn't understand about the pollen."

He chuckled. It couldn't be helped and Sophie's visage turned stern. "Don't laugh at me. It's not my fault we aren't told anything."

Bram hauled her into his arms, breasts crushed to his chest, and he nuzzled her neck. Sea salt now fragranced the lavender fields and he lapped it from her skin. "What would *you* like to do, Sophie?" With one hand on her waist, he lifted her face with the other. "What does your body say it would like to do, right now."

"I'd like to…touch your bare arms, as I did that night in Vauxhall. But I want to continue up to your shoulders and neck. I want to see your chest bare and…touch it. Kiss it."

"Then I would say you should follow your instincts, as they are serving you well indeed."

"Would you like that then?" she asked tentatively.

"Sophie, your hands on me, anywhere at all, reduce me to a gibbering wreck."

A shy smile curved her lips. "And yours on me have a similar effect." She dallied with his shirt laces. "By the way, what's rule thirty-two?"

"I think," he whispered, "it would be better to show you."

He kissed her, gently, their lips dancing over each other, never quite becoming deep or fierce, but simply exploring, relishing.

But gentle could not sustain. The kiss roused, sparked, tongues met and breaths exchanged as they tangled closer. Bram's hands clutched at her open dress, pulling the scratchy fabric from her shoulders and tasting the delicate skin revealed.

The longing that had swept Bram from the very first touch of her hand at that ridiculous ball a year ago suddenly overwhelmed him. He forced himself to slow, to be patient, as he lowered her dress and it sank to the floor in a brown heap.

SOPHIE FELT both shy and wanton all at the same time.

They loved each other, freely and without burden, but she'd never stood before a man in purely her chemise and stays before. Her waist was not as trim as she wished and what about those wide hips? She would never again complain about her breasts, however, as Bram seemed intensely enamoured.

"Turn around, Sophie."

Goodness.

She twisted and felt Bram's nimble fingers tugging at the tight laces of her stays, until finally, with a deep breath, they loosened and joined the dress on the wooden boards, leaving only a gaping chemise.

Her hair was swept aside and soft lips ravished her nape. It did not cause a shiver. No, it instead racked her body with an intense fever until craving coiled in her stomach. Arms clasped around her waist, pulling her hard against his firm body.

Fervid utterances whispered into her ear as potent hands roamed, and she forgot all about wide hips. The schooner rocked gently and their bodies swayed with the motion, murmuring timbers a cadence to Bram's vehement and impassioned words.

"Exquisite. Luscious. Mine," he crooned.

Before she could respond in kind, the chemise was parted; tanned fingers, his scarred knuckles, brushed over her bare breasts, cupping and caressing. A gasp eluded her at this act of possession, breath taken, to be replaced by surging pleasure that jolted her body.

He twirled her to face him, and she gazed into his eyes. Blue Kelmarsh sapphires blazing with desire, intention and want.

They lurched to the sumptuous bed, kissing, feeling, hands nomadic in their desire to discover.

It creaked as they fell together, sinking into a soft mattress that smelled of pure sea air. With coming twilight, the world fell hushed; a call of gulls before dark the lone sound to punctuate the night.

Sprawled on her back, Bram straddled her hips and then slowly removed his shirt.

It was on purpose, she knew that. She'd wanted to see his chest and so he acquiesced.

Magnificent.

Muscles bulged in places she couldn't name and although not as tanned as his arms, his body gleamed with health and vigour.

She reached out and touched, watched his eyelids lower in pleasure as she traced lines, hollows, a fine deep scar. But it seemed he could only bear so much and soon took his revenge. Urgent hands discarded her last remnant of clothing, his head dipping and his mouth finding its prize. Lips, tongue and teeth grazed the tips of her breasts and she arched to the ecstasy.

Now his whole body pressed and she loved the contrast – rough fingers on her smooth stomach, that hard male part of him pressing against her soft thigh, the leather buckskins abrading her skin as he parted her legs to cradle his body. At the overwhelming rightness of his position, she vaguely started to comprehend the flower analogy.

"Bram," she pleaded.

"I know, my love. Soon."

Muscles tightened in his jaw, and he groaned anew as his searching hands caressed her womanly core – rhythmic and steady. Primal and essential.

"I can't…" She didn't know what, only that the sensation was too extreme, too searing, coiling within her, tighter and tighter. But then the touch departed.

A fervid cerulean sea gazed down, turbulent and wild. "Trust me, Sophie," he growled as she must have whimpered her displeasure. "Call me selfish but I want to be deep inside you when it happens."

At his nonsensical words, she reached for him again, but he shook his head and moved to the side. His blasted boots were obviously still on as cursing broke out and something crashed to the wooden boards, before a very naked Bram landed beside her.

She tried to peer down, to see what was about to happen, but he caught her lips in an unyielding kiss. "Not yet. I want you to feel."

And she did. He ground his hips against her, that hard prodding of before now blunter, hotter, more direct. It pushed adamantly against her core, reburgeoning all the sensations of moments ago. But now Bram's sounds of virile pleasure added to the torment, heightening the raw pulsing of her body.

"God, it's nearly upon you, love…" The words groaned in her ear and all she could do was clutch onto his buttocks so he wouldn't cease, score her nails on his beautiful back. Bram's breath panted loud as he suddenly reared, adjusting his position.

All she could see was shadow and skin, sliding and touching, as Bram lifted her thigh and began a slow repeated thrusting. She loved the sight of his slim hips moving over hers, his taut stomach with its line of chestnut hair descending to their joined skin, but most of all she loved the firm pressure, the fullness, and her moan deepened as Bram slowly made them one.

The pinch of pain was expected, but the strange tightness was unforeseen, as was the slow push, pull and drag that led her to clench in demanding need.

"Sophie? Can I… How does that feel?" Bram whispered, strained, and she realised he held himself back in deference to her maidenly body.

"It feels…nice."

"Good," he murmured. "That's good, but let's see if we can make it better." A bold tongue lashed her breast again, and she cried out against the onslaught as gradually his pace quickened, his body now held above hers on tense forearms.

"Bram," she gasped and the words seemed to release an invisible hold on his restrained movements. He lunged, deep, mouth ravishing hers, and she arched against the savage pounding he now inflicted. That feeling of before, that spiralled pleasure, reclaimed her body, but this time more powerful as his firm hands clutched at her hips and the rhythm intensified.

He muttered unintelligible words into her ear, grunts interspersed with teasing nips on her neck and mouth. She pushed back, lifted a thigh, rocked against his plundering, and heard him groan a curse as that small movement allowed him to slip even deeper within.

Tight, her whole being felt so tight with rushing frenzy and when she could bear it not a moment longer, Bram ground his powerful body against her, and she seemed to splinter within.

Pure pleasure rammed her, hips bucking against their will, and she cried out her tormentor's name as her body seized and gripped in a relentless, brutal embrace. Limbs knotted around him, never to let go.

But still he wouldn't cease, his own body lunging in uncontrolled jabs. "Yes, Sophie, yes," he growled. "Hold me."

She caught a glimpse of Bram's face before he buried it into her neck, roaring. Blemished knuckles lashed themselves to the white sheets as his pelvis slammed into hers, shuddering, and he repeated her name over and over again against her damp skin.

Their movements slowed, with Bram maintaining lazy sporadic thrusts. He laved her neck with kisses whilst her own fingers roamed his broad shoulders and slim waist, sneaking down for an occasional brush of his smooth buttocks. They both seemed loath to discontinue and although his exhausted body was heavy, it was not enough to complain about – more like a weighty blanket.

Eventually, warm breath tickled her ear. "Did you enjoy pollination, my love?"

She laughed, causing Bram to grimace and roll over, dragging her with him so that she sprawled across his chest.

"Marry me, my flower. I love you so deeply."

Levering herself up with the coverlet held to her breast, she seized his gaze. Darkness had now descended on the river but a low moon shone bright through the small windows, flashing square patterns of silver across their bodies.

"Most certainly, now that I've discovered *all* your secrets," she teased.

"Ah. Actually, there is one other."

She frowned. More? "What would that be?"

Bram reached up to tangle his hand at her nape, and she was forced to meet his lips in a beguiling kiss.

"That as soon as I saw you," he said, his mouth still touching hers, "my life was no longer my own. Remember Almack's? I vaguely recall saying something ridiculous about me hunting and pursuing you, but that was a lie unto myself. It's always been quite the reverse, Sophie. Since I met you, I have been your captured wolf."

"And what should I do with him? This wolf I've captured and love so impossibly much, have always loved." She returned the kiss, rubbing her lips against his, feeling his stubble abrade them. From somewhere above deck came distant shouts and the gathering of sails, but she honestly could not have cared less if they'd taken a wrong turn on the river and were headed to the Orient.

Bram, however, would probably disagree – his breath becoming shallow again. "I'm hoping you'll take him to the country, far away from ships, let him read to you, paint you and...pollinate you. Maybe feed him raw bones every now and then."

"My very own tamed wolf?" she said, creeping her hand lower, a flush rising at her own audacity.

She suddenly found herself flipped onto her back, Bram's legs insinuating between hers, hands brushing the still tender breasts, a feral light to his eye.

Hmm. Not *that* tame then.

The End

The End

ALSO BY EMILY WINDSOR

RULES OF THE ROGUE SERIES

An Earl in Wolf's Clothing (Book 1)

From the hallowed halls of London's Almack's to the
unkempt taverns of Drury Lane, from whispered words in
glittering theatres to seductive encounters at Vauxhall
Gardens – an earl must pursue his love.
A determined lady. An even more determined gentleman.
Let the pursuit begin…

Merry Christmas, my Viscount (Book 2)

Seduce a rogue? By Christmas Eve? What a troubling
resolution for the most proper widow Mrs Lily Mereworth
to be left with… How? And more importantly, who?
Ghost stories on a windy night, swordplay down the Great
Portrait Gallery, a lady and a spymaster with no thought to
love… Merry Christmas.

Let Sleeping Dukes Lie (Book 3)

"Strait-laced. Ruthless. Arrogant." – The Duke of
Rakecombe has forever spurned love...and with good
reason.
"Forthright. Impudent. Capricious saucebox." – The fiery
Miss Aideen Quinlan refuses to be spurned, unable to erase
the memory of the duke's vehement kiss...
An unlikely couple, an unquenchable passion.
Resistance is futile.

Marquess to a Flame (Book 4)

The Marquess of Winterbourne has long been guided by his
Rules of the Rogue, but as spy for the Crown, his next mission
will break every single one. Sent to the wilds of Cornwall to
beguile secrets from a lady, the last thing this rogue expects
is to unearth his own buried heart.

CAPTIVATING DEBUTANTES SERIES

Captivated by the Viscount

My Captive Earl

Her Noble Captive

ABOUT THE AUTHOR

Emily grew up in the north of England on a diet of historical romance and strong tea.

Unfortunately, you couldn't study Georgian slang or the Regency London Season, so she did the next best thing and gained a degree in Classics and History instead. This 'led' to an eight-year stint in engineering.

Having left city life, she now lives in a dilapidated farmhouse in the country where her days are spent writing, fixing the leaky roof, battling the endless vegetation and finding pictures of well-tied cravats.

Happy Reading,
Love,
Emily
x

f facebook.com/AuthorEmilyWindsor
p pinterest.com/EmilyWindsorBks
BB bookbub.com/authors/emily-windsor
g goodreads.com/EmilyWindsor
a amazon.com/author/emilywindsor

Made in the USA
Las Vegas, NV
10 February 2024

85595274R00156